THE COPPER GAUNTLET

MAGISTERIUM

BOOK TWO

THE COPPER GAUNTLET

HOLLY BLACK *and* CASSANDRA CLARE

WITH ILLUSTRATIONS BY
SCOTT FISCHER

SCHOLASTIC INC.

FOR URSULA ANNABEL LINK GRANT,
HALF FIVE-YEAR-OLD, HALF FIRE

↑ ≈ △ ○ @

CHAPTER ONE

CALL REMOVED A small circle of oily pepperoni from his slice of pizza and slid his hand under the table. Immediately, he felt a wash of Havoc's wet tongue as the Chaos-ridden wolf inhaled the food.

"Don't feed that thing," his father said gruffly. "It's going to bite your hand clean off one of these days."

Call petted Havoc's head, ignoring his dad. Lately, Alastair wasn't happy with Call. He didn't want to hear about his time at the Magisterium. He hated that Call had been picked as an apprentice by Rufus, Alastair's former master. And he'd been ready to tear out his hair ever since Call had come home with a Chaos-ridden wolf.

For Call's whole life, it had been just him and his father, and his father's stories about how evil his former school was — the same school that Call now attended, despite Call's hardest efforts to not get admitted. Call expected his father to be angry when he had gotten back from his first year of the Magisterium, but he hadn't anticipated how it would *feel* to have his father so angry. They used to get along so effortlessly. Now everything felt . . . strained.

Call hoped this was just because of the Magisterium. Because the other option was that Alastair knew Call was secretly evil.

The whole being-secretly-evil thing distressed Call, too. A lot. He'd started making a list in his head — any evidence of him being an Evil Overlord went into one column and any evidence against it went into another. He'd taken to referring to the list before making any and all decisions. Would an Evil Overlord drink the last cup of coffee in the pot? Which book would an Evil Overlord take out from the library? Was dressing in all black a definite Evil Overlord move, or a legitimate choice on laundry day? The worst part was that he was pretty sure his father was playing the same game, totaling and retotaling Call's Evil Overlord Points whenever he looked in Call's direction.

But Alastair could merely suspect. He couldn't be sure. There were some things only Call knew.

Call couldn't stop thinking about what Master Joseph had told him: that he, Callum Hunt, possessed the soul of the Enemy of Death. That he *was* the Enemy of Death, destined for evil. Even in the cozy yellow-painted kitchen where he and his dad had eaten thousands of meals together, the words rang in Call's ears.

The soul of Callum Hunt is dead. Forced from your body, that soul shriveled up and died. Constantine Madden's soul has taken root and grown, newborn and intact. Since then, his followers have labored to make it seem like he wasn't gone from the world, so that you would be safe.

"Call?" his father asked, staring at him oddly.

Don't look at me, Call wanted to say. And at the same time he wanted to ask, *What do you see when you look?*

He and Alastair were splitting Call's favorite pizza, pepperoni and pineapple, and ordinarily they would have been chatting about Call's latest escapade in town or whatever fix-it project Alastair was currently working on in his garage, but Alastair wasn't talking now and Call couldn't think of anything to say. He missed his best friends, Aaron and Tamara, but he couldn't talk about them in front of his father because they were part of the world of magic that Alastair hated.

Call slid off his chair. "Can I go out in the backyard with Havoc?"

Alastair frowned down at the wolf, a once-adorable pup that had now grown into a rangy teenage monster, taking up a lot of the real estate underneath the table. The wolf looked up at Call's dad with Chaos-ridden eyes, tongue lolling from his mouth. He whined gently.

"Very well," said Alastair with a long-suffering sigh. "But don't be long. And keep away from people. Our best bet of keeping the neighbors from making a fuss is to control the circumstances under which Havoc is seen."

Havoc jumped up, toenails clacking over the linoleum as he made for the door. Call grinned. He knew that having the rare devotion of a Chaos-ridden beast counted for a lot of Evil Overlord Points, but he couldn't regret keeping him.

Of course, that was probably a problem with being an Evil Overlord. You didn't regret the right things.

Call tried not to think about it as he stepped outside. It was a warm summer afternoon. The backyard was full of thick green overgrown grass; Alastair wasn't very meticulous about keeping it trimmed, being the sort of person who was more interested in keeping the neighbors away than sharing lawn-mowing tips. Call amused himself by throwing a stick to Havoc and having him retrieve it, tail wagging, eyes sparkling. He would have run alongside Havoc if he could have, but his damaged leg kept him from moving too fast. Havoc seemed to understand this, and rarely scampered too far out of reach.

After Havoc had done some fetching, they crossed the street together toward a stretch of park and Havoc ran off toward some bushes. Call checked his pockets for plastic bags. Evil Overlords definitely didn't clean up after their own dogs, so each walk counted as a mark in the good column.

"Call?"

Call spun around, surprised. He was even more surprised when he saw who was speaking to him. Kylie Myles's blond hair was pulled back by two unicorn clips and she was holding on to a pink leash. On the other end of it was what appeared to be a small white wig, but might have been a dog.

"You — uh," Call said. "You know my name?"

"I feel like I haven't seen you around lately," Kylie replied, apparently deciding to ignore his confusion. She pitched her voice low. "Did you transfer? To the ballet school?"

Call was seized by hesitation. Kylie had been with him at the Iron Trial, the entrance exam for the Magisterium, but he had passed and she had failed. She'd been removed to another room by the mages and he hadn't seen her since. She clearly remembered Call, since she was looking at him with a puzzled expression, but he wasn't sure exactly what she thought had happened to him. Her memories had certainly been altered before she'd been released back into the general population.

For a wild moment, he imagined telling her everything. Telling her how they'd been trying out for a *magic* school and not a *ballet* school, and how Master Rufus had picked him, even though he'd scored way worse than she had. Would she believe him if he told her about what the school was like and what it felt like to be able to shape fire in his hands or fly up into the air? He thought about telling her that Aaron was his best friend and also a Makar, which was *a very big deal* because it meant he was one of the few living magicians who could work magic with the element of chaos.

"School's okay," he mumbled, shrugging, not sure what else to say.

"I'm surprised you got in," she said, glancing at his leg and then falling into an awkward silence.

He felt a familiar rush of anger and remembered exactly what it had felt like to go to his old school and have no one believe he could be good at any physical stuff. For as long as Call could remember, his left leg had been shorter and weaker than the other. Walking on it caused him pain, and none of the innumerable surgeries he'd endured had helped much. His father had always said he'd been born this way, but Master Joseph had told him something different.

"It's all about the upper body strength," Call said loftily, not sure what that really meant.

She nodded, though, wide-eyed. "What's it like? Ballet school?"

"Harsh," he said. "Everyone dances until they collapse. We eat only raw-egg smoothies and wheat protein. Every Friday we have a dance-off and whoever is left standing gets a chocolate bar. Also we have to watch dance movies constantly."

She was about to say something in return, but she was interrupted by Havoc pushing out of the bushes. He was carrying a stick between his teeth, and his eyes were wide and coruscating — shades of orange, yellow, and hellfire red. As Kylie stared, her own eyes popping, Call realized how huge Havoc must look to her, how very obviously not a dog or any kind of normal pet he was.

Kylie screamed. Before Call could say another word, she bolted out of the yard and tore down the street, her white mop of a dog barely keeping pace with her.

So much for making nice with the neighbors.

By the time Call got home, he'd decided that between lying to Kylie and scaring her off, he had to take away all the good points he'd gotten for picking up after Havoc.

The Evil Overlord column was winning the day.

"Is everything all right?" his father asked, seeing the look on Call's face as he closed the door.

"Yeah, fine," Call said dejectedly.

"Good." Alastair cleared his throat. "I thought we might go out this evening," he said. "To the cinema."

Call was startled. They hadn't done much since he'd come back for the summer. Alastair, day after day, seeming sunken in gloom, had been wearing a path from the TV room to the garage, where he fixed up old cars and made them shine like new, then sold them to collectors. Sometimes Call grabbed his skateboard and skated halfheartedly around the town, but nothing seemed like much fun compared to the Magisterium.

He'd even started missing the lichen.

"What movie do you want to see?" Call asked, figuring

that Evil Overlords didn't consider the movie choices of others. That had to count for something.

"There's a new one. With spaceships," his dad said, surprising Call with his choice. "And perhaps we could drop that monster of yours at the pound on the way. Trade it in for a nice poodle. Or even a pit bull. Anything not rabid."

Havoc looked up at Alastair balefully, his eerie eyes swirling with color. Call thought of Kylie's wig dog.

"He's not rabid," Call said, rubbing Havoc's neck ruff. The wolf slid down and rolled on his back, tongue lolling, so Call could scratch his belly. "Can he come? He could wait for us in the car with the windows down."

Frowning, Alastair shook his head. "Absolutely not. Tie it up out in the garage."

"He's not an *it*. And I bet he'd like popcorn," Call said. "And gummi worms."

Alastair checked his watch, then pointed to the garage. "Well, perhaps you can bring some back for it."

"*Him!*" With a sigh, Call led Havoc out into Alastair's workshop in the garage. It was a big space, bigger than the largest room in the house, and it smelled of oil and gasoline and old wood. The chassis of a Citroën rested on blocks, tires missing and seats removed. Stacks of yellowed repair manuals were piled on antique stools, while headlights dangled down from the rafters. A coil of rope hung above an assortment of wrenches. Call used the rope to fasten a loose knot around the wolf's collar.

He knelt down in front of Havoc. "We'll be back at school soon," he whispered. "With Tamara and Aaron. And then everything will go back to normal."

The dog whined like he understood. Like he missed the Magisterium as much as Call did.

↑ ≈ △ ○ ◎

Call had a hard time keeping his mind on the movie, despite the spaceships, aliens, and explosions. He kept thinking about the way they watched movies at the Magisterium, with an air mage projecting the images onto a cave wall. Because the movies were controlled by the mages, anything could happen in them. He'd seen *Star Wars* with six different endings, and movies where the kids from the Magisterium were projected onto the screen, fighting monsters, flying cars, and turning into superheroes.

In comparison, this movie seemed a little flat. Call concentrated on the parts he would have done differently as he downed three Extreme! Sour Apple Slushies and two large tubs of buttered popcorn. Alastair stared at the screen with an expression of mild horror, not even turning when Call offered him some peanut clusters. As a consequence of having to eat all the snacks himself, Call was buzzing with sugar by the time they got back to Alastair's car.

"Did you like it?" Alastair asked.

"It was pretty good," Call said, not wanting Alastair to feel like he didn't appreciate his dad dragging himself to a movie he would never have gone to see on his own. "The part where the space station blew up was awesome."

There was a silence, not quite long enough to be uncomfortable, before Alastair spoke again. "You know, there's no reason for you to go back to the Magisterium. You've learned the basics. You could practice here, with me."

Call felt his heart sink. They'd had this conversation, or variations of it, a hundred times already, and it never went well. "I think I should probably go back," Call said as neutrally as possible. "I already went through the First Gate, so I should finish what I started."

Alastair's expression darkened. "It's not good for children to be underground. Kept in the dark like worms. Your skin growing pale and gray. Your Vitamin D levels dropping. The vitality leeching from your body . . ."

"Do I look *gray*?" Call rarely paid attention to his appearance beyond the basics — making sure his pants weren't inside out and his hair wasn't sticking up — but being *gray* sounded bad. He cast a surreptitious glance at his hand, but it still appeared to be its usual pinky-beige color.

Alastair was gripping the wheel in frustration as they turned onto their street. "What is it about that school that you like?"

"What did *you* like about it?" Call demanded. "You went there, and I know you didn't hate every minute. You met Mom there —"

"Yes," Alastair said. "I had friends there. That was what I liked about it." It was the first time Call could remember him saying he'd liked anything about mage school.

"I have friends there, too," said Call. "I don't have any here, but I do there."

"All the friends I went to school with are dead now, Call," said Alastair, and Call felt the hair rise up on the back of his neck. He thought of Aaron, Tamara, and Celia — then had to stop. It was too awful.

Not just the idea of them dying.

But the idea of them dying because of him.

Because of his secret.

The evil inside him.

Stop, Call told himself. They were back at their house now. Something about it looked wrong to Call. Off. Call stared for a minute before he realized what it was. He'd left the garage door closed, Havoc tied up inside, but now it was open, a big black square.

"Havoc!" Call grabbed at the door handle and half fell out onto the pavement, his weak leg twanging. He could hear his father calling his name, but he didn't care.

He half limped, half ran to the garage. The rope was still there, but one end of it was frayed, as though sawed through by a knife — or a sharp wolf tooth. Call tried to imagine Havoc all alone in the garage, in the dark. Barking and waiting for Call to answer. Call started to feel cold all through his chest. Havoc hadn't been tied up a lot at Alastair's, and it had probably freaked him out. Maybe he'd chewed the rope and thrown himself against the door until it opened.

"Havoc!" Call called again, louder. "Havoc, we're home! You can come back now!"

He whirled around, but the wolf didn't come out of the bushes, didn't emerge from the shadows that were starting to gather between the trees.

It was getting late.

Call's father came up behind him. He looked at the torn rope and the open door and sighed, raking a hand through his gray-black hair. "Call," he said gently. "Call, it's gone. Your wolf's gone."

"You don't know that!" Call shouted, spinning to face Alastair.

"Call —"

"You always hated Havoc!" Call snapped. "You're probably glad he's gone."

Alastair's expression hardened. "I'm not glad you're upset, Call. But yes, that wolf was never meant to be a pet. It might have killed or really hurt someone. One of your friends or, God forbid, you. I just hope it runs off into the woods and doesn't head into town to start snacking on the neighbors."

"Shut up!" Call told him, although there was something vaguely comforting about the idea that if Havoc ate someone, Call might be able to find him in the commotion. Call pushed that thought firmly out of his mind, consigning it into the Evil Overlord column.

Thoughts like that didn't help anything. He had to find Havoc *before* awful stuff happened. "Havoc's never hurt anyone," he said instead.

"I'm sorry, Call," Alastair said. To Call's surprise, he sounded sincere. "I know you've wanted a pet for a long time. Maybe if I'd let you keep that mole rat . . ." He sighed again. Call wondered if his dad had kept him from having a pet because Evil Overlords shouldn't have pets. Because Evil Overlords didn't love anything, especially not innocent things, like animals. Like Havoc.

Call imagined how scared Havoc had to be — he hadn't been on his own since Call had found him as a puppy.

"Please," Call begged. "Please help me look for Havoc."

Alastair nodded once, a sharp jerk of his jaw. "Get in the car. We can call for him as we take a slow drive around the block. He might not have gotten far."

"Okay," Call said. He looked back toward the garage, feeling as though he was overlooking something, as though he'd see his wolf, if he just stared hard enough.

But no matter how many times they went around the block and no matter how many times they called, Havoc didn't come out. It got darker and darker and they went home. Alastair made spaghetti for dinner, but Call couldn't force any of it down. He got Alastair to promise to help make LOST DOG posters for Havoc the next day, even though Alastair believed a picture of Havoc would do more harm than good.

"Chaos-ridden animals aren't meant to be pets, Callum," Alastair said after clearing away Call's untouched plate. "They don't care about people. They *can't*."

Call didn't say anything to that, but he went to bed with a lump in his throat and a feeling of dread.

↑ ≈ △ ○ @

A high-pitched whining noise roused Call out of a restless sleep. He shot upright in bed, grabbing for Miri, the knife he always kept on his nightstand. He slid his legs off the bed, wincing as his feet touched the cold floor.

"Havoc?" he whispered.

He thought he heard another whine, distant. He peered out the window but all he could see were shadowy trees and darkness.

He slipped out into the hallway. His dad's bedroom door was shut and the line between it and the floor was dark. Though he could still be awake, Call knew. Sometimes Alastair stayed up all night fixing things in his workshop downstairs.

"Havoc?" Call whispered again.

There was no answering noise, but gooseflesh spiraled up Call's arms. He could *feel* that his wolf was nearby, that Havoc was anxious, was scared. Call moved in the direction of the feeling, though he couldn't explain it. It led him down the hall to the top of the cellar stairs. Call swallowed hard, gripped Miri, and started to descend.

He'd always been a little creeped out by the basement, which was full of old auto parts, broken furniture, dollhouses, dolls that needed repairing, and antique tin toys that sometimes whirred to life.

A bar of yellow light peeked out from under the doorway that led through to another of Alastair's storage rooms, full of even more junk he hadn't gotten around to fixing yet. Call gathered his courage and limped across the room, pushing the door open.

It didn't budge. His father had locked it.

Call's heart sped.

There was no reason for his dad to lock away a bunch of old, half-repaired stuff. No reason at all.

"Dad?" Call called through the door, wondering if Alastair was in there for some reason.

But he heard something very different stir on the other side. Fury rose up in him, terrible and choking. He took his little knife and tried to press it into the gap on the door, tried to push back the bolt.

After a tense moment, the tip of Miri pressed the right place and the lock sprung. The door opened.

The back of the cellar was no longer the way Call remembered it. The clutter had been removed, leaving space for what looked like a very spare mage's office. A desk stood in one corner, piles of old and new books surrounding it. There was a cot in the other. And in the center of the floor, bound by shackles and gagged with a horrible-looking leather muzzle, was Havoc.

The wolf lunged toward Call, whining, only to be snapped back by his chains. Call sank to his knees, fingers ruffling Havoc's fur as he felt for the release on the collar. He was so happy to see Havoc and so overwhelmed with rage at what his father had done that for a moment he missed the most important detail.

But as he scanned the room for where Alastair kept the key, he finally saw what he should have noticed first.

The cot against the far wall had shackles attached to it as well.

Shackles just the right size for a boy who was about to turn thirteen.

CHAPTER TWO

CALL COULDN'T STOP staring at the shackles. His heart felt like it was too small in his chest, desperately pumping away without making the blood move in his veins. The shackles were forged out of iron, inscribed with alchemical symbols, obvious mage-work, sunk deep into the wall behind them. Once they were clapped on, it would be impossible to get free. . . .

Behind Call, Havoc made a whimpering sound. Call forced himself to look away, to concentrate on freeing his wolf. The muzzle was easy to get off, but the moment he did so, Havoc started barking wildly, as though trying to tell Call the story of how he'd wound up chained in the basement.

"Shhhhhh," Call said, grabbing Havoc's nose in panic, trying to keep him quiet. *Don't wake up Dad.*

Havoc whimpered as Call tried to pull himself together. The floor of the storage room was concrete, and Call reached down into it for a jolt of earth magic to break the wolf's chains.

The earth magic, when it came, felt weak: Call's concentration was all over the place and he knew it. He just couldn't believe his father would pretend to be sorry about Havoc being missing and drive him around, letting him call for Havoc when he knew the whole time where he was, after he had chained him in the basement.

Except he couldn't have chained Havoc in the basement himself. He'd been with Call the whole time. So someone else must have done it. A friend of his father's? Call's mind whirled. Alastair didn't have any friends.

His heart sped up at the thought, and the intense combination of fear and magic split Havoc's chains — the wolf was free. Call darted across the room to Alastair's desk and grabbed at the papers there. They were all covered in his dad's fine spidery handwriting: pages of notes and drawings. There was a sketch of the gates of the Magisterium, and of a pillared building Call didn't know, and of the airplane hangar where the Iron Trial had been held. But most of the drawings were of a weird mechanical thing that looked like an old-fashioned armored metal gauntlet, covered with strange symbols. It would have been cool if something about it hadn't sent a chill of creepiness up Call's spine.

The drawings sat beside a book explaining a weird, upsetting ritual. The tome was bound in cracked black leather, and the contents were horrifying. They explained how chaos magic could be harvested and used by someone other than a Makar — through the removal of a chaos creature's still-beating heart. Once in possession of the gauntlet and the heart, chaos magic could be pushed out of a Makar, destroying the Makar completely.

But if they weren't chaos mages, if they weren't Makars, they'd survive.

Looking at the shackles on the cot, Call could guess who was going to be experimented on. Alastair was going to use chaos to perform a dark form of magical surgery on Call, one that would kill him if he really was the Enemy of Death and possessed the Enemy's Makar ability.

Call had thought Alastair suspected the truth about him, but it looked like he'd moved beyond suspicion. Even if Call survived the magical surgery, he'd know this was a test he was supposed to fail. He possessed Constantine Madden's soul and his own father wanted him dead because of it.

Beside the book was a note in Alastair's spidery handwriting: *This has to work on him. It must.* "Must" was underlined several times, and next to it was written a date in September.

It was the date Call was supposed to return to the Magisterium. People in town knew he was home for the summer and probably figured he was returning to ballet school around the same time the local kids went back to public school. If Call had just disappeared in September, no one would have thought anything of it.

Call turned around to look at the shackles again. He felt sick to his stomach. September was only two weeks away.

"Call."

Call whirled around. His father was standing in the doorway, dressed — as though he'd never planned on sleeping. His glasses were pushed up on his nose. He looked totally normal, and a little sad. Call stared in disbelief as his dad reached out a hand to him.

"Call, it's not what you think —"

"Tell me you didn't lock up Havoc here," Call said in a low voice. "Tell me none of this stuff is yours."

"I'm not the one who chained him up." It was the first time Alastair had called Havoc a *him* and not an *it*. "But my plan is necessary, Call. It's for you, for your own good. There are terrible people in the world and they'll do things to you; they'll use you. I can't have that."

"So you're going to do something terrible to me first?"

"It's for your own good!"

"That's a lie!" Call shouted. He let go of Havoc, who growled. His ears were flat to his head and he was glaring at Alastair through swirling, multicolored eyes. "Everything you've ever said was a lie. You lied about the Magisterium —"

"I didn't lie about the Magisterium!" Alastair snapped. "It was the worst place for you! It *is* the worst place for you!"

"Because you think I'm Constantine Madden!" Call shouted. "You think I'm the Enemy of Death!"

It was as if he'd stopped a tornado midspin: There was a sudden, charged, horrible silence. Even Havoc didn't make a sound as Alastair's expression crumbled and his body sagged against the doorway. When he replied, he spoke very softly. It was worse, in a way, than the anger. "You *are* Constantine Madden," he said. "Aren't you?"

"I don't know!" Call felt adrift, bereft. "I don't remember being anyone but me. But if I really am him, then you're supposed to help me know what to do about it. Instead, you're locking up my dog and . . ."

Call looked over at the boy-size shackles and swallowed the rest of his words.

"When I saw the wolf, that's when I *knew*," said Alastair, still in the same quiet voice. "I guessed before, but I could convince myself that *you* couldn't possibly be like *him*. But Constantine had a wolf just like Havoc, back when we were your age. The wolf used to go everywhere with him. Just like Havoc does with you."

Call felt a cold shiver pass across his skin. "You said you were Constantine's friend."

"We were in the same apprentice group. Under Master Rufus." It was more than Alastair had ever said about his time at the Magisterium before. "Rufus chose five students at my Iron Trial. Your mother. Her brother, Declan. Constantine Madden. Constantine's brother, Jericho. And me." It hurt him to tell Call this — Call could see. "By the end of our Silver Year, only four of us were alive, and Constantine had started wearing the mask. Five years later, everyone was gone but him and myself. After the Cold Massacre, he was rarely seen."

The Cold Massacre was where Call's mother had died. Where his leg had been destroyed. It was where Constantine Madden had removed the soul of the child called Callum Hunt and put his own soul into the child's body. But that wasn't even the worst thing Call knew about it. The worst thing was what Master Joseph had told him about his mother.

"I know what she wrote in the snow," Call said now. "She wrote '*Kill the child*.' She meant me."

His dad didn't deny it.

"Why didn't you kill me?"

"Call, I'd never hurt you —"

"Seriously?" Call grabbed for one of the drawings of the gauntlet. "What's this? What were you going to use it for? Gardening?"

Alastair's expression turned grim. "Call, give that here."

"Were you going to chain me up so I wouldn't struggle

when you pulled out Havoc's heart?" Call pointed at the shackles. "Or so I wouldn't struggle when you used it on me?"

"Don't be ridiculous!"

Alastair took a step forward, and that's when Havoc leaped at him, snarling. Call shouted, and Havoc tried to arrest himself midjump, twisting his body desperately. He hit Alastair side-on, knocking him backward. Alastair crashed into a small table that broke under him. Wolf and man slammed against the floor.

"Havoc!" Call called. The wolf rolled off Alastair and resumed his place at Call's side, still snarling. Alastair pushed himself up onto his knees and gradually stood, his balance unsteady.

Call lurched automatically toward his father. Alastair looked at him and there was something on his face that Call had never expected to see:

Fear.

It made Call furious.

"I'm leaving," he spat. "Havoc and I are leaving and we're never coming back. You missed your chance to kill us."

"Call," Alastair said, holding out a warning hand. "I can't let you do that."

Call wondered whether there had been something off for Alastair every time he'd ever looked at Call, some creeping horrible sense of wrongness. He'd always thought of Alastair as his dad, even after what Master Joseph had told him, but it was possible that Alastair no longer thought of Call as his son.

Call looked down at the knife in his hand. He remembered the day of the Trial and wondered whether Alastair had thrown Miri *to* him or *at* him. *Kill the child.* He remembered Alastair writing to Master Rufus to ask him to bind Call's magic.

Suddenly, everything Alastair had done made a horrible kind of sense.

"Go on," Call said to Havoc, tipping his head toward the door that led to the sprawling mess of the rest of the basement. "We're getting out of here."

Havoc turned and padded away. Call began to carefully back out after his wolf.

"No! You can't go!" Alastair lunged for Call, grabbing his arm. His father wasn't a big man, but he was lean and long and wiry. Call slipped and went down hard on the concrete, landing the wrong way on his leg. Pain shot up his body, making his vision swim. Over Havoc's barking, Call heard his father saying, "You can't go back to the Magisterium. I have to fix this. I promise you I *will* fix it —"

He means he's going to kill me, Call thought. *He means I'll be fixed when I'm dead.*

Fury overcame him, fury at all the lies Alastair had told and was telling even now, at the cold knot of dread he'd been carrying around since Master Joseph had told him who he truly was, at the thought that everyone he cared about might hate him if they knew.

Rage poured out of him. The wall behind Alastair cracked suddenly, a fissure traveling up the side of it, and everything in the room began to move. Alastair's desk went flying into one wall. The cot exploded toward the ceiling. Alastair looked around, stunned, just as Call sent the magic toward him. Alastair flew up into the air and hit the broken wall, his head making an awful thudding sound before his entire body slumped to the ground.

Call stood up shakily. His father was unconscious, unmoving, his eyes closed. He crept a little closer and stared. His father's chest was still rising and falling. He was still breathing.

Letting your rage get so out of control that you knocked out your father with magic definitely went in the bad column of the Evil Overlord list.

Call knew he had to get out of the house before Alastair woke up. He staggered out of the room, pushing the door closed behind him, Havoc at his heels.

In the main basement there was a wooden chest full of puzzles and old board games with missing pieces sitting to one side of an odd assemblage of broken chairs. Call shoved it in front of the storage room door. At least that would slow down Alastair, Call thought, as he made his way up the steps.

He darted into his bedroom and threw on a jacket over his pajamas, shoving his feet into sneakers. Havoc pranced around him, barking softly, as he stuffed a canvas duffel bag with some random extra clothes, then went into the kitchen and grabbed a bunch of chips and cookies. He emptied out the tin box on top of the fridge where Alastair kept the grocery money — about forty dollars in crumpled ones and fives. He shoved it into the bag, sheathed Miri, and dropped the knife on top of his other belongings before zipping everything up.

He hoisted the bag up on his shoulder. His leg was aching and he felt shaky from the fall and the recoil of the magic that was still echoing through his body. The moonlight pouring in through the windows lit up everything in the room with white edging. Call stared around, wondering if he'd ever see the kitchen again, or the house, or his father.

Havoc gave a whine, his ear cocked. Call couldn't hear anything, but that didn't mean Alastair wasn't waking up. Call shoved down his wayward thoughts, grabbed Havoc by the ruff, and crept quietly out of the house.

↑ ≋ △ ○ @

The streets of the town were empty in early-morning darkness but Call stuck to the shadows anyway, in case Alastair decided to drive around looking for him. The sun would be rising soon.

About twenty minutes into his escape, his phone rang. He nearly leaped out of his skin before he managed to silence it.

The caller ID said it was coming from the house. Alastair was definitely awake and had made it out of the basement. The relief Call felt quickly turned to fresh fear. Alastair called again. And again.

Call turned off his phone and threw it away, in case his dad could trace his whereabouts through it like detectives did on TV.

He needed to decide where he was headed — and fast. Classes at the Magisterium didn't start for two weeks, but there was always someone around. He was sure Master Rufus would let him bunk down in his old room until Tamara and Aaron showed up — and would protect him from his father, if it came to that.

Then Call imagined himself with just Havoc and Master Rufus to keep him company, rattling around the echoing caverns of the school. It seemed depressing. Anyway, he wasn't sure how he could get all the way to a remote cave system in Virginia on his own. It had been a long, dusty drive home to North Carolina in Alastair's antique Rolls-Royce at the beginning of the summer, a trip he had no idea how to retrace.

He'd texted back and forth with his friends, but he didn't know where Aaron stayed when he wasn't at school; Aaron had been cagey about his location. Tamara's family lived right outside of DC, though, and Call was sure that more buses ran to DC than to anywhere near the Magisterium.

He already missed his phone.

Tamara had sent him a present for his upcoming birthday — a leather dog collar and leash for Havoc — and it had come with her return address on it. He remembered the address because her house had a name — *the Gables* — and Alastair had laughed and said that was what really rich people did, name their houses.

Call could go there.

With more purpose than he'd felt in weeks, Call started toward the bus station. It was a little building with two benches outside and an air-conditioned box where an elderly lady sat and doled out tickets from behind the glass. An old man was already sitting on one of the benches, hat tipped over his face like he was napping.

Mosquitoes buzzed in the air as Call approached the old woman.

"Um," he said. "I need a one-way bus ticket to Arlington."

She gave him a long look, pursing coral-painted lips. "How old are you?" she asked.

"Eighteen," he told her, hoping he sounded confident. It seemed very possible that she wouldn't believe him, but sometimes old people weren't good at judging age. He tried to stand up in a way that made him seem extra tall.

"Mmm," she said finally. "Forty dollars for one adult non-refundable ticket. You're in luck — your bus leaves in a half hour. But there's no dogs, unless that's a service animal."

"Oh, yeah," Call said, with a quick look down at Havoc. "He's totally a service dog. He was *in* the service — the navy, actually."

The woman's eyebrows went up.

"He saved a man," Call said, trying out the story as he counted the cash and pushed it through the slot. "From drowning. And sharks. Well, just the one shark, but it was a pretty big one. He's got a medal and everything."

She stared at him for a long moment, then her gaze went to the way Call was standing. "So you need a service dog for your leg, huh?" she said. "You should have just said." She slid his ticket across to him.

Embarrassed, Call grabbed the paper and turned away without answering. The purchase had taken almost all his money, leaving him with only a dollar and some change. With that, he bought himself two candy bars at the vending machine and settled down to wait for the bus. Havoc flopped near his feet.

As soon as he got to Tamara's house, he promised himself, things were going to get better. Things were going to be just fine.

CHAPTER THREE

O N T H E B U S , Call dozed on and off with his face pressed against the window. Havoc had curled up at his feet, which was cozy, and also kept anyone from trying to sit next to him.

Restless dreams flitted through Call's mind as he slept. He dreamed about snow and ice and the dead bodies of mages scattered across a glacier. He dreamed he was looking in the mirror at his own face, but it wasn't his face anymore, it was Constantine Madden's. He dreamed he was bound to a wall in shackles, with Alastair about to cut out his heart.

He woke with a shout, only to find himself blinking at the bus conductor, who was leaning over him, his lined face concerned. "We're in Arlington, kid," he said. "Everyone else is already off the bus. Is there someone here to pick you up?"

Call muttered something like "Sure" and stumbled off the bus, Havoc at his heels.

There was a pay phone on the corner. Call stared at it. He

had the vague idea that you could use them to call information and get people's numbers, but he had no idea how. He'd always used the Internet for that sort of thing. He was about to start toward the phone when a red-and-black taxi pulled up to the curb, depositing a bunch of rowdy kids from a fraternity onto the pavement. The driver got out, unloading their luggage from the trunk.

Call jogged over to it, ignoring the twinge in his leg. He leaned in the window. "Do you know where the Gables is?"

The taxi driver raised an eyebrow. "Pretty fancy place, yeah. Big old house."

Call felt his heart lift. "Can you take me there? And my dog?"

The driver frowned at Havoc. The wolf was sniffing the wheels of the taxi. "You call that thing a dog?"

Call wondered if he should mention the service thing again. "Havoc's a rare breed," he said instead.

The man snorted. "That I believe. Sure, get in. So long as neither of you gets carsick, you'll be better passengers than the frat kids."

A few moments later, Call was sliding into the backseat, Havoc hopping in next to him. The cushions were torn, showing the foam padding underneath, and Call was pretty sure a spring was sticking into his back. The cab didn't seem to have any seat belts or shock absorbers, either — they banged and rattled along the street, with Call being thrown from side to side like a pinball. Despite Call's promises, Havoc was starting to look a bit nauseous.

Finally, they reached the top of a hill. Before them was a tall iron fence, the massive and ornate gate standing open. A neatly trimmed lawn stretched out on the other side like a sea of green. He could see uniformed people hurrying across it carrying trays. He squinted, trying to figure out what was going on. Maybe Tamara's parents were having a party?

Then he spotted the house, on the end of a winding driveway. It was grand enough to make Call think of the manor houses on the BBC programs Alastair liked to watch. It was the kind of place that dukes and duchesses lived in. Call had known Tamara was *rich*, but he'd thought of her as having money the way some of the kids at his old school did — kids who had new phones or the good sneakers that everyone else wanted. Now he realized he had no idea what kind of rich she really was.

"That'll be thirty bucks," said the cabbie.

"Uh, can you take me up to the house?" Call asked, intent on finding Tamara. She could definitely afford to loan him the money.

"You've got to be kidding me," the cabbie said, heading up the driveway. "I'm keeping the meter running."

A few other cars were pulling in behind the taxi, gleaming black and silver BMWs, Mercedes, and Aston Martins. There was definitely a party going on — people milling around in the garden at the side of the house, separated from the long stretch of green by low boxwood hedges. Call could see twinkling lights and hear far-off music.

He slid out of the car. A broad-shouldered white man with a shaved head, wearing a black suit and shiny shoes, was consulting a list of names and waving people inside the house. The guy didn't look anything like Tamara's father, and for a moment Call panicked, thinking he'd come to the wrong place.

Then Call realized the guy had to be a butler — or something like that. A butler who looked at Call with such hostility as to remind him that he was only wearing pajamas under his jacket, that his hair was probably still sticking up from the bus ride, and that he was being followed by a large and unsuitable-for-garden-parties wolf.

"Can I help you?" the butler asked. He wore a name tag that said STEBBINS on it in elegantly scripted letters.

"Is Tamara here?" Call asked. "I have to talk to her. I'm one of her friends from school and —"

"I am very sorry," Stebbins said in a clipped way that made it clear he wasn't sorry at all. "But there is an event going on. I can check to see if your name is on the list, but otherwise, I'm afraid you'll have to come back later."

"I *can't* come back later," insisted Call. "Please, just tell Tamara I need her help."

"Tamara Rajavi is a very busy young lady," Stebbins said. "And that animal needs to be on a leash or you need to remove it from the premises."

"Excuse me." A tall, elegantly dressed woman with completely silver hair stepped out of a Mercedes and came up the steps behind Call. She flashed a cream-colored invitation in one black-gloved hand and Stebbins was suddenly all smiles.

"Welcome, Mrs. Tarquin," he said, swinging the door wide. "Mr. and Mrs. Rajavi will be delighted to see you —"

Call made a break for it, darting around Stebbins. He heard the man shout after him and Havoc, but they were busy racing down the huge marble hallway, lined with gorgeous carpets, toward wide glass doors that opened onto a patio and the party.

Fancy-looking people covered a square of lawn surrounded by high hedges. There were rectangular pools and massive stone urns full of roses. Hedges were cut into the shapes of alchemical symbols. Women wore long flowered dresses and beribboned hats, while the men were in pastel suits. Call couldn't pick out anyone he knew, but he slid past a bush in the shape of a large fire symbol and tried to get away from the house, to where the knots of people were thicker.

One of the servers, a sandy-haired kid holding a tray of glasses filled with what looked like champagne, hurried to intercept Call.

"Excuse me, sir, but I think someone is looking for you," the waiter told him, jerking his head back toward the doorway, where Stebbins stood, pointing right at Call and speaking angrily to another server.

"I know Tamara," Call said, looking around frantically. "If I could just talk to her —"

"I'm afraid this party is invitation-only," said the waiter, looking as if he felt a little sorry for Call. "If you could come with me —"

Finally, Call caught sight of someone he knew.

A tall Asian boy was standing in a small group of other kids about Call's age. He was dressed in a crisp cream-colored linen suit, his dark hair perfectly styled. Jasper deWinter.

"Jasper!" Call yelled, waving his hand around frantically. "Hey, Jasper!"

Jasper looked over at him and his eyes widened. He headed toward Call. He was carrying a glass of fruit punch in which chunks of real fruit floated. Call had never been so relieved to see anyone. He started reconsidering all the bad things he'd ever thought about Jasper. Jasper was a hero.

"Mr. deWinter," said the waiter. "Do you know this boy?"

Jasper took a sip of punch, his brown eyes traveling up and down Call, from his tangled hair to his dirty sneakers.

"Never seen him before in my life," he said.

Call's positive feelings about Jasper evaporated in a whoosh. "Jasper, you liar —"

"He's probably just one of the local kids trying to get in here on a bet," Jasper said, narrowing his eyes at Call. "You know how curious the neighbors tend to get about what goes on at the Gables."

"Indeed," murmured the waiter. His sympathetic look was gone, and he was glaring as if Call were a bug floating in the punch.

"Jasper," Call said through his teeth, "when we get back to school, I'm going to murder you for this."

"Death threats," said Jasper. "What is this world coming to?"

The waiter made a clucking noise. Jasper grinned at Call, clearly enjoying himself.

"He does look a bit raggedy," Jasper went on. "Maybe we should give him some popcorn shrimp and fruit punch before we send him back on his way."

"That would be very kind of you, Mr. deWinter," said the waiter, and Call was about to do something — explode, possibly — when he suddenly heard a voice shouting his name.

"Call, Call, *Call*!" It was Tamara, bursting through the crowd. She was wearing a flowered silk dress, though if she'd had a beribboned hat, it had fallen off. Her hair was out of its familiar braids, tumbling down her back in curls. She threw herself at Call and hugged him hard.

She smelled nice. Like honey soap.

"Tamara," Call tried to say, but she was squeezing him so hard that it came out as "Ouuuffgh." He patted her back awkwardly. Havoc, delighted to see Tamara, pranced in a circle.

When Tamara let Call go, the waiter was staring at them with his mouth open. Jasper stood frozen, his expression cold. "Jasper, you're a toad," Tamara said to him, with finality. "Bates, Call is one of my very good friends. He is *absolutely* invited to this party."

Jasper turned on his heel and stalked away. Call was about to yell something insulting after him when Havoc started to bark. He lunged forward, too fast for Call to grab him. Call heard the other guests gasp and exclaim as they moved away from the bounding wolf. Then he heard someone shout "Havoc!" and the crowd parted enough that Call could see Havoc standing up on his hind legs, his paws against Aaron's chest. Aaron was grinning and running his hands through Havoc's ruff.

The hubbub among the guests increased: People were babbling in alarm, some of them practically yelling.

"Oh, no," Tamara said, biting her lip.

"What is it?" Call had already started forward, eager to get to Aaron. Tamara caught his wrist.

"Havoc's a Chaos-ridden wolf, Call, and he's climbing all over their Makar. Come on!"

Tamara tugged him forward, and indeed it was a lot easier for Call to make his way through the crowd with Tamara steering him like a tugboat. Guests were screaming and running in the other direction. Tamara and Call arrived at Aaron just as two very elegant adults, looking worried, also reached him — a handsome man in an ice-white suit and a beautiful, severe-looking woman with long dark hair studded with flowers. Her shoes had clearly been made by a metal mage: They looked as if they'd been cast of silver, and they rang like bells when she walked. Call couldn't even imagine how much they'd cost.

"Get *off*!" snapped the man, shoving at Havoc, which was kind of a brave thing to do, Call thought, even though the only thing Aaron was in real danger of was being licked to death.

"Dad, Mom," Tamara managed, out of breath. "Remember, I told you about Havoc? He's fine. He's safe. He's like . . . our mascot."

Her father looked at her as though she had explained no such thing, but her interruption gave Aaron time to squat down and grab hold of Havoc's collar. He sank his fingers into the wolf's fur, rubbing his ears. Havoc's tongue lolled out of his mouth with pleasure.

"It's amazing how he responds to you, Aaron. He becomes positively tame," Tamara's mother said, beaming at Aaron. The rest of the party had started oohing and clapping, as though Aaron had performed some miracle, as though Havoc behaving normally was a sign that their Makar would triumph over the forces of the Chaos-ridden.

Call, standing behind Tamara, felt invisible and annoyed about it. No one cared that Havoc was *his* dog and had spent the summer being perfectly tame for *him*. No one cared that he and Havoc had gone to the park every Friday for the past two months and played Frisbee until Havoc accidentally bit the Frisbee in half or that, once, Havoc had licked a little girl's ice-cream cone gently instead of biting off her whole hand the way he would have if Call hadn't told him not to, which was definitely a point for him because an Evil Overlord would never have done that.

No one cared unless Aaron was involved. Perfect Aaron, in an even crisper suit than the one Jasper was wearing and a new, stupid-looking haircut that meant his hair was falling into his eyes. Call noted with some satisfaction that there were dirty paw prints near one of the fancy jacket pockets.

Call knew he shouldn't feel the way he did. Aaron was his friend. Aaron didn't have any family, not even a father who was trying to kill him. It was good that people liked Aaron. It meant that Havoc got to stay at the party and that someone would probably lend Call thirty dollars without much fuss.

When Aaron grinned at Call, his whole face lighting up, Call forced himself to smile back.

"Why don't you find your friend some party clothes?" Tamara's mother said, with an amused nod at Call. "And, Stebbins, do go pay for the taxi he came in. It's been idling by the gate for ages now." She smiled at Call. He wasn't sure what to make of her. She seemed friendly and warm, but Call thought there was something about her friendliness that wasn't quite real. "But hurry back. The glamours start soon."

Aaron shooed Havoc toward the house. "Call can borrow some of my clothes," he said.

"Yeah, come tell us what happened," Tamara said, leading the way. "Not that we're not happy to see you, but what are you doing here? Why didn't you call to say you were coming?"

"Is it because of your dad?" Aaron asked, giving him a sympathetic look.

"Yeah," Call said slowly. They walked through the huge glass doors and through a marble-tiled room filled with rich, jewel-colored rugs. As they climbed up a ridiculous, marvelous ironwork staircase, Call spun out a story about how Alastair had forbidden him to go back to the Magisterium. That part was true enough; Tamara and Aaron knew Alastair had always hated the idea of Call going to mage school. It was possible to embroider it until it became the reason they'd had a big fight and even the reason that Call had been afraid his father was going to lock him up in the basement and keep him there. He added that Alastair hated Havoc and was mean to him, for extra sympathy.

By the time he was done, Call had almost convinced himself it was true. It seemed like a way more believable story than the truth.

Tamara and Aaron made all the right sympathetic noises and asked dozens of questions so that he was almost relieved when Tamara left so Call could change. She took Havoc with her. Call followed Aaron into the room where he was staying and flopped down on the giant king-size bed in the center. The walls were covered with expensive-looking antique objects that Call suspected Alastair would have killed to get his hands on: big carved metal plates, tiles painted with angular patterns, and framed scraps of bright silk and metal. There were grand windows looking down onto the lawns below. Above the bed was a chandelier dangling blue crystals in the shape of bells.

"This is some place, huh?" Aaron said, clearly still a bit dazed by it himself. He went over to the imposing wooden wardrobe in the corner and swung it open. He pulled out white pants, a jacket, and a shirt, and brought them over to Call.

"What?" he said self-consciously, when Call didn't move to take them from him.

Call realized he'd been staring. "You didn't mention that you were staying at Tamara's house," he said.

Aaron shrugged. "It's weird."

"That doesn't mean it has to be a secret!"

"It wasn't a secret," said Aaron hotly. "There was just never a time to bring it up."

"You don't even look like you," Call said, taking the clothes.

"What do you mean?" Aaron sounded surprised, but Call didn't see how he could be. Call had never seen him in any clothes as fancy as the ones he was wearing now, not even when he'd been declared the Makar in front of the whole Magisterium and the Assembly. His new shoes probably cost hundreds of dollars. He was tan and healthy. He smelled like aftershave despite not needing to shave. He'd probably spent the whole summer running around outside with Tamara and eating really balanced meals. No pizza dinners for the Makar. "Do you mean the clothes?" Aaron tugged at them self-consciously. "Tamara's parents insisted I take them. And I felt really weird wandering around here in jeans and T-shirts when everyone else always looks so . . ."

"Rich?" said Call. "Well, at least you didn't show up in your pajamas."

Aaron grinned. "You always know how to make an entrance," he said. Call figured he was thinking of when they'd met at the Iron Trial and Call had exploded a pen all over himself.

Call took the new clothes and went into the bathroom to change. They were, as he had suspected they would be, too big. Aaron had a lot more muscles than he did. He settled for rolling the sleeves of his jacket up practically to his elbows and running wet fingers through his hair until it was no longer standing up in crazy spikes.

When he came back into the bedroom, Aaron was standing near the windows, looking down at the lawn. There was a big fountain in the middle of the grass and some children had gathered around it, throwing in handfuls of some kind of substance that made the water flare up in different colors.

"So you like it here?" Call asked, doing his best not to sound resentful. It wasn't Aaron's fault he was the Makar. None of it was Aaron's fault.

Aaron pushed some of his blond hair out of his face. The black stone in the band on his wrist, the one that signified that Aaron could work chaos magic, glittered. "I know I wouldn't be here if I wasn't the Makar," he said, almost as if he knew what Call had been thinking. "Tamara's parents are nice. Really nice. But I know it wouldn't be like this if I was just Aaron Stewart from some foster home. It's good for them, politically, to be close to the Makar. Even if he is only thirteen. They said I could stay as long as I liked."

Call felt his resentment starting to trickle away. He wondered how long Aaron had waited to hear that, that he could stay somewhere as long as he liked. He thought it probably had been a long time. "Tamara's your friend," he said. "And not because of politics or who you are. She was your friend before anyone knew you were the Makar."

Aaron flashed a smile. "And you were, too."

"I thought you were okay," Call conceded, and Aaron smiled again.

"It's just that being the Makar at school meant one thing," he said. "But this summer, it's been doing tricks and going to parties like this one. Being introduced to lots of people and everyone being really impressed to meet me and treating me like I'm special. It's . . . fun." He swallowed. "I know I really didn't want to be the Makar when I found out, but I can't help feeling like my life could be pretty great. I mean, if it wasn't for the Enemy. Is it bad that I feel that way?" His eyes searched Call's face. "I can't ask anyone else but you. No one else would give me a straight answer."

And just like that, Call's resentment dissolved. He remembered Aaron sitting on the couch in their room at school, still white-faced and shocked from being dragged up in front of the whole Magisterium so the Masters could announce that he was the one great hope who would lead them all against the Enemy.

There *was* an enemy, Call knew now. It just wasn't who they thought it was. And there *were* people who wanted Aaron dead. They wouldn't stop. Unless the Enemy told them to stop . . .

If Call was the Enemy, well, then Aaron was safe, right? If Master Joseph needed Call to mount an attack, then Master Joseph was out of luck. Call would never do anything to hurt his friends. Because he *had* friends. And that was definitely not something that Evil Overlords had, was it?

Abruptly, he thought of his father slumped unconscious on the floor. He would never have thought he'd do anything to hurt his father, either.

"It's not bad to think being the Makar is fun," Call said finally. "You should have fun. So long as you don't forget that 'if it wasn't for the Enemy' is a pretty big if."

"I know," Aaron said softly.

"And as long as you don't get conceited. But you don't have to worry about that, because you've got me and Tamara to remind you that you're still the same loser you were before."

Aaron gave a crooked smile. "Thanks."

Call wasn't sure if Aaron was being sarcastic or sincere. He opened his mouth to clarify when Tamara yanked open the door and glowered at them. "Are you guys done? Honestly, Call, how long does it take to get dressed?"

"We're ready," Aaron said, coming away from the window.

Outside, Call could see magic sparking over the lawn.

CHAPTER FOUR

CALL UNDERSTOOD WHY neighbor kids would want to sneak into the party. When he came back through the doors with Aaron, Tamara, and a freshly brushed Havoc on a new leash, he took in the full scope of the event and was amazed.

Cloth-covered tables were heaped with platters of food — tiny chicken sausages in pastry, fruit cut into the shapes of moons and stars and suns, salads of herbs and pickled tomatoes, blocks of gooey cheese and crackers, popcorn shrimp on tiny skewers, blackened scallops, seared tuna, gelatin molds with chunks of meat suspended in them, and chilled tins of tiny black beads resting in bowls of ice that Call thought was probably caviar.

Lion-size ice sculptures of manticores flapped crystalline wings that sent a cooling breeze into the air, ice frogs leaped from table to table, and ice pirate ships soared into the sky before running aground on ice rocks. At a central table an ice fountain ran with red punch instead of water. Four ice peacocks perched on the edges of the sculpture, using sparkling claws to ladle the drink into ice cups for passing guests.

Beside the banquet stood a line of topiaries trimmed into tidy shapes — flowers, symbols, patterns, and letters. Bright flowers ringed each trunk, but the brightest sight of all was an arched folly with a waterfall of liquid fire. It flamed and sparked onto the grass where barefoot girls in party frocks ran back and forth putting their hands into the sparks, which ran up and down their skin without seeming to burn them. As if to drive home the point, a painted sign hung in the air above the waterfall. It read CHILDREN, PLEASE PLAY WITH THE FIRE.

Call kind of wanted to run back and forth in it, too, but he wasn't sure if he was allowed or if it was just for little kids. Havoc nosed in the grass for dropped bits of food. Tamara had tied a pink bow around his neck. Call wondered if Havoc felt humiliated. He didn't seem to be.

"You've been going to parties like this all summer?" Call asked Aaron.

Aaron looked a little uncomfortable. "Pretty much."

"I've been going to parties like this all my life," Tamara said, dragging them along. "They're just parties. They get boring fast. Now come on, the glamours are actually cool. You don't want to miss them."

They went past the topiaries and the fire waterfall, past the tables and the clumps of partygoers to a wide stretch of lawn, where a small group had gathered. Call could tell they were mages not just by the subtle bands that glittered on their wrists but also from their air of confidence and power.

"What's going to happen?" Call asked.

Tamara grinned. "The mages are going to show off."

As if he'd heard her, one of the mages, a compactly built

man with light brown skin, raised his hand. The area around the mages started to crowd as Mr. and Mrs. Rajavi called over the rest of the partygoers.

"That's Master Cameron," Tamara whispered, looking at the mage, whose hand had begun to glow. "He teaches at the Collegium. He does the best tricks with —"

Suddenly, a wave rose from the mage's hand. It was as if the grass were the sea instead, goaded into producing a tidal wave. It grew and grew and grew until it towered above them, shadowing the party, large enough to crush the house and flood the grounds. Call sucked in a breath.

The air smelled of brine. Inside the wave, he could see things moving. Eels and sharks snapping their jaws. Salt spray splashed Call's face as the whole thing crashed down . . . and disappeared.

Everyone burst into applause. Call would have clapped, too, if he hadn't been holding Havoc's leash in one hand. Havoc was whining and nosing his fur. He hated being wet.

"Water," Tamara finished with a laugh. "Once, when it was really hot, he came over and made a massive sprinkler right next to the pool. We all ran through it, even Kimiya."

"What do you mean, even Kimiya?" came a teasing voice. "I like water as much as anyone else!" Tamara's older sister, wearing a silver dress and sandals, had come up behind them. Holding her hand was Alex Strike, who was heading into his fourth year at the Magisterium and was Master Rufus's frequent assistant. He was dressed down in jeans and a T-shirt, with a bronze band at his wrist, since he hadn't gotten his silver one yet. He grinned at Call.

"Hey, squirt," he said.

Call smiled a little awkwardly. Alex had always been nice to him, but he hadn't known Alex was dating Tamara's older sister. Kimiya was really pretty and popular, and Call always felt as if he were about to fall over or set himself on fire when he was around her. It made sense that two popular people were together, but it also made him more conscious of a lot of other things — his limp, his messy hair, the fact he was standing there in Aaron's borrowed clothes.

Master Cameron finished his display with a flourish — sparkling droplets that shot out toward the guests. Everyone squealed, anticipating getting wet, but the water evaporated a few feet above the heads of the crowd, turning into wisps of colored vapor. Mr. and Mrs. Rajavi led the applause as another mage stepped forward, this one a tall woman with a magnificent crown of silver hair. Call recognized her as the woman who had brushed past him imperiously on the front steps.

"Anastasia Tarquin," said Tamara in a whisper. "She's Alex's stepmother."

"That she is," Alex confirmed. His expression as he watched her was neutral. Call wondered if he liked her. When Call had been younger, he'd wished his dad would get married again so he could have a stepmother; it seemed better than no mother at all. Only when he was older had he stopped to wonder what would have happened if his dad had married someone he didn't like.

Anastasia Tarquin raised both hands imperiously, holding thin metal rods in each. When she let them go, they lined themselves up in the air in front of her. She twitched her fingers, and one of them vibrated, sending out a single perfect note of music. Call jumped in surprise.

Alex looked over at him. "Cool, huh? When you master metal, you'll be able to get it to vibrate to whatever frequency you want."

The other metal rods were trembling now, each one of them like a different guitar string being plucked, sending out a torrent of music. Call liked music as much as the next person, but he'd never really *thought* about it before, about how alchemical magic could be used not just to build up and defend, or to attack and battle, but to make art. The music was like rain breaking through the humid air; it made him think of waterfalls and snow and ice floes far out in the ocean.

When the last note of the music died away, the metal rods dropped, falling to the earth and melting into it like rainwater sinking into mud. Mrs. Tarquin bowed and stepped back amid a shower of applause. As she moved away, she winked in Alex's direction. Maybe they got along after all.

"And now," said Mr. Rajavi, "perhaps our very own Makar, Aaron Stewart, would favor us with a demonstration of chaos magic?"

Call felt Aaron stiffen beside him as everyone clapped enthusiastically. Tamara turned and patted Aaron on the shoulder. He looked at her for a second, biting his lip, before he straightened up and made his way to the center of the mages' circle.

He looked very small there.

Doing tricks and going to parties. That's what Aaron had told Call, but Call hadn't thought he'd meant actual *tricks*. Call had no idea what a chaos mage could do that was pretty or artistic. He remembered the rolling, devouring darkness the other Chaos-ridden wolves had disappeared into; remembered the chaos elemental pocked with wide, wet mouths; and shuddered with a feeling that was part dread and part anticipation.

Aaron lifted his hands, fingers spread wide. Darkness rolled in.

A hush spread over the party as more people joined the crowd, staring at their Makar and the growing shadows around him. Chaos magic came from the void, came from nothing. It was creation and destruction all rolled into one, and Aaron commanded it.

For a moment, even Call was a little afraid of him.

The shadows congealed into the twin shapes of two chaos elementals. They were thin, sleek creatures that resembled whippets made entirely of darkness, smaller than the one in Master Joseph's lair had been. Still, their eyes glittered with the madness of the void.

Gasps went up all around the party. Tamara clutched Call's arm.

For his part, Call gaped. This didn't seem like a trick. Those things seemed dangerous. They were regarding the crowd as though they'd like nothing better than to devour everyone watching and pick their teeth with the bones of the people over by the food.

They began to slip sinuously over the grass.

Okay, Aaron, Call thought. *Dismiss them. De-summon them. Do something.*

Aaron lifted his hand. Threads of darkness began to spiral out from his fingers. His brow was furrowed in concentration. He reached out —

Havoc began to bark wildly, startling Call and Aaron both. Call saw the moment that Aaron's concentration got away from him, the shadows vanishing from his fingertips.

Whatever he'd been meaning to do didn't happen. Instead, one of the chaos elementals sprang into the air, toward Tamara's mother. Her eyes went wide, her mouth opening in astonished terror. Her hand flew out, fire igniting in the center of her palm.

Aaron fell to his knees, flinging out both hands. Darkness exploded outward, surrounding the elemental. The creature disappeared, along with its twin. The chaos elementals were gone, scattered into shadows that melted away into the sunshine. Call became conscious of the fact that it was a summer day again, a summer day at a fancy garden party. He wasn't sure if there'd ever been any real danger.

Everyone began laughing and clapping. Even Mrs. Rajavi looked delighted.

Aaron was breathing hard. His face looked pale, with a hectic flush on his cheeks as though from illness. He didn't look like someone who'd just done a trick. He looked like someone who'd almost gotten his friend's mother eaten.

Call turned to Tamara. "What was that?"

Her eyes sparkled. "What do you mean? He did a great job!"

"He could have been killed!" Call hissed at her, stopping himself from adding that her mom could probably have been killed, too. Aaron was on his feet now, pushing his way through the crowd toward them. He wasn't making very fast progress, since everyone seemed to want to move closer to touch him and congratulate him and pat him on the back.

Tamara scoffed. "It was just a party trick, Call. All the other mages were standing by. They would have interfered if anything had gone wrong."

Call could taste coppery anger in the back of his throat. He knew, and Tamara knew, too, that mages weren't infallible.

They didn't always interfere to stop things in time. No one had interfered to stop Constantine Madden when he'd pushed his chaos magic so far that it had killed his brother and nearly destroyed the Magisterium. He'd been so injured and scarred by what had happened that he'd always worn a silver mask afterward, to cover his face.

He must have hated how he looked.

Call put up his hand to touch the uninjured skin of his own face just as Aaron got to them, flushed and wild-eyed. "Can we go sit down somewhere?" he said, quietly enough for his words not to reach the crowd. "I need to catch my breath."

"Sure." Call scrambled to position himself a little in front of Aaron as he leaned down to Havoc. "Pull me over to the fountain," he told the wolf in a whisper, and Havoc yanked him forward. The crowd parted hastily to let Havoc by, and Call, Tamara, and Aaron followed in his wake. Call was aware of Alex looking after them sympathetically, though Kimiya had already turned her attention to the next mage's trick.

Colored sparks rose in the air behind them as they rounded a hedge shaped like a shield and discovered a fountain. This one was round, made of yellow stone, and had an aged look that made Call think it must have been brought from somewhere else. Aaron sat down on the lip of it, scrubbing his hands through his wavy blond hair. "I hate my haircut," he said.

"It looks fine," said Call.

"You don't really think that," said Aaron.

"Not really," Call said, and gave Aaron what he hoped was a supportive smile. Aaron looked worried. Maybe it hadn't been that supportive. "You okay?"

Aaron took a deep breath. "I just —"

"Have you heard?" An adult voice floated through the air, through the leaves. It was deep and bass; Call had heard it before. "Someone broke into the Collegium last week. They tried to steal the Alkahest."

Call and Aaron stared at each other, and then at Tamara, who had gone very still. She put her finger to her lips, quieting them.

"Someone?" replied a light, female voice. "You mean the minions of the Enemy. Who else? He means to start up the war again."

"No broken Alkahest is going to save him once our Makar is trained and ready" came the reply.

"But if he's able to repair it, the tragedy of Verity Torres could repeat itself," cautioned a third voice, this one a man's, sharp with nervousness. "Our Makar is young, like she was. We need time. The Alkahest is too powerful for us to take an attempt to steal it lightly."

"They're moving it to a more defensible location." The woman's voice again. "They were fools to keep it on display in the first place."

"Until we're sure it's secure, the safety of our Makar must be our highest priority," the first speaker said.

Aaron had gone still where he sat, the burbling water of the fountain loud in Call's ears.

"I thought having a Makar around was supposed to make *us* safer," said the nervous voice. "If we're busy guarding him, who's guarding us?"

Call stood up, struck by the thought that they were about a second away from overhearing one of the mages say something bad about Aaron. Something even worse than just speculating about the Enemy's plans for killing him.

Call wished he could tell Aaron that he was pretty sure the Enemy of Death hadn't tried to steal the Alkahest — whatever that was — and also wasn't currently planning anything worse than revenge on Jasper.

Of course, he had no idea what Master Joseph was up to. So maybe the minions of the Enemy of Death *were* behind the attempted theft, which was less reassuring. Master Joseph had plenty of power on his own. He'd been managing without Constantine Madden for thirteen years, however much he said he needed Call.

"Come on," Tamara said loudly, grabbing Aaron's arm and hauling him to his feet. She must have been thinking along the same lines as Call. "I'm starving. Let's go get something to eat."

"Sure," Aaron said, although Call could tell his heart wasn't in it. Nonetheless, he followed Call and Tamara to the buffet table and watched while Call piled three plates with towers of shrimp and scallops, sausages and cheese.

People kept coming up to Aaron, congratulating him on his control of the chaos elementals, wanting to invite him to things or tell him a story about their involvement in the last war. Aaron was polite, nodding along with even the dullest anecdotes.

Call made Tamara a cheese plate, mostly because he was sure that Evil Overlords didn't make other people cheese plates. Evil Overlords didn't care if their friends were hungry.

Tamara took the cheese plate, shrugged, and ate a dried apricot off it. "This is so boring," she whispered. "I can't believe Aaron isn't dead from boredom."

"We have to do something," Call said, throwing a breaded shrimp up into the air and catching it in his mouth. "People like Aaron act all nice until suddenly they explode and banish some annoying geezer into the void."

"That's not true," Tamara said, rolling her eyes. "You might do that, but Aaron wouldn't."

"Oh, yeah?" Call raised his eyebrows. "Take a good look at his face and say that again."

Tamara studied Aaron for a long moment. Aaron was trapped in conversation with a skinny old mage in a pink suit, and his eyes looked glazed. "Fine. I know where we can go." She dumped the plate Call had made her and grabbed hold of Aaron's sleeve. He turned toward her in surprise and then shrugged helplessly at the adult talking to him as she dragged him away from the conversation and toward the house.

Call abandoned his half-finished food on a stone banister and hurried after them. Tamara gave him a brilliant, crazy grin as they pulled Aaron inside, Havoc trotting behind.

"Where are we going?" Aaron said.

"Come on." Tamara led them through the house until they reached a library lined with richly bound books. Mullioned windows set with colored glass let in sparkling beams of light, and deep-red rugs covered the floor. Tamara crossed the room toward a massive fireplace. A stone urn stood at each side, carved out of multicolored agate. Each one had a word inscribed on it.

Tamara took hold of the first one and twisted it around so that the word faced them. *Prima*. She moved to the second urn and twisted it until the second word faced them as well. *Materia*.

Prima materia, Call knew, was an alchemical term. It meant the very first substance of the world, the substance that everything that wasn't chaos — earth, air, fire, water, metal, and souls — came from.

A sharp click sounded, and a section of the wall swung open onto a well-lit stone hallway.

"Whoa," Call said.

He wasn't sure where he'd been expecting Tamara to take them — to her room, maybe, or to a quiet corner of the house. He hadn't expected a secret door.

"When were you going to tell me about this?" Aaron said, turning to Tamara. "I've been living here for a month!"

Tamara looked delighted at having kept a secret from him. "I'm not supposed to show anyone. You're lucky to be seeing it now, *Makar*."

Aaron stuck his tongue out at her.

Tamara laughed and ducked into the hallway, reaching up to pull a torch down from the wall. It glowed a bright gold green and gave off a faint smell of sulfur. She set off down the corridor, pausing when she realized the boys weren't right on her heels. She snapped her fingers, her curls swinging. "Come on," she said. "Move it, slowpokes."

They looked at each other, shrugged, and headed after her.

As they walked, Havoc huffing along after them, Call realized why the hallways were so narrow — they ran through the whole house like veins beside bone, so anyone in any of the public rooms could be spied upon. And at regular intervals there were small hatches that opened into what looked like air ducts, covered by ornate ironwork registers.

Call opened one and peered down into the kitchen, where the staff were making up fresh pitchers of rosewater lemonade and placing tiny squares of tuna onto individual leaves that rested on large glass platters. He opened another and saw Alex and Tamara's sister cuddling on a sofette beside two brass statues of greyhounds. As he watched, Alex leaned in and kissed Kimiya.

"What are you doing?" Tamara called back, under her breath.

"Nothing!" Call slid the hatch closed. He went a little farther without succumbing to temptation but paused when he heard Tamara's parents. As he paused, he heard Mrs. Rajavi say something about the guests at the party. Call knew he should follow Tamara, but he itched to eavesdrop.

Aaron stopped and turned to look at Call. Call made a beckoning gesture and Aaron and Tamara joined him at the hatch. Aaron slid it open quietly with nimble fingers and they all peered down.

"We probably shouldn't . . . ," Tamara began, but curiosity seemed to overcome her objections partway through her sentence. Call wondered how often she did this by herself and what secrets she'd learned that way.

Tamara's mother and father were standing in their study, a mahogany table between them. On it was a chess set, though Call didn't see the usual knights, rooks, and pawns; instead there were shapes he didn't recognize.

"— Anastasia, of course," Mr. Rajavi finished. They'd come in in the middle of his sentence.

Mrs. Rajavi nodded. "Of course." She picked up an empty glass sitting on a silver tray, and, as they watched, it filled itself with some pale liquid. "I just wish there was a way not to invite the deWinters to these things. That family believes that if they pretend long enough it's still the glory days of magical enterprise, maybe no one will notice how threadbare their clothing or their conversation has become. Thank goodness Tamara cooled on their son once school began."

Mr. Rajavi snorted. "The deWinters still have friends on the Assembly. It wouldn't do to put them off entirely."

Aaron looked disappointed that they were just gossiping, but Call was delighted. Tamara's parents were awesome, he decided. Anyone who wanted to keep Jasper out of a party was A-OK by him.

Mrs. Rajavi made a face. "They're clearly trying to throw their youngest son into the path of the Makar. Probably hoping that if they become friends, some of the glory will rub off on him, and their family by extension."

"From what Tamara has said, Jasper has failed to endear himself to Aaron," said Mr. Rajavi drily. "I don't think you have anything to worry about, dear. Tamara is the one in Aaron's apprentice group, not Jasper."

"And Callum Hunt, of course." Tamara's mother took a sip from her glass. "What do you think of him?"

"He resembles his father." Mr. Rajavi frowned. "Unfortunate about Alastair Hunt. He was a promising metal mage when he studied under Master Rufus."

Call froze. Aaron and Tamara were both looking at him with apprehensive expressions as Mr. Rajavi went on.

"He was driven mad by the death of his wife in the Cold Massacre, they say. Putters about not using magic, wasting his life. Still, there's no reason not to extend a welcome to his son. Master Rufus must have seen something in him if he chose him as an apprentice."

Call felt Tamara's hand on his arm, pulling him away from the hatch. Aaron closed it behind them and they moved on down the hall, Call with his fingers tangled in Havoc's ruff for reassurance. His stomach felt a little hollow, and he was relieved when they came to a narrow door, which opened silently into what looked like another study.

The gold-green light of the torch showed big comfortable couches in the center of the room, a coffee table, and a desk. Along one wall was a bookshelf, but the tomes here weren't the beautifully bound and curated volumes Call had seen in the library. These looked older, dustier and more worn. A few spines were ripped. Some were just manuscripts, tied with stained string.

"What's this place for?" Call asked as Havoc jumped up on one of the couches, circling a few times before dropping into a napping position.

"Secret meetings," Tamara said, her eyes sparkling. "My parents don't think I know about it, but I do. There are books about dangerous magical techniques in here, and all sorts of records dating back years. There used to be a time when mages were allowed to make money off magic, when they had huge businesses. Then they passed the Enterprise Laws. You weren't allowed to use your magic to make money in the normal world anymore. Some families lost everything."

Call wondered if that was what had happened to Jasper's family. He wondered if the Hunt family had made money like that, too — or if his mother's family had. He realized he knew almost nothing about them.

"So how *do* mages make money?" Aaron asked, looking around the room, clearly thinking about the massive estate they were in and the party they'd just attended.

"They can either work for the Assembly or they can get a regular job," Tamara said. "But if you had money from before, you could invest it."

Call wondered how Constantine Madden had made his money but then figured he probably hadn't thought the Enterprise Laws applied to him once he went to war against the other mages. Which brought Call right back around to the reason he'd come to Tamara's in the first place: "Do you think any of the people at the party are headed back to the Magisterium?" Call asked. "Maybe I could get a ride with one of them?"

"A ride? To the Magisterium? But no one's even there," Aaron said.

"Someone's got to be there," said Call. "And I've got to stay somewhere. I can't go home."

"Don't be ridiculous," Tamara said. "You can stay here until school starts. We can swim in the pool and practice magic. I already worked it out with my parents. We set up a spare room for you and everything."

Call reached over to pat Havoc's head. The wolf didn't open his eyes. "You don't think your parents mind?"

They'd all heard her parents talking about him, after all.

Tamara shook her head. "They're happy to have you," she said in a voice that made it clear they welcomed Call for good reasons and less good reasons.

But it was somewhere to stay. And they hadn't said anything bad about him, not really. They'd said Master Rufus must have chosen him for a reason.

"You could call Alastair," Aaron said. "So he won't worry. I mean, even if he doesn't want you to go back to the Magisterium, he's got to want to know you're safe."

"Yeah," Call said, thinking of his father slumped against the wall of the storage room, wondering how dedicated he was to chasing after Call and killing him. "Maybe tomorrow. After we find out more dirt on Jasper. And eat all the food at the buffet. And swim in the pool."

"And we can get some magic practice in," said Aaron with a grin. "Master Rufus won't know what hit him. We'll be through the Second Gate before everyone else."

"As long as it's before Jasper," said Call. Tamara laughed.

Havoc rolled onto his back, snoring gently.

CHAPTER FIVE

SPENDING TIME AT the Gables gave Call a new appreciation for what it was like to be rich.

A bell woke him in the morning for breakfast, which was eaten in a big sunny room overlooking the garden. Though Tamara's parents ate simple breakfasts of bread and yogurt, that didn't stop them from putting on an impressive spread for their guests. There was fresh-squeezed juice on the table and hot food like eggs and toast, instead of dry cereal and milk. There was butter in creamy little pats, instead of a crumb-encrusted brick that got brought out meal after meal. Havoc had his own bowls, with chopped meat in them, although he wasn't allowed to sleep in the house. He slept in the stables, on fresh hay, and made the horses nervous.

Call had a hard time believing he was staying at a place where there was a stable with horses out back.

There were clothes, too — bought in Call's size from a

department store, and ironed before being hung in the wardrobe in Call's room. White shirts. Jeans. Swim trunks.

Tamara must have grown up like this. She talked to the butler and the housekeeper with an easy familiarity. She called for iced tea by the pool and dropped towels on the grass and left them, certain someone would come and pick them up.

Tamara's parents had even been willing to tell Alastair that Call was on a trip with them and they'd bring him directly to the Magisterium once they got back. Mrs. Rajavi reported that Alastair had sounded perfectly pleasant on the phone and wanted Call to have a good time. Call didn't actually think that Alastair had been happy to get the call, but the Rajavis were powerful enough that he didn't think Alastair would come after him so long as he was in their care. And once he was at the Magisterium, he'd definitely be safe.

He wasn't sure what he'd do at the end of the school year, but that was far enough in the future that he didn't need to worry about it.

Despite Call's uneasiness about his father, he let the days slip by in long sunshine-filled hours of swimming and lying on the grass and eating ice cream. He'd been self-conscious the first time he'd come out to the seashell-shaped pool in his trunks, realizing Aaron and Tamara had never seen his bare legs before. His left was thinner than his other leg, and covered in scars that had faded over the years from angry red to light pink. They weren't so bad, he'd thought anxiously, sitting and looking at them in his room. Still, they weren't anything he liked to show people.

Neither of them had seemed to notice, though. They'd just laughed and splashed him and pretty soon Call was sitting out on the lawn with them and Alex and Kimiya, soaking up the sun and drinking iced mint tea with sugar. He was actually sort of getting a tan, which hardly ever happened. Not that that was unexpected, considering that he went to school underground.

Sometimes Aaron would play tennis with Alex, whenever Alex could be pried away from Kimiya's face. Magical tennis seemed a lot like regular tennis to Call, except that every time the ball went wide, Alex summoned it back with a snap of his fingers.

Though they'd promised to practice magic, they didn't get a lot of practicing in. Once or twice they went out beside the house and called up fire, shaping it into burning orbs that could be safely handled, or used earth magic to pull iron filaments up out of the dirt. Once, they practiced heaving big stones out of the ground, but when one flew perilously close to Aaron's head, Mrs. Rajavi came out and scolded them for endangering the Makar. Tamara just rolled her eyes.

One afternoon — late, when the hazy air was full of droning bees — Call was walking from the breakfast room toward the staircase and overheard Mr. Rajavi speaking in one of the parlors. His voice was low, but as Call crept forward, he heard him cut off by an exclamation from Alex. Alex wasn't yelling, but the rage in his voice carried. "What exactly are you trying to say, sir?"

Call edged closer, not sure what kind of conversation he was eavesdropping on. He told himself that he was doing it in case it turned out they were talking about Aaron, but in fact, he was more worried they'd discovered something about *him*.

Could Alastair have said something else to Mrs. Rajavi on the phone, something she hadn't told Call? The magical world already thought Alastair was nuts, but whatever he said about Call would have the advantage of being true.

"We've enjoyed having you as our guest," Mrs. Rajavi was saying. "But Kimiya is still young and we think you're both moving too fast."

"We're just asking you to take a break for the school year," Mr. Rajavi said.

Call let out a breath. They weren't talking about Aaron or Call or anything important. Just dating.

"And this doesn't have anything to do with the fact that my stepmother opposed your last Assembly proposal, right?" Alex sounded furious. Call decided that maybe it was important after all.

"Watch yourself," Mr. Rajavi said. "Remember what I told you about respect?"

"What about respecting what your daughter wants?" Alex asked, his voice rising. "Kimiya? Tell him!"

"I can't believe this is happening," Kimiya said. "I just want everyone to stop yelling at one another." After many years of arguing with his own father, culminating in the terrible argument that he couldn't even think about without feeling sick to his stomach, Call knew this wasn't going anywhere good. Taking a deep breath, he pushed open the door to the room and looked at the four of them with the most confused expression he could muster.

"Oh, hey," Call said. "I'm sorry. This house is so big that I keep getting turned around."

"Callum," Mrs. Rajavi said, forcing a smile.

Kimiya looked ready to cry. Alex looked ready to hit someone; Call recognized the expression.

"Oh, hey, Alex," Call said, trying to think of a good reason to drag him out of there before he did something he regretted. "Can you come with me for a second? Aaron wanted to, uh, ask you something."

Alex turned that furious expression on Call, and for a moment Call wasn't sure he'd made the right decision. But then Alex nodded and said, "Sure."

"I'm glad we had this talk," Mr. Rajavi told him.

"Me, too," Alex said between gritted teeth. Then he walked out, forcing Call to scramble to catch up.

Alex stalked out onto the lawn, heading toward the stone fountain. When he got to it, he kicked it hard and yelled something Alastair had forbidden Call to ever utter.

"I'm sorry," Call said. In the distance, he could see Aaron and Tamara throwing sticks to Havoc on one of the far lawns. Fortunately, they were out of earshot.

"Aaron doesn't really want to see me, does he?" said Alex.

"Nope," said Call. "Sorry again."

"So why'd you pull me out of there?" Alex didn't look angry now, just curious.

"Nothing good was going to happen," Call said firmly. "That wasn't the kind of fight that anybody wins."

"Maybe," Alex said slowly. "They just — they make me so angry. They're all about putting on a show. Like they're perfect and everyone else is less."

Call frowned. "What do you mean?"

Alex cut a glance toward Aaron and lowered his voice even further. "Nothing. I don't mean anything at all."

Alex clearly thought that Call couldn't understand. It would be useless to explain that it might seem like Tamara's parents liked him, but they wouldn't if they knew the truth. They might not even like Aaron if he wasn't the Makar. But

Alex would never believe that a little kid like Call had big enough secrets to matter to anyone, even if he did.

↑ ≈ △ ○ ◎

It was only a few days later that Call had to pack up his new clothes and get ready to head back to school. He stuffed himself with sausages and eggs at breakfast, knowing it was going to be a while before he saw non-lichen-based food again. Aaron and Tamara were already wearing their green second-year Magisterium uniforms, while Alex and Kimiya were in fourth-year white and glowering at each other.

Call sat there in his jeans and T-shirt, feeling very out of place.

Alex gave Call a pointed look, as if to say, *You'll never be good enough for them either.*

Mr. Rajavi looked at his watch. "Time to go," he said. "Call?"

"Yeah?" Call turned toward Tamara's father.

"Take care of yourself." There was something in his voice that made Call unsure if the words were kindly meant, but maybe he was just letting Alex get to him.

Everyone headed for the foyer, where Stebbins, his bald head gleaming, was assembling their bags. Aaron and Call both had new duffels, while Tamara and Kimiya had matching sets of snakeskin luggage. Alex had a suitcase with his initials, ATS, on it. He picked it up and headed for the door.

Once outside, Alex started down the driveway. Call realized with a jolt that a white Mercedes was waiting at the end of the drive, its motor running. Alex's stepmother had come.

Kimiya gave a little gasp. Stebbins looked wistful.

"Nice car," Call said.

"Shut up," Tamara muttered. "Just because you're obsessed with *cars*." She gave Stebbins an odd warning look, which Call didn't have a chance to parse. Too many other things were happening at once.

Kimiya was chasing after Alex, oblivious to the fact that everyone was now gawking at the two of them. "What's wrong?" she asked when she caught up to him. "I thought you were going to ride with us on the bus!"

He stopped in the middle of the drive and turned on her. "I'm *keeping my distance*, just like your dad wanted. Anastasia is taking me to the Magisterium. Summer's over. We're done."

"Alex, don't be like this," she said, looking stunned by his anger. "We could talk about it —"

"We've talked enough." He sounded as if he were choking on hurt. "You should have stuck up for me. You should have stuck up for *us*," he told her, hoisting his bag up on his shoulder. "But you didn't." He spun away, stalking off down the driveway.

"Alex!" Kimiya shouted. But he didn't respond. He reached the Mercedes and climbed inside. It sped away, sending up a cloud of dust.

"Kimiya!" Tamara started to run toward her sister, but her mother caught her by the wrist.

"Give her a moment," she said. "She probably wants to be left alone."

Mrs. Rajavi's gaze was bright and hard. Call decided he had never been so uncomfortable in his life. He kept remembering Alex saying, "Kimiya, tell them," and Kimiya not saying what he'd obviously wanted her to say. She had to be afraid of her parents. Call wasn't sure he blamed her.

After a few minutes, a yellow school bus pulled through the gates of the Gables. Kimiya came back into the house, wiping her eyes against her sleeve and sniffing brokenly. She grabbed her luggage without looking at anyone.

When her mother reached out to put a hand on her shoulder, Kimiya shrugged it off.

Call knelt down to unzip his bag to make sure he had everything. He zipped it back up, but not before Mrs. Rajavi had caught sight of his knife, glinting atop his clothes.

"Is that Semiramis?" she asked.

Call nodded, zipping the bag up hastily. "It was my mother's."

"I know. I remember when she made it. She was a very skilled metal mage." Tamara's mother cocked her head to the side. "Semiramis is named for an Assyrian queen who turned into a dove when she died. Callum means *dove*, too. Doves stand for peace, which is what your mother wanted more than anything else."

"I guess she must have," Call said, feeling even more uncomfortable that her scrutiny had turned to him, and also a little sad that this woman had known more about his mother than he did.

Mrs. Rajavi smiled down at him, brushing a lock of his ink-black hair out of his eyes. "She must have loved you very much. And you must miss her."

Call bit the inside of his cheek, remembering the words his mother had carved in the ice of the cave where she died.

She must have spent a long time picking out the name Callum. She'd probably made a list, argued back and forth over a half dozen favorites with Alastair before settling on

Callum. Callum, which stood for doves and peace and the end of the war. And then Constantine Madden had killed her child and stolen that small body for himself. Call was the opposite of everything she'd ever hoped for.

Call realized he was biting down so hard that the inside of his mouth was bleeding.

"Thank you, Mrs. Rajavi," he forced himself to say. Then, barely even seeing where he was going, he boarded the bus. Havoc followed, flopping down in the aisle so everyone else had to step over him.

There were a few kids already seated. Aaron was up near the front. He shoved over, leaving room for Call to flop down next to him and watch as Mr. and Mrs. Rajavi kissed Tamara good-bye.

Call thought about Tamara's stories about her parents and about the third sister who'd become one of the Devoured. He remembered how stern and cold they'd seemed at the Trial. Were they pretending to be the perfect family for Aaron's benefit, trying to act like the fantasy parents he'd never had?

Whatever impression they were trying to make, Call wasn't sure they succeeded. Kimiya sat in the back and cried all the way to the Magisterium.

↑ ≈ △ ○ ◎

Call remembered the first time he'd ever arrived at the Magisterium and how alien and strange the caves had seemed, glowing with bioluminescent moss, underground rivers lapping at silty shores, and shimmering stalactites hanging from the ceilings like fangs.

Now it seemed like home. A laughing, chattering group of

students poured in through the gates. People ran around hugging one another. Jasper came across the room to hug Tamara, even though, Call thought with annoyance, it had been barely two weeks since he'd seen her. Everyone crowded around Aaron, even the fourth and fifth years with their silver and gold wristbands, clapping him on the back and ruffling his hair.

Call felt a hand on his shoulder. It was Alex, who'd made it to the Magisterium before their slow bus. "Just remember," he said, looking over at Aaron. "No matter how much of a fuss everyone makes over him, you're still his best friend."

"Right," Call said. He wondered if Alex was upset over the breakup, but he didn't look it.

Someone was running toward Call through the crowd. "Call! Call!" It was Celia, her mass of dirty-blond hair tamed into a ponytail. She looked delighted to see him, beaming all over her face. Alex moved away with an amused smile.

"Did you have a good summer?" Celia asked. "I heard you were at Tamara's. Was it awesome? Were you there for the party? I heard the party was great. Did you see the mage tricks? Were there really frozen manticores?"

"They were ice manticores . . . not, like, actual manticores that had been frozen." Call felt dizzy trying to keep up. "I mean, I think. Are manticores real?"

"That sounds so cool. Jasper told me all about it."

"Jasper's a —" Call looked at Celia's beaming face and decided not to pursue the topic of Jasper. Celia liked everyone; she couldn't seem to help it. "Yeah. So how come you weren't there?"

"Oh." Celia blushed and ducked her head. "It's nothing. My parents don't really get along with Tamara's. But I like Tamara," she added hurriedly.

"It would be okay if you didn't," he said.

She looked confused, and Call wanted to kick himself. What did he know about what was okay and what wasn't? He was the person who kept a mental list of potentially evil behaviors. Was it okay if she didn't like Tamara? Wasn't Tamara his best friend, along with Aaron?

Havoc suddenly barked and put his paws up on Celia's shirt, cutting off the discussion. Celia giggled.

"Callum Hunt!" It was Master Rufus, striding toward them through the crowd. "Keep your chaos wolf silent, please." He gave Havoc a beady eye and Havoc slid to the ground, looking chastened. "Tamara, Aaron, Call, come with me to your rooms."

Aaron grinned at Call as they slung their duffels over their shoulders and followed behind Master Rufus through the tunnels. They knew their way, and Call found that he was no longer unnerved by the dripping stalactites and the quiet cool of the caves.

Tamara paused to look into a pool where pale fish darted back and forth. Call thought he saw a crystalline shape scamper over the wall behind her. Was it Warren? Or some other elemental? He frowned, remembering the little lizard.

Finally, they were in front of their old rooms. Master Rufus stepped back to allow Tamara to wave her new copper wristband in front of the door. It unlocked instantly, allowing them into the chambers.

The rooms were just as they'd been when they arrived for their Iron Year. The same chandelier carved with designs of flame, the same half circle of desks, the same duo of plush sofas facing each other, and the same massive fireplace. Symbols picked out in mica and quartz shimmered when the light hit them, and three doors adorned with each of their names led to their bedrooms.

Call let out a long sigh and dropped onto one of the couches.

"There will be dinner in the Refectory in a half hour. Then you'll put away your things and go to bed early. The first years arrived yesterday. Tomorrow, lessons begin in earnest," said Master Rufus, with a long look at each one of them. "Some say that the Copper Year of apprenticeship is the most grueling. Do you know why?"

The three of them glanced at one another. Call had no idea what answer Master Rufus was looking for.

Master Rufus nodded at their silence, clearly pleased. "Because now that you know the basics, we'll be going out on missions. Classes here will be confined to keeping up with your maths and sciences as well as a few new tricks, but the real learning will be out in the field. We'll begin this week with some experiments."

Call had no idea what to make of their new curriculum, but the fact that Master Rufus was delighted about it could only be a bad sign. Going out of the stuffy, damp Magisterium classrooms sounded like fun, but Call had been wrong before. During one of their "outside exercises" he'd nearly drowned under a pile of logs, and Jasper of all people had pulled him out.

"Get settled in," said Master Rufus with his usual regal nod, and swept out of their chambers.

Tamara dragged her suitcase toward her room. "Call, you'd better put on your uniform before dinner — they should have left one for you in your room, like last year. You can't show up to the Refectory in jeans and a T-shirt that says DOCTOR MON-KEY KNOWS WHAT YOU DID."

"What does that mean, anyway?" Aaron asked.

Call shrugged. "I don't know. I got it at the Salvation Army store." He stretched. "Maybe I'll take a nap."

"I'm not tired. I'm going to the library," Aaron said, abandoning his bag and starting for the door.

"You want to find out about the Alkahest," Call guessed. It was clearly some kind of weapon, but none of them had been able to piece together exactly what it was or what it did. No one seemed to want to answer any questions about it in anything but the vaguest possible terms. And the library at the Rajavis' house hadn't held any answers either.

Call hated to admit it, but he'd been relieved. The more they talked about the Alkahest and the Enemy and his possible plans, the more Call felt like he was going to get caught.

"I need to be able to protect people," Aaron said. "And I can't do that if I don't even understand the threat."

Call sighed. "Can't we look up stuff after we unpack?"

"You don't have to come," Aaron said. "I'm not going to be in any danger on my way to the library."

"Don't be stupid," Tamara said. "Of course we're coming. Call has just got to put on his uniform."

"Yeah," he said with obviously forced enthusiasm, heading for his room and throwing his duffel on the bed.

He had a little trouble getting his feet into the big boots they all wore around the Magisterium to protect them from rocks and water — and on occasion, lava — but he figured he'd get used to them again. When he headed back to the common room, Aaron and Tamara were perched on the back of the sofa, sharing a bag of Ruffles. Tamara held it out to him.

Call grabbed the bag, shoving a fistful of chips into his face, and started toward the door. They followed, and Havoc ran after them, barking. By the time they spilled out into the hallway, Havoc was in the lead. "Library!" Call told him. "Library, Havoc!"

On the way, Call vowed to be helpful. After all, what made Evil Overlords bad was how they acted, not their secret thoughts. There was no such thing as a helpful Evil Overlord.

It was a huge relief to be able to walk around the corridors of the Magisterium openly with Havoc, instead of hiding him in the bedroom. The other students cast them glances that were a mixture of respect, fear, and admiration when they saw the Chaos-ridden wolf loping ahead of them.

Of course they were impressed by Aaron, too, the black gem stark in his wristband. But Havoc belonged to Call.

Not that that was what anyone thought. *Aaron's wolf,* he heard the students whisper to one another as they passed. *Look at the size of that thing. He must be pretty powerful to control it.*

"You forgot your wristband," Aaron said with a sideways grin, dropping Call's new copper wristband into his hand. "Again. Don't make me always have to remind you."

Call rolled his eyes, sliding the wristband on. It felt good on his wrist. Familiar.

They reached the library, which was shaped like the inside of a conch shell: a spiral room that narrowed as it went down until it reached a flat lower level where long tables had been set up. Since classes hadn't started yet, the place was empty.

"Where do we start?" Call wondered aloud, looking around the vast expanse of books that stretched down and away.

"Well, I'm no library expert, but *A* for *Alkahest* seems like a safe bet," said Tamara, skipping ahead. She was obviously thrilled to be back.

As it turned out, the library was divided into sections and subsections. They eventually turned up a book entitled *Alkahests and Other Indices of Magick* on a top shelf that required Aaron to stand on a chair to reach it.

They brought the book over to one of the long tables, and Aaron carefully cracked it open. The spine shed dust.

Call tried to read over Aaron's shoulder, catching every few words. An alkahest, the book said, was a universal solvent, a substance that dissolved all things, from gold to diamonds to chaos magic. As Call frowned, not sure what that had to do with what they'd overheard, Aaron flipped the page and they saw a drawing of the Alkahest, which wasn't a substance at all, but an enormous glove — a gauntlet, really — made from copper.

Forged from a combination of all the elemental forces, the gauntlet was a weapon created for one purpose — to push the ability to control chaos out of a Makar. Instead of controlling the void, the Makar would be destroyed by it. The gauntlet could be wielded by any mage, but it required the living heart of a chaos creature to give it power.

Call sucked in a long breath. He'd seen the exact same gauntlet in the drawing in his father's creepy basement ritual room. The Alkahest had been the reason Alastair had wanted to cut out Havoc's heart.

Alastair must have tried to steal the gauntlet from the Collegium.

Call's head swam. He gripped the edge of the table to keep himself upright. Aaron flipped the page.

There was a black-and-white photograph of the gauntlet in a glass case, probably in its resting place in the Collegium. A brief history was recorded in a sidebar beside the picture. It had been created by a group of researchers who'd called themselves the Order of Disorder. Master Joseph and Constantine Madden had once been part of their number, hoping to plumb the depths of chaos magic and to find a way to allow more mages to access the void. When Constantine Madden broke away and became the Enemy of Death, the Order had hoped their Alkahest could stop him.

Apparently, the Alkahest had fallen into the Enemy's hands near the end of the war, allowing the Enemy's minions to kill Verity Torres on the battlefield while Constantine Madden led more of his forces to the mountain in La Rinconada for the Cold Massacre.

The book said that the Order of Disorder still existed, researching Chaos-ridden animals, though no one was sure who their leaders were now.

"The mages will figure out who tried to take it," Tamara said. "And it's in a safer place now."

"If one of Constantine Madden's people get ahold of it, the next time I see the gauntlet, it'll be pointed at me." Aaron exhaled a long, worried breath. "Let's see if this book says anything about destroying the Alkahest."

Call wanted to say something, to reassure Aaron that it wasn't the minions of the Enemy who were after the gauntlet; it was just Call's dad.

But before he could decide to do it, Master Rufus made his way down the nautilus stairs of the library. All three of his apprentices turned to look guiltily in his direction, even though there was nothing for them to look guilty about. They were in a *library, researching.* Rufus ought to have been thrilled.

He didn't look thrilled. He looked worried. Peering over Tamara's shoulder, he frowned and said, "Aaron, the Alkahest is locked up. The Assembly had it moved to a vault designed by metal mages during the last war. It's underground, beneath a place you've been before, and completely secure."

"I just wanted to know more about it," Aaron said.

"I see." Master Rufus folded his arms over his chest. "Well, I am not here to interrupt your studies. I am here to speak with Callum."

"Me?" Call asked.

"You." Master Rufus took a few steps away from the others and Call followed him reluctantly.

"Havoc, stay," Call muttered. He wasn't sure what the mage was going to tell him, but he could tell it wasn't going to be good.

"Your father is here to see you," the Master announced.

"What?" Call shouldn't have been stunned, but he was. "I thought parents weren't allowed to come to the Magisterium."

"They're not." Master Rufus peered down at Call, as though he was trying to discern the answer to some question. "But the Magisterium is not in the habit of kidnapping students, either. I assumed you arrived here in the standard manner; Alastair informed us that he didn't speak with you before you left your home. He said you ran away."

"He doesn't want me to be here," said Call. "He wants me to stay away from the Magisterium."

"As you know," said Rufus gently, "such a thing is not possible for a mage who has passed the First Gate. You must complete your training."

"I want to," said Call. "I don't want to go back with him. I don't have to, do I?"

"No," said Master Rufus, but the way he said the word, the answer didn't seem quite as definite. "But as I said, it's not our intention to steal children away from their parents. I thought he'd gotten more used to the idea of you being my apprentice."

"Not really," Call said.

"I'll go with you, if you like," said Master Rufus. "When you talk to him."

"I don't want to talk to him," Call blurted out. Part of him wanted desperately to see his father — wanted to make sure he was okay after the horror of seeing him slam against a wall. But he knew he couldn't. It would be impossible for them to have a conversation that didn't involve the words *Constantine* or *murder me* or *Alkahest*. There were just too many secrets that people might overhear.

"I want you to tell him to leave," Call told his teacher.

Master Rufus looked for a long time at Call. Then he sighed. "All right," he said. "I'll do as you ask."

"You don't look like you want to," Call said.

"Alastair was my student once," said Rufus. "I hold him in regard still. I had hoped that your attendance here would begin to soften his hatred for mages and the Magisterium."

Call couldn't think of anything to say to that. Not without telling Master Rufus things he couldn't possibly tell him. He just shook his head. "Please make him go away," he whispered.

Master Rufus nodded and turned to leave the library. Call glanced back over at Aaron and Tamara. They were both leaning on the table, their faces tinted green by the lamps. They were staring at him worriedly. He thought about going back over to them, but he didn't feel like facing their questions. Instead, he turned and raced out of the library as fast as his leg would let him.

CHAPTER SIX

CALL WANDERED THROUGH the halls of the Magisterium, heading down toward the cool lakes and rivers that ran through the caves. Eventually, he stopped by the side of one, took off his boots, and stuck his feet into the silty water.

He wondered again about whether he was a good person. He'd always figured he was okay, like most people. Not terrible, but not great, either. Normal.

Definitely not a murderer.

But Constantine Madden was a murderer. He was an evil madman who'd created monsters and tried to cheat death. And Call was Constantine. So didn't that mean he was responsible for everything Constantine had ever done, even if he didn't remember it?

And now Call was letting Aaron worry and plan to face a threat that didn't even exist, because he was selfish.

Call kicked the water, sending droplets flying against the

wall and scattering the pale, eyeless fish that had gathered around his toes.

Just then, a lizard dropped down from the ceiling onto the stone beside Call.

"Augh!" Call yelled, jumping to his feet. "What are you doing here?"

"Live here," said Warren, tongue flicking out to lick an eyeball. "Watch you."

Because that wasn't creepy at all.

Call sighed. The last time he'd seen the lizard, Warren had led Call, Tamara, and Aaron into the room of one of the Devoured, a mage who'd used so much fire magic that he'd become a fire elemental. The warning of the Devoured rang in Call's ears: *One of you will fail. One of you will die. And one of you is already dead.*

Now Call knew which one of those he was. Callum Hunt was already dead.

"Go away," he warned the lizard. "Go away or I'll drown you in the river."

Warren gave him a goggle-eyed look before scuttling halfway up the wall. "Not the only thing that's watching," he said before disappearing into the darkness.

With a sigh, Call picked up his boots and padded barefoot back to his chambers. There, he flung himself down on one of the couches and stared into the fireplace, concentrating on not thinking about anything awful, until Tamara and Aaron returned, Havoc trotting after them. Aaron was carrying a big plate of lichen.

Despite himself, Call's stomach growled at the fried-chicken smell coming off the mass of green stuff.

"You didn't go to dinner," Tamara said. "Rafe and Kai say hello."

"Is everything okay?" Aaron asked.

"Yup," Call said, taking a big forkful of lichen and adding another lie to his growing Evil Overlord list.

↑ ≈ △ ○ @

Classes started the next morning. For the first time, they had a dedicated classroom. Or class-cave, he guessed. It was a big room with uneven rocky walls, and a circular depression in the center. The circle was a sunken bench, around which they could sit for lessons. There was also a pool for practicing water magic and providing a counterweight for fire. Additionally, there was a pit of churned-up dirt. And — probably just for Aaron — there was a metal plinth on which rested a gleaming black stone, symbol of the void.

Aaron, Tamara, and Call flopped onto the bench while Master Rufus smoothed out a space of wall. As he gestured, sparks flew from his fingers, tracing letters over the stone. "Last year, you walked through the Gate of Control. You mastered your magic. That is the first step toward being a true mage. This year, we will begin to work on your mastery of the elements themselves."

He began to pace. Rufus often paced when he was thinking.

"Some Masters, if they had a chaos mage in their group, would separate out that student from the others. They would teach him or her on their own, believing that a chaos mage might otherwise disrupt the balance of their apprentice group."

"What?" Aaron looked horrified.

"I won't do that," Rufus said, frowning at them. Call wondered what it was like for him, being the Master who'd turned out to have a Makar in his group. Most Masters would kill for the chance, but most Masters weren't Rufus. He'd taught Constantine Madden, and that had gone horribly wrong. Maybe he didn't want to take any more chances. "Aaron will stay with the group. I understand that Call will be your counterweight?"

Aaron looked over at Call as though he was expecting Call to take back the offer.

"Yeah," Call said. "I mean, if he still wants."

That made Aaron give him a lopsided grin. "I want."

"Good." Master Rufus nodded. "So we'll work on counterweight exercises, all of us. Earth, air, water, and fire. Aaron, I want you to be proficient in those before you attempt to use Call as your counterweight."

"Because I could hurt him," Aaron said.

"You could *kill* him," Master Rufus cautioned.

"You won't, though," Tamara told Aaron. Call frowned, wondering how close the two of them had gotten over the summer, and if that was another reason Aaron hadn't mentioned staying at Tamara's house.

Tamara looked over at Call, her expression oddly intense. "I won't let anything bad happen to you."

"I am sure no one thinks you would hurt a friend *on purpose*," Master Rufus said, glancing toward Call. "And we're going to make sure that none of you hurts anyone by *accident*, either."

Call let out a breath. That was exactly what he wanted to learn. How not to hurt anyone, even by accident.

Aaron looked horrified. "Can I just not have a counter-weight, if the counterweight might *die*?"

Master Rufus looked at him with something that might have been pity. "Chaos magic takes a terrible toll on a Makar, and it's not always easy to see when you're using too much of it. You *need* a counterweight for your own safety, but it would be better if you never used one."

Call tried to smile at Aaron encouragingly, but Aaron wasn't looking at him.

Master Rufus went on to outline the rest of the year's studies. They were going to go on missions in the forest surrounding the Magisterium and do small tasks — move the paths of streams, put out fires, make observations of their surroundings, and bring back items for further study. A few of their missions would include other apprentice groups, and, eventually, all of the Copper Year students would be sent together to capture rogue elementals.

Call thought about camping under the stars with Tamara and Aaron and Havoc. It sounded great. They could make s'mores — or at least toast some lichen — and tell ghost stories. Until their Copper Year ran out and summer started again, they could pretend the rest of the world and all its expectations didn't exist.

↑ ≈ △ ○ ◉

That night, Call was on his way to the Mission Gate with Havoc when Celia caught up to him. She had changed out of the uniform they had to wear during school hours and was wearing a fuzzy pink skirt and a pink-and-green-striped blouse.

"Are you headed to the Gallery?" she asked, a little out of breath. "We could go together."

He usually loved the warm pools and fizzy drinks and movies of the Gallery, but he wasn't sure he wanted to be around so many people right then. "I was just taking Havoc for a walk."

"I'll come along." She smiled at him as if she really thought that standing outside in the muggy mosquito-infested dark with him was just as much fun as the Gallery. She bent to pet Havoc's head.

"Uh, okay," Call said, unable to hide his surprise. "Great."

They went outside and watched as Havoc nosed around patches of weeds. Fireflies lit the air like sparks from a fire.

"Gwenda snuck a pet in this year," Celia said abruptly. "Fuzzball. She says that since you guys get to keep a wolf, her ferret should be no big deal. The ferret's not even Chaos-ridden. Jasper's allergic, though, so I don't know if she'll be able to keep her, no matter what she says."

Call grinned. Anything that was bad for Jasper had to be good for the world. "I think I like Fuzzball."

It turned out that Celia was a font of information. She told Call which apprentice had a weird rash, who got cave lice, which Iron Year supposedly wet the bed. Celia knew about Alex and Kimiya breaking up and about Alex sulking. She also claimed that Rafe was a cheater.

"On tests?" Call asked, confused.

"No," Celia said, laughing. "He kissed one girl *on the mouth* after he told another girl that he liked her. It's Susan DeVille, who cheats on tests. She writes the answers on her wrist in invisible ink and then uses magic to turn it purple."

"You know everything," Call said, amazed. He had no idea that apprentices were telling one another that they liked one another. "What about Jasper? Tell me something bad about Jasper."

She gave him a reproachful look. "Jasper's nice. I don't know anything bad about him."

Call sighed in disappointment, just as Havoc trotted back toward them with an enormous leaf-covered branch in his mouth. He dropped it at Call's feet, tail wagging, as though he'd brought over a regular-size stick he hoped Call would throw.

After a moment of awed silence, both Call and Celia began to laugh.

After that, Celia joined him for Havoc's evening walk most nights. Sometimes Tamara and Aaron came, too, but since Tamara took Havoc for morning walks and Aaron got extra Makar work piled on top of his regular studies, mostly they begged off.

One day toward the end of September, someone else joined Call on the path outside school. He thought for a second when he saw a boy loping toward him in jeans and a sweater — the hot weather had cooled off and there was a definite chill in the air — that it was Aaron, but as he got closer, Call realized it was Alex Strike.

He looked disheveled and a little pale, though it could just have been his summer tan fading. Call stood on the path waiting as Alex approached, holding Havoc's leash. Call was definitely puzzled. Since school started, Alex hadn't so much as smiled across the Refectory at him, and if Alex had been doing errands for Master Rufus, Call hadn't seen him. He'd assumed Alex was avoiding them all because of Kimiya, and also because, well, Alex was one of the most popular kids in school and probably didn't have a lot of time for Copper Years.

But now Alex was definitely seeking him out. He raised a hand in greeting as he got close to Call and Havoc. "Hey, Call." He bent down to pet the wolf. "Havoc. Long time no see."

Havoc whined, looking mortally offended.

"I figured you were avoiding us," Call said. "Because of Kimiya."

Alex straightened up. "Do you ever not say what you're thinking?"

"That seems like a trick question somehow," Call mused. Havoc yanked at his leash and Call started along the path, following the wolf. Alex trotted after him.

"It was actually Kimiya I wanted to talk to you about," Alex said. "You know we broke up. . . ."

"Everyone knows," said Call, zipping up his hoodie. It had rained recently and the trees were dripping.

"Did Tamara say anything about Kimiya to you? Whether she's still angry at me?"

Havoc jerked on his leash. Call let him go, and Havoc bounded after something — probably a squirrel. "I don't think Tamara's ever mentioned Kimiya and you to me," he said, puzzled. His first instinct was to tell Alex that there was no point asking him anything, because he knew nothing about girls and less about dating, and Tamara never mentioned her sister's romantic choices. Also, Kimiya was so pretty that she probably had another boyfriend by now.

But his second instinct told him that his first instinct was

Evil Overlordish. Evil Overlords didn't help others with their love lives.

He, Call, could.

"Tamara has kind of a temper," Call said. "I mean, she gets mad easily. But she doesn't stay mad. So if Kimiya is like her, she probably isn't still angry. You could try talking to her."

Alex nodded but didn't look as if Call was saying anything he hadn't thought of.

"Or you could try *not* talking to her," Call said. "When I don't talk to Tamara, she comes and hits me, so that would be a way that Kimiya might come to you first. Plus, once she hits you, it breaks the ice."

"Or my shoulder," said Alex.

"I mean, if it doesn't work, then, like they say, 'If you love someone, set them free. Don't lock them up underground in a cavern.'"

"I don't think that's the saying, Call."

Call looked at Havoc bounding along the ridge. "Just don't show her who you really are," he said. "Pretend you're a person she might love, and then she'll love you. Because people just love who they think other people are, anyway."

Alex whistled. "When did you get so cynical? Do you get it from your dad?"

Call frowned, no longer feeling inclined to be very helpful. "This has nothing to do with my dad. Why bring him up?"

Alex stepped back, raising his hands. "Hey, all I know is what people say. That he was friends with the Enemy of Death once. He was in his mage group. And now he hates magicians and everything having to do with magic."

"So what if he does?" Call snapped.

"Has he ever reached out to anyone?" Alex asked. "Any mages? Anyone he used to be friends with?"

Call shook his head. "I don't think so. He has a different life now."

"It sucks when people are lonely," Alex said. "My step-mother was lonely when my dad died, until she got on the Assembly. Now she's happy running everyone's life."

Call wanted to deny that Alastair wasn't happy with his new non-magical, antique-geek friends. But he remembered the tightness in his father's jaw, how quiet he'd been over the years, the haunted way he looked sometimes, as though his burdens were almost too much to bear.

"Yeah," Call said finally, snapping his fingers. Havoc rushed down the hill toward him, claws scraping on the wet ground. He tried to not think of his dad, alone, at home. Of what his dad had thought when Master Rufus came to tell him that Call didn't want to even see him. "It does."

He thought about it the next day, as he listened to Master Rufus's lecture on advanced elemental usage. Master Rufus paced back and forth in the front of the classroom, explaining how rogue elementals were dangerous and usually had to be put down, but occasionally mages also found them useful to bind into service.

"Flying depletes our magical energies," Master Rufus said. "For example."

Aaron stuck up his hand, a public-school reflex. "But doesn't controlling elementals also use up magical energy?"

Master Rufus nodded. "Interesting question. Yes, it does deplete energy, but not continuously. Once you've bound an elemental, keeping them requires less energy. Almost all mages keep one or two elementals in their service. And schools like the Magisterium have many."

"What?" Call looked around, half expecting some watery wyvern to burst through the rock wall.

Master Rufus raised a brow. "How do you think your uniforms get cleaned? Or your rooms, for that matter?"

Call hadn't much thought about it before, but found himself unnerved. Was some creature like Warren scrubbing his underwear? He was mightily creeped out. But maybe that was species-ist. Maybe he needed to be more open-minded.

He remembered Warren munching down eyeless fish. Maybe not.

Master Rufus went on, warming to his subject. "And of course, the elementals we use in exercises — but also some for defense. Ancient elementals, sleeping deep in the caves, waiting."

"Waiting for what?" Call asked, wide-eyed.

"For the summons to battle."

"You mean if the war starts up again," said Aaron tonelessly, "they'll be sent out to fight the Enemy."

Master Rufus nodded.

"But how do you get them to do what you want?" Call demanded. "Why would they agree to sleep for such a long time and then be woken up just to fight?"

"They are bound to the Magisterium by ancient elemental magic," said Rufus. "The first mages who ever founded the academy captured them, bound their powers, and laid them to rest many miles below the earth. They rise at our bidding and are controlled by us."

"How is that different from the Enemy and his

Chaos-ridden?" Tamara asked. She'd somehow turned one of her braids into a lopsided bun with a pen, which now stuck out of her hair.

"Tamara!" Aaron said. "It's completely different. The Chaos-ridden are evil. Except Havoc," he added hastily.

"So what are these things? Good?" Tamara asked. "If they're good, why keep them locked up underground?"

"They are neither evil nor good," Rufus explained. "They are immensely powerful, like the Greek Titans, and they care nothing about human beings. Where they go, destruction and death follow — not because they wish to kill, but because they don't recognize or care what they do. Blaming a great elemental for destroying a town would be like blaming a volcano for erupting."

"So they have to be controlled for everyone's good," Call said. He could hear the doubt and suspicion in his own voice.

"One of the metal elementals, Automotones, escaped after Verity Torres's battle with the Enemy," said Rufus. "He tore a bridge apart. The cars on it plunged into the water. People drowned before he was returned to his place below the Magisterium."

"He wasn't punished?" Tamara sounded particularly interested in this.

Rufus shrugged. "As I said, it would be like punishing a volcano for erupting. We need these creatures. They are all we have to match the force of Constantine's Chaos-ridden."

"Can we see one?" Call asked.

"What?" Rufus paused, pen in hand.

"I want to see one." Even Call wasn't entirely sure why he was asking. There was something that compelled him about the idea of a creature that was neither evil nor good. That never had to worry about how to behave. A force of nature.

"In a few weeks, you will be starting missions," said Rufus. "You will be on your own outside the Magisterium, traveling, carrying out projects. If you complete those successfully, I see no reason why you couldn't view a sleeping elemental."

There was a knock on the door, and after Rufus said it was okay to enter, it was pushed open. Rafe came inside. He'd looked a lot happier since Master Lemuel had left the Magisterium, but Call wondered if he'd been scared to come back to school after Drew's death. "Master Rockmaple sent you this," he said, holding out a folded-over paper to Master Rufus.

Master Rufus read it, then crumpled it in one hand. It burst into flame, blackening to ash. "Thank you," he said to Rafe with a nod, as though setting correspondence on fire was a perfectly reasonable thing to do. "Tell your Master I will see him at lunch."

Rafe left, wide-eyed.

Call desperately wished he could see whatever was on that paper. The problem with having a horrible secret was that any time anything happened, Call worried it had something to do with him.

But Master Rufus didn't even look in his direction when he resumed the lesson. And when nothing happened the next day or the day after, Call forgot to be worried.

And as the weeks went by and the leaves on the trees began to blaze with yellow and red and orange, like conjured fire, it became easier and easier for Call to forget he had a secret at all.

CHAPTER SEVEN

A S THE WEATHER turned nippy, Call started wearing hoodies and sweaters on his walks with Havoc. Havoc had never really experienced fall and was having a deliriously good time hiding in piles of leaves with only his spotted paws sticking up.

"Does he think we can't see him?" Celia asked curiously one day, after Havoc had leaped down the side of a hill and crashed into a huge leaf pile. Just his tail was visible, sticking out of the end of the pile.

"I can only see his tail," Call said. "He's doing pretty well, really."

Celia giggled. Call had gone from thinking it was weird that Celia laughed at everything he said to thinking it was kind of awesome. She was wearing a red fuzzy sweater and looked pink-cheeked and pretty.

"So how did your dad react when you brought Havoc

home?" she asked, gathering up a handful of leaves from the ground: yellow, gold, and russet.

Call chose his words carefully. "Not well," he said. "I mean, we live in a small town. It would be kind of hard to keep any pet a secret, and even though no one knows what Chaos-ridden is, they do know what a big wolf is."

"Yeah." Celia's eyes rounded with sympathy. "He must have been worried someone would hurt Havoc."

Celia was so *nice*, Call thought. It never even occurred to her that Alastair might want to hurt Havoc himself. Which was impressive considering that the only time she'd seen Alastair, at the Iron Trial, he'd been wild-eyed and waving a knife around. Reflexively, Call touched Miri's hilt where it stuck up above the inside pocket of his jacket.

"That was your mom's knife, right?" Celia asked shyly.

"Yeah," Call said. "She made it when she was a mage at school here." He swallowed around the hard lump in his throat. He tried not to think about his mother too much, about whether she would have been kinder to Havoc, whether she would have loved him no matter what fingerprints were on his soul.

"I know she died at the Cold Massacre," Celia said. "I'm so sorry."

Call cleared his throat. "It's all right. It was a long time ago. I never really knew her."

"I never knew my aunt, either," she said. "I was a baby when she was killed at the Cold Massacre. But if I ever got a chance to take revenge, I'd —"

She broke off, looking embarrassed. Havoc had freed himself from the leaves and was trotting up the hill, twigs caught in his fur.

"You'd what?" Call said.

"I'd kill the Enemy of Death myself," she told him with finality. "I hate him so much."

Call felt like he'd been punched in the stomach. Celia was looking down at the leaves in her hands, letting them scatter over the ground like confetti. He could tell that her lips were trembling, that she was a second away from crying. Someone else, a better friend, would have stepped forward to put an arm around her, maybe pat her shoulder. But Call stood paralyzed. How could he offer to comfort Celia over something he'd done himself?

If she found out the truth, she'd hate him.

↑ ≈ △ ○ ◉

That night, Call had a dream. In it, he was skateboarding around his old town with Havoc, who had his own green-and-gold skateboard with spiky wheels. They were both wearing sunglasses, and whenever they passed someone on the street, that person broke into spontaneous applause and threw handfuls of candy to them, as though they were in a Halloween parade.

"Hello, Call," Master Joseph said, appearing suddenly in the middle of the street. Call tried to skate past him when everything went white, as though they were standing on a blank sheet of paper. Havoc was gone.

Master Joseph smiled at Call. He wore long Assembly robes and clasped his hands behind his back.

Call began to back away. "Get out of my dream," he said, looking around wildly for something, anything he could use as a weapon. "Get out of my head!"

"I'm afraid I can't do that," Master Joseph said. There was a dark stain across the front of his robes. It looked like dirty water. Call remembered him cradling the dead body of his son, Drew, how water had gotten all over Master Joseph and how he had cried with ugly sobs.

After, he'd gotten to his feet and called Call "Master." He'd said it was all right that Drew was dead, because Call was Constantine Madden, and if Constantine Madden wanted Drew dead, then he must have a good reason.

"This isn't real," Call insisted, pointing to his leg, which wasn't scarred or thin and didn't hurt at all. "Which means you're not real."

"Oh, but I am," said Master Joseph. He snapped his fingers and snow began to fall, dusting Call's hair and catching in his lashes. "As real as this. As real as the terrible choice Alastair Hunt must make."

"What? What choice?" Call asked, drawn into the argument despite himself.

Master Joseph went on as if Call hadn't spoken. "Why do you remain at the Magisterium, where they will only despise you? You could be with the man who has raised you and with me, your loyal friend. You could be safe. We could begin to rebuild your empire. If you agreed, I could take you tonight."

"No," Call said. "I'll never go with you."

"Oh, you will," Master Joseph told him. "Maybe not yet, but you will. I know you, you see, much better than you know yourself."

Call woke up with the cold sting of snow still on his face and shuddered. He put his hand to his cheek. It came away wet. He tried to tell himself it was just a dream, but dreams didn't melt on your skin.

The next class, Call raised his hand before Master Rufus could start a lecture. Master Rufus's eyebrows rose. Tamara looked surprised, although Aaron was too busy searching for something in his satchel to pay any attention.

"You don't need to do that," Master Rufus said. "There are only three of you here."

"It's a habit," Call said, wiggling his fingers a little, a trick anyone who needed to be called on to get a bathroom pass knew well.

Master Rufus sighed. "All right then, Call. What is it that you need?"

He dropped his hand. "I want to know how to prevent people from finding us."

Master Rufus rubbed a hand over his face, as though a bit flummoxed by this request. "I'm not sure I understand what you mean — or why you need to know that. Is there something you'd like to tell me?"

Tamara looked approvingly at Call. "That's smart. If we knew how to hide better, then Aaron would be safer."

Call might not have been smart enough to think of that, but he was smart enough to keep his mouth shut.

Aaron finally looked up at the mention of his name, blinking a few times as though trying to figure out what they'd been talking about.

"The element of air is what allows us to communicate over great distances," Master Rufus said. "So it is the element of earth that blocks those communications. You can enchant a stone to protect the person who wears it or carries it. Now tell me why we chose to build the school where we did."

"So being under all this rock would make it easy to protect the school from being found?" Aaron asked. "But what about that tornado phone thing you let Call use?"

And what about my dream? Call thought but did not say.

Master Rufus nodded. "Yes, the earth around the Magisterium is enchanted. There are areas of access so we can have some contact with the outside world. Perhaps we should make our Makar a stone specifically enchanted against scrying. Gather around and I will show you how. But Call and Tamara, if I find that you're using this to sneak around or to hide something, you will be in a world of trouble. I will lock you up underground like one of those elementals we discussed."

"What about Aaron? How come he isn't included in that lecture?" Tamara demanded, brows furrowed.

Master Rufus looked in Aaron's direction and then back at Tamara and Call. "Because individually, you and Call might be trouble — but together, the pair of you are even worse."

Aaron snickered. Call tried not to look in Tamara's direction. He was afraid that if he did, he'd discover she was upset that Master Rufus thought she was anything like Call.

↑ ≈ △ ○ ◎

The day that everything started to unravel for Call wasn't all that different from many other days. Call was outside with Master Milagros's group — Jasper, Nigel, Celia, and Gwenda.

They were practicing sending bolts of fire at one another. Call's sleeve was already singed and, with his leg, he was having to do a lot of deflecting to avoid getting burned. Aaron, who Call had suddenly realized was a corrupt and evil-hearted cheater, was jumping out of the way half the time instead of bothering with magic.

Eventually, Call sat down on a log, breathing hard. Jasper looked over at him as though considering whether to set his seat on fire, but seemed to decide against it when Tamara sent a blast of heat in his direction.

"The important thing," Master Rufus said, sitting down beside Call, "is to always control the circumstances. Other people will *react* to them, but if you *control* them, you'll have the upper hand."

That sounded disturbingly like something Alastair had said to him just that past summer. *Our best bet of keeping people from making a fuss is controlling the circumstances under which Havoc is seen.* It was easy to think of Alastair's training at the Magisterium as not affecting him at all, but Master Rufus had been his teacher, too.

"What does that mean?" Call asked.

Master Rufus sighed. "If you can't jump the way the others can, lead them to a terrain where they'll have the same disadvantage. Up a tree. In a stream. Or even better, lead them to a terrain where you'll have the advantage. Create your own advantage."

"There's no terrain where I have the advantage," Call muttered, but he kept thinking about what Master Rufus had said all through the rest of the day, while eating purple tubers in the Refectory, while walking Havoc, and then as he stared up at the uneven rock ceiling of his room that night.

He kept thinking about his father *controlling the circumstances* and seeking a *terrain where he'd have the advantage*. He kept thinking about the chains in his father's house and the drawing of the Alkahest on his father's desk. He kept coming to the same disturbing conclusion.

He'd been pretty sure that his father was the one who'd tried to steal the Alkahest, but that had meant it was his father who *failed*. But what if the failure had been deliberate?

What if Alastair had failed, knowing that the mages would move the Alkahest out of the Collegium to a more secure location? What if he already knew the secure place that they were very likely to use — a terrain where he'd have the advantage?

Back at the house, beside the drawings of the Alkahest, there'd been a map of the layout of the airline hangar where the Trial had been held.

Call hadn't wondered where Alastair had gotten that from, until now. Tamara's parents said that Alastair was a great metal mage and Master Rufus had said that the Alkahest was safe, in a vault created by metal mages, below a place the kids had been before. The airplane hangar was made almost entirely of metal. Maybe Alastair — being a great metal mage — had been one of the people who'd helped build it, one of the people who knew exactly how to get into the hangar and to the vault that might be below it.

If all that was true, then Alastair hadn't failed to steal the Alkahest. If all that was true, the Alkahest was more vulnerable than ever.

Call lay awake for a long time that night, staring into the dark.

Call went through much of the next day in a daze. He couldn't pay attention in class when Master Rufus was trying to teach them how to levitate objects using metal and earth magic, and he dropped a lit candle on Tamara's head. He forgot to walk Havoc, which had unfortunate results for the rug in his bedroom. In the Refectory, he got distracted by the fact that Celia was waving at him — and nearly tripped Aaron.

Aaron stumbled, catching himself on the edge of one of the stone tables bearing enormous cauldrons of soup. "All right," he said firmly, taking Call's plate out of his hands. "That's enough."

Tamara nodded fervently. "Way past enough."

"What?" Call was alarmed; Aaron had become very businesslike, piling food briskly onto Call's plate. Huge mountains of food. "What's going on?"

"You're being all weird," said Tamara, who had piled her plate high as well. "We're going back to the room to talk about it."

"What? I'm not — I don't —" But Call was caught up in his friends' determination like a dust mote in a windstorm. Carrying plates, Tamara and Aaron marched him out of the Refectory, back down the corridors to their room, and pushed him inside still protesting.

They put their plates down on the table and went to grab cutlery. Seconds later they were gathered around the food, forking up lichen pizza and mossy mashed potatoes.

Hesitantly, Call picked up his fork. "What do you mean I'm weird?"

"Distracted," Tamara said. "You keep dropping things and forgetting things. You called Master Rufus Jasper and you called Jasper Celia. And you forgot to walk Havoc."

Havoc barked. Call looked at him darkly.

"Plus you keep staring off into space like someone died," Aaron said, handing Call a fork. "What's going on? And don't say 'Nothing.'"

Call looked at them. His friends. He was so tired of lying. He didn't want to be like Constantine Madden. He wanted to be a good person. The idea of telling them the truth felt awful, but being good wasn't supposed to be fun, right?

"Promise you won't tell anyone?" Call asked them. "You absolutely promise and swear on — on your honor as a mage?"

Call was kind of proud of that one, since he'd just made it up. Both Call and Tamara looked impressed.

"Absolutely," said Tamara.

"Definitely," said Aaron.

"I think it was my dad who tried to steal the Alkahest," Call confessed.

Aaron dropped a plate of lichen onto the table. "*What?*"

Tamara looked absolutely horrified. "Call, don't joke around."

"I'm not," Call said. "I wouldn't. I think he tried to steal it from the Collegium and I think he's going to try to steal it again. This time, he might succeed."

Aaron gaped at him. "Why would your father do that? How do you know?"

Call told them what he'd found in the basement, how Havoc had been chained up, how he'd found the open books with the illustrations of the Alkahest in them. He told them about the map of the airplane hangar, too.

"He was going to cut out Havoc's heart to power the device?" Tamara asked, looking green.

At his name, the wolf looked up at Call and whined. Call nodded.

"But you didn't see it anywhere? The Alkahest itself?" Aaron asked.

Call shook his head. "I didn't know it was a real thing. I didn't know what he was doing or what he wanted Havoc for." He didn't mention the boy-size shackles on the wall. He was prepared to tell some of the truth but not all of it. He wasn't sure where that fell on the Evil Overlord spectrum, but he didn't care.

"Why would your dad want to kill Aaron?" Tamara demanded.

"He wouldn't," Call said quickly. "I am totally, completely sure my dad isn't working for the Enemy of Death."

"But then why would he — ?" Tamara shook her head. "I don't get it. Your dad hates magic. Why would he be trying to power an Alkahest if he wasn't trying to . . ."

Call was starting to panic. Why wouldn't Tamara believe him? Some small part of him knew that missing the piece of the story where Call was the Enemy of Death, it was hard to come up with a reason Alastair might want the Alkahest that *didn't* have to do with Aaron.

"He hates the Magisterium," Call said, balling his hands into fists under the table. "Maybe he just wants to freak out the mages. Scare them."

"Maybe he wants to kill the Enemy," suggested Aaron. "Maybe he's trying to get rid of him so you will be safe."

"The Enemy's been around for dozens of years," said Tamara. "And Alastair just got this idea? And it's a coincidence that the minute a new Makar shows up, he starts working on a Makar-killing device?"

"Maybe he's trying to get rid of *me* so Call will be safe," Aaron said, his green eyes darkening. "I nearly got both of you killed when they kidnapped me, and Call did agree to be my counterweight. That's dangerous."

"Like Call said, Alastair hates mages," said Tamara. "I don't think he cares about the war. If he brings the Magisterium down, then Call won't have to go here anymore, and that's what he wants more than anything." She bit nervously on her thumbnail. "We have to tell someone."

"What?" Call sat bolt upright. "Tamara, I swear, Alastair is not working for the Enemy!"

"So what?" Tamara said, an edge to her voice. "He's trying to steal a dangerous magical device. Even if your dad just wanted to keep it around so he slept better at night, the Alkahest is too valuable and too deadly. What if the Enemy knew he had it? He'd kill your dad and take the Alkahest. Telling the other mages will help protect him."

Call hurled himself to his feet and began to pace back and forth. "No. I'll go to my dad and tell him I know his plan. That way he won't be able to go through with it, and the Alkahest will stay safe."

"That's too risky," Aaron said. "Your dad was going to cut out Havoc's heart. I don't think you should go anywhere near him alone. He threw a knife at you, remember?"

"He was throwing it *to* me," Call said, even though he no longer knew if he believed that.

Tamara let out a long breath. "I know you don't want to get your dad in trouble, but he did this to himself."

"He's my *dad*," said Call. "I should be the one to decide." He looked at Tamara. Her dark eyes were fixed on him. Call took a deep breath and played his last card. "You swore you'd keep my secret. You swore on your honor."

Tamara's voice broke. "Call! What if you're wrong about him wanting to hurt Aaron? What if you're wrong about your father? You might be. We don't always know our family members the way we think we do."

"So you were lying," Call said. "You lied to my face. You don't have any honor."

Aaron got to his feet. "Guys, come on —"

"Look, I'm going to tell Master Rufus," Tamara said. "I know you don't want me to, and I know I said I wouldn't, but I have to."

"You don't have to," Call told her, his voice rising. "And if you cared about other things besides getting ahead in the Magisterium, you wouldn't. You're supposed to be my friend. You're supposed to keep your word."

"Aaron's your friend!" she shouted. "Don't you even care what the Enemy might do to him?"

"If Call says his dad isn't working for the Enemy, I believe him," Aaron said hurriedly. "I'm the one in danger, so it should be my choice —"

Tamara's face was scarlet and there were tears in her eyes. Call realized that no matter what, she would always choose Aaron over him. "You'll just let yourself be put in danger!" she yelled. "It's who you are! And Call knows it." She whirled on Call. "How dare you take advantage of that. I will tell Master

Rufus. I will. And if something happens to Aaron because of the Alkahest, then it's — it's your fault!"

She turned and bolted out of the room. Call realized he was breathing as hard as if he'd been running. And in another second, he *was* running, racing after Tamara.

"Havoc," he yelled. "Come on! Get her! I mean, don't hurt her. Only maim her a little!"

Havoc gave a howl, but Aaron — after giving Call a thoroughly disgusted look — grabbed for his collar. The Makar threw himself on the wolf while Call skidded out into the corridor just in time to see Tamara's braids whipping around the end of the hall. He started after her, but he knew that with his leg, he could never catch up.

Fury bloomed inside his chest as he ran. Tamara was untrustworthy and terrible. He'd expected his friends to be angry, but not to *betray* him. Fiery darts of pain shot up his leg; he slipped and fell to his knees, and for a moment — just a moment — he thought of what exactly he would do if he could have two working legs, if he could leave the pain behind him. What would he do for that? Would he kill for it? Would he stop caring about his Evil Overlord list?

"Call?" There was a hand on his shoulder, and then on his arm, pulling him to his feet. Alex Strike, looking put-together as usual, his uniform pristine, seemed concerned. "What are you doing?"

"Tamara —" Call gasped.

"She went toward Rufus's office," said Alex, pointing at a set of iron-and-copper double doors. "Are you sure you should —"

But Call was already darting around him. He knew exactly

where Rufus's office was. He pounded down the last corridor and threw open the door.

Tamara was standing in the center of the room, on the middle of a circular rug. Rufus was leaning against his desk, backlit by the glow of lamps behind him. He looked very grave.

Call skidded to a halt. He looked back and forth between Tamara and Rufus.

"You can't," he said to Tamara. "You can't tell him."

Tamara straightened her shoulders. "I have to, Call."

"You *promised*," Call said raggedly. He'd half thought that Aaron might have followed him, but Aaron hadn't, and he felt suddenly and horribly alone, facing both Tamara and Rufus as if they were enemies. He felt a flash of rage toward Tamara. He'd never wanted to be angry at her, or hide things from Rufus. He'd never wanted to be in this position. And he'd never wanted to think he couldn't trust Tamara.

"It seems that something serious is happening here," said Rufus.

"Nothing," Call said. "Nothing's wrong."

Rufus looked back and forth, from Call to Tamara. Call knew which one of them would be trusted. He even knew which one of them should be trusted.

"Fine," said Tamara. "I'll just say it. Alastair Hunt is the one who tried to steal the Alkahest, and if we don't stop him, he'll try again."

Master Rufus raised his thin eyebrows. "How do you know that?"

"Because," Tamara said, even as Call fixed her with eyes like daggers, "Call said so."

CHAPTER EIGHT

THE MAGES SENT Tamara back to her room. She
went without looking at Call, her head down, her shoulders hunched. He didn't say anything to her. He had to stay
behind and answer endless questions about what he'd seen
and hadn't seen, about how Alastair had been behaving and
whether he'd ever spoken about Constantine Madden. Call
was asked whether he knew that his father and Constantine had
once been friends, and especially about whether Alastair
had ever spoken about Call's mother, Sarah, in a way that suggested he wanted to bring her back from the dead.

"Is that possible?" Call asked. But nobody would give him
a straight answer.

Call could tell that while Aaron — and even maybe
Tamara — might have believed Alastair wasn't in league with
the Enemy, all the Masters were sure he was a traitor. Or crazy.
Or a crazy traitor.

If Call had wanted to discredit Alastair, to make it impossible for anyone to believe him if he claimed Call had the soul of Constantine Madden, he couldn't have done a better job. That part should have made him happy, but it didn't. Nothing did. He was furious with himself and even more furious with Tamara.

It was late when they finally dismissed him, and Master Rufus led him back to his room.

"I understand now why you did not wish to see your father when he came for you," Master Rufus said.

Call didn't respond. Adults had an amazing knack for stating the obvious, and also for telling you whenever they figured anything out.

"You need to know that you are not in trouble, Callum," said Rufus. "No one would have expected you to break your father's secrecy, but this burden should never have been set on your shoulders."

Call stayed silent. He'd been talking for hours and he had nothing more to say.

"Your father became very eccentric after the war. Maybe none of us was willing to see how extreme his behavior had become. Working with the elements as we do has many dangers. We can bend the world to our desires. But the toll on the mind can be great."

"He's not insane," Call snapped.

Master Rufus paused and peered down at Call for a long moment. "I would be very careful about saying that where someone could overhear you," Master Rufus told him. "Better the world thinks he's mad than believes him to be in league with the Enemy."

"Do you think he's insane?" Call demanded.

"I cannot imagine Alastair in league with Constantine," Rufus answered after a pause. "I taught them both. They were indeed friends. No one was more betrayed by Constantine's eventual descent into evil than Alastair was. No one was more determined to bring Constantine down — even more so after Sarah was killed. There is no greater betrayal than that of a friend."

Call looked at Rufus, feeling dizzy. He thought of Aaron, who had been born to defeat Call. Destined for it, even if he didn't know it.

"Some people are meant to be friends, and some to be enemies," said Rufus. "Eventually the universe rights itself."

"Everything in balance," Call muttered. It was an alchemical saying.

"Exactly." Rufus laid a hand on Call's shoulder, which was surprising enough to make Call jump. "Will you be all right?"

Call nodded and slipped into his rooms. They were empty; both Tamara and Aaron had gone to their bedrooms, the doors shut tightly. He went into his own room and lay down on the bed fully clothed. Havoc was already asleep on the blankets. Call drew Miri from her sheath and held her up where he could see her, could see the whorls and swirls of folded metal in the blade. *Peace.*

He let his hand fall to the side and closed his eyes, too exhausted to even bother to undress.

↑ ≈ △ ○ @

He woke the next day to the wretched screaming of the first bell, which meant he was already late for breakfast. He hadn't eaten much the night before and he felt queasy, as though he'd been punched several times in the stomach instead of just skipped a meal.

He pulled on a fresh uniform and tugged on his boots.

Neither Tamara nor Aaron was waiting for him in the common space of their rooms. Either they'd decided they hated him or they didn't even know he'd returned the night before.

With his Chaos-ridden wolf trailing after him, Call began his stiff-legged walk to the Refectory. It was teeming with apprentices. Gray-clad Iron Year students milled around, still making faces over the fuzziness of the piles of different colored lichen and gaping at large mushroom slices toasting on a grill. A few of the Silver and Gold Year apprentices sat in clumps, back from missions and looking around as contemptuously as if they were already Masters.

Aaron was sitting at a table with some of the other Copper Years. Celia was there, along with Gwenda, Rafe, Laurel, and Jasper. The plates in front of them were clean.

Tamara was at another table with Kimiya and her friends. Call wondered if she was telling them all about Alastair and Call and what a hero she was, but at this point there was nothing Call could do about it. With a sigh, he started to put together a plate of stewed purple tubers that smelled a bit like porridge for himself and some bacony lichen for Havoc. He ate standing up, so he wouldn't have to sit next to anyone. He wasn't sure he'd be welcome anywhere.

When the second alarm sounded, Call headed toward where Master Rufus was sitting with the other Masters.

"Ah," Master Rufus said, summoning Tamara and Aaron toward him with a wave of his hand. "Time to begin our lessons."

"Hurrah," said Call sarcastically. Master Rufus gave him a quelling look and rose to lead them out of the Refectory. Call, Aaron, and Tamara trailed after him like the tail of a reluctant and miserable comet.

"You okay?" Aaron asked, bumping shoulders with Call as Master Rufus led them down a set of stone stairs carved into the rock. The steps wound down and around in a spiral. Little glowing salamanders skittered across the ceiling. Call thought once again of Warren.

"That depends," Call said. "Are you on my side or hers?"

He glanced over at Tamara, whose lips tightened. She looked as if she was thinking about pushing Call down the steps.

Aaron was visibly upset. "Does there have to be sides?"

"When she turns my father in, yeah, there has to be sides!" Call hissed. "Nobody who was really my friend would do that. She promised to keep a secret and she lied. She's a liar."

"And no one who was really Aaron's friend would protect someone who was trying to kill him!" Tamara snapped.

"And again, *liar*, if you were really my friend, you'd believe me when I said that wasn't what Alastair was trying to do!"

A look worse than anger crossed Tamara's face. It was pity. "You're not objective, Call."

Neither are you! Call started to yell, but Master Rufus had whirled around and was looming over all of them menacingly.

"Not one more word about Alastair Hunt out of any of you," he said. "Or you'll be sorting sand instead of having dinner."

Call had spent his first week at the Magisterium sorting

sand and privately thought he'd rather take on a chaos elemental. He shut his mouth, and so did Aaron and Tamara. Tamara looked grim and Aaron looked despondent. He was biting at his fingernails, which was something he did only when he was really upset.

"Now," said Master Rufus, turning around. Call realized that they'd made their way into a large grotto without his even noticing. The walls were covered in springy blue moss the color of the sky. Master Rufus began to pace, his hands behind his back. "We all know that in order to use an element, you require a counterweight, something that keeps you in balance so an element won't take control of you. Right?"

"It keeps you from being Devoured. Like that fire guy," Aaron said, referencing the monstrous, burning being they had met in the deep caverns below the Magisterium.

Master Rufus made a pained face. "Yes, the being that was once Master Marcus. Or, as you put it, 'that fire guy.' But there is more to it, no?"

"It's an opposite," Tamara said, tossing her braids. "So it pulls you in the other direction. Like the counterweight for fire is water."

"And the counterweight for chaos is?" said Rufus, looking hard at Aaron.

"Call," Aaron said. "I mean, *my* counterweight is Call. Not everyone's is Call. But the counterweight for chaos is a person. Just . . . not always Call."

"Eloquent as always," said Rufus. "And is there a problem with a counterweight?"

"It's hard to find one sometimes?" Aaron was clearly guessing, although Call thought he had to be right. Finding fire seemed like it would be hard. Maybe adult mages all carried lighters.

"It limits your power," Tamara said. Master Rufus nodded in her direction, indicating that she'd given the superior answer.

"Limiting your power is part of how it keeps you safe," he said. "Now, what is the *opposite* of a counterweight?"

Tamara answered that, too, showing off. "What we did with the sand last year."

Call wanted to make a face at her, but he was pretty sure he'd get caught. That was the problem with three-person classrooms.

Master Rufus nodded. "Sympathetic acceleration, we call it. Very dangerous because it draws you deeper into the element. It gives you power, but the price can be very high."

Call hoped this wasn't the beginning of a lecture about how he had been a problem back then and was still a problem now.

But Master Rufus moved on. "What I'd like you all to do is to practice using your counterweights. First, gather up something to represent each of the elements. Aaron, this is going to be especially challenging for you, as you have chosen Call for your counterweight."

"Hey!" Call said.

"I meant only that working with a human counterweight is challenging. Now, go, find your counterweights."

Call walked around the edge of the grotto, finding a rock. Air was all around him, so he figured he had that covered. Fire and water were harder, but he used magic to turn some of the water from the silty cave pool into an orb he kept floating near his head. Then he took a vine and resolved to light it on fire with magic when the time came.

He went back to where the others were standing. Of course, they'd completed the exercise before he had.

"Very good," said Master Rufus. "Let's start with air magic. I am going to use air magic to send each one of you up into the air — but keep hold of your counterweight. It's going to be your only contact with earth magic. Come down once you feel you need to use the counterweight."

One by one, they were sent up into the air. Call could feel it whistling around him, the exhilarating lure of flying making him giddy. Flying was his favorite part of magic. In the air, his leg never bothered him. He began to use air magic, forming patterns of color, making clouds and then flying through them. The more magic he expended, the more he understood how someone could be Devoured. It seemed to him that becoming part of the air wouldn't take much. He could relax into it and be blown along like an errant leaf. All his worries and fears would be blown away, too.

All he had to do was drop his bit of rock.

"Call." Master Rufus was looking up at him. "The exercise is over."

Call twisted around to see that Tamara and Aaron were already on the ground. He reached down to his stone and let the weight of its connection to earth fill him, lowering him slowly until he was standing again, his leg aching as always.

Rufus gave Call a measured look. "Well done, everyone," he said. "Now, Aaron, we're going to try an exercise involving chaos. Something small."

Aaron nodded, looking nervous.

"You shouldn't be worried," said Rufus, indicating that they should clear a space in the center of the room. "If I understand correctly, you defeated many Chaos-ridden when you fought Master Joseph last year."

"Yes, but . . ." Aaron bit at a fingernail. "I did it without a counterweight."

"No, you didn't. Call was there."

"It's true," Tamara said. "Call was practically holding you down."

"You may have used his magic instinctively," said Rufus. "The counterweight of chaos is a human being because the counterweight of the void is the soul. When you use chaos magic, you seek a human soul to balance you. Without a counterweight, you can easily use up your own magic and die."

"That sounds . . . bad," Aaron said. He moved into the center of the room, and after a second, Call joined him. They stood awkwardly, shoulder to shoulder. "But I don't want to hurt Call."

"You won't." Master Rufus strode to the corner of the grotto and returned carrying a cage. In the cage was an elemental — a lizard with curved spines running along its back. Its eyes were bright gold.

"*Warren?*" Call said.

Master Rufus set the cage on the ground. "You will make this elemental disappear. Send it into the realm of chaos."

"But it's *Warren*," Call objected. "We know that lizard."

"Yeah, I'm really not sure I want to do . . . that," said Aaron. "Can't I disappear a rock or something?"

"I'd like to see you work with something more substantial than that," said Rufus.

"Warren does not want to be disappeared," said the lizard. "Warren has important things to tell you."

"Hear that? He's got important things to tell us," said Aaron.

"He's also a liar," pointed out Tamara.

"Well, you'd know all about being a liar, wouldn't you?" Call snapped.

Tamara's cheeks pinked but she ignored him. "Remember when Warren took us to the wrong cave and the Devoured almost killed us?"

Aaron cut his eyes sideways toward Call. "I don't want to do it," he whispered.

"You can't," Call muttered under his breath.

"I have to do *something*." Aaron sounded slightly panicked.

"Disappear the cage," Call replied, keeping his voice to a near whisper.

"What?"

"You heard me." Call grabbed Aaron's arm. "Do it."

Master Rufus's eyes narrowed. "Call —"

Aaron's hand shot out. A dark tendril uncoiled in his palm, then exploded outward, surrounding the cage, hiding Warren from sight. Call felt a slight pull inside himself, as if there were a rubber band inside his rib cage and Aaron was twanging it. Was that what it meant to be a counterweight?

The smoke began to clear. Call dropped his hand, just in time to see Warren's tail disappear through a crack in the grotto wall. The cage was gone, the space where it had stood empty.

Rufus raised his eyebrows. "I didn't mean for you to send the cage into chaos as well, but — good job."

Tamara was staring at the place where Warren's cage had disappeared. Under other circumstances, Call would have shot her a reassuring look, but not now. "What's the limit to Aaron's power?" she asked suddenly. "Like, what can he do? Could he send the whole Magisterium into the void?"

Master Rufus turned toward her, bushy eyebrows drawing together in surprise. "There are three things that make mages great. One is their fine control, another is their imagination, and the third is their well of power. One of our challenges is to discover the answer to your question. What can Aaron do before he needs his counterweight to pull him back? What can Call do? What can you do? There is only one way to find out — practice. Now, let's try working with earth."

Call sighed. It looked like they wouldn't be finished for a long while.

↑ ≈ △ ○ @

After the exercises were finally over, the three apprentices walked back from the grotto. Call was exhausted and had fallen behind the others. His leg hurt, his head hurt, and he dawdled near a pool of eyeless fish.

"You guys have it easy," he told them as they swam lethargically, pale in the moss-lit gloom.

The surface of the water was suddenly broken and a fish was swept up into the air by a long pink tongue. Call looked up to see Warren hanging from a stalactite.

The elemental blinked down at him. "The end is closer than you think," he said.

"What?" Call asked, thinking he'd misheard.

"The end is closer than you think," the lizard repeated. Then he darted up the rocky formation to the ceiling of the cave.

"Hey, we helped you!" Call called after him, but Warren didn't return.

↑ ≈ △ ○ @

At dinner, Call sat with Aaron, Jasper, and Celia, while Tamara, once again, joined her sister. Call could practically feel waves of ice radiating off her back every time he glanced at her.

"Why do you keep looking over at Tamara?" Celia asked, spearing a bright yellow mushroom with her fork.

"Because she told the mages to investigate his dad," Jasper said. Call startled, turning to glare at him. Jasper smiled angelically.

"Investigate him for what?" Celia's eyes were round.

Call didn't say anything. If he started explaining or manufacturing excuses, it would only make things worse. Instead, he wondered how Jasper knew any of this. Maybe he and Tamara were back to being thick as thieves. It served Tamara right to be stuck with someone like Jasper.

Jasper was about to make another comment, but Aaron warned him off with a "Shut it."

"I don't know what he did," Jasper admitted. "But I heard some of the mages talking. They were saying the search party they sent to find him didn't turn up anything. Apparently, he's disappeared."

"Disappeared?" Celia echoed, looking over at Call, waiting for him to say something.

Call frowned at his plate, small cracks appearing at the edges of the pottery from the force of his rage. He was a second-year mage, he'd walked through the Gate of Control; he knew he shouldn't be losing it like this. And yet he didn't want to stop Jasper from talking, not when Jasper seemed to know more about what was happening with Alastair than he did.

"Yeah, I guess someone warned him," Jasper went on, his gaze sliding over to Call, the implication of his words clear.

"Call didn't warn anyone," Aaron said. "He was with us the whole time. And stop acting like you know anything, when you really don't."

"I know more than you do," Jasper said with a sneer in Aaron's direction. "I know he's not to be trusted."

A shiver went up Call's spine, because Jasper was right.

Call couldn't even trust himself.

↑ ≈ △ ○ ☺

That night, Call flopped down on the couch in the common room. Rufus had assigned them some reading about the robber-baron era of mage politics, which had lasted until only a couple of decades back, but Call couldn't concentrate. The words swam on the page, the edges of the book occasionally sparking into tiny flames he quickly put out. Anger and fear had scorched the spine with black ash that smeared darkly over his fingers.

Tamara had made herself scarce after dinner, and Aaron had gone to the library to do his homework. He'd invited Call to come along, but that was because Aaron was nice and couldn't help doing nice things. Call knew he was better off alone. Just him and Havoc on the couch, the wolf curled up on his feet, panting softly, his coruscating eyes glowing in the dim room.

Just as he was pretty sure he was about to set fire to the book again, the door opened. It was Alex Strike, brown hair messy as usual — Call felt for him about that one — and an odd expression on his face.

Call shoved the history book under a cushion and sat up, careful not to dislodge Havoc. Because he was Rufus's assistant, Alex was one of the only people besides Rufus to have access to the room. Still, he'd never come in like this before.

"What's going on?" Call asked.

Alex sat down on the couch opposite Call, glancing at the closed doors of Tamara's and Aaron's rooms. "Are your roommates out?"

Call nodded, uncertain where this was going. Maybe he was in trouble. Maybe Alex had a message from Rufus. Maybe there was some kind of Magisterium second-year hazing ritual that involved being tied to a stalactite overnight.

"It's about your dad," Alex said. "I know about the Alkahest. I know the mages are looking for him."

Call glanced down at Havoc, who growled low in his throat. "Does *everyone* know?" Call asked, thinking of Jasper.

Alex shook his head. "Not how serious things are."

"My dad didn't do it," Call said. "Not like they're saying. He's not in league with the Enemy. He's not in league with anyone."

A strange expression passed over Alex's face, like maybe he'd only just then realized how dangerous it was to be talking to Call about this. "I believe you," he said finally. "Which is why you need to get word to your dad to stay hidden. If they find him, they're going to kill him."

"What?" Call said, although he'd heard the words perfectly clearly.

Alex shook his head. "The Alkahest is *gone*. If he's the one who got it, they're not going to bother with prison. He'll be dead as soon as they find him. That's why I figured you ought to know. Warn him, before it's too late."

Call wondered how Alex knew this stuff and then remembered his stepmother was on the Assembly. So instead he asked, "Why are you helping me?"

"Because you helped me," he said. "Gotta go."

Call nodded and Alex slipped out.

If Alastair were murdered by the mages, it would be Call's fault. He had to do something, but the more he thought about it, the more he was sure that there was no safe way to get Alastair a message. Master Rufus would be watching for that — would use it to catch Alastair if he could. But if Call could find his dad in time, maybe he could warn him in person.

Thinking of Alastair made Call remember the room in the basement, set up for a ritual, and the small, boy-size cot in the corner. It made Call remember how Havoc had whined and the sound his father's head had made when it hit the wall.

If he found his father and his father had the Alkahest, what would Alastair do with it?

Call knew he had to focus. Call knew his dad better than anyone. He should be able to guess where Alastair was hiding. It would be a place that was out of the way, one he knew really well. A place the mages wouldn't think to look. One that wasn't easily traceable back to him.

Call sat up straight.

Alastair bought a lot of broken-down antique cars to strip for parts — way too many to store in the garage of the house or in his shop, so he'd rented the dilapidated barn of an elderly lady about forty miles from where they lived . . . and paid her in cash. That barn would be a perfect hideout — Alastair had even slept there sometimes, when he was working late into the night.

Call slid off the couch, causing Havoc to tumble to the ground with an annoyed grunt. He reached down to stroke the wolf's head. "Don't worry, boy," he said. "You're coming with me."

He headed into his bedroom and pulled his canvas duffel out from under the bed. He stuffed it quickly with clothes, tossed Miri in, and, after a moment of thought, returned to the main room to add what was left of the Ruffles chips. He'd need to have something to eat on the road.

He was just swinging the bag over his shoulder when the door opened again and Tamara and Aaron came in. Aaron was carrying a pile of books, his and Tamara's, and she was laughing at something he'd said. For a moment, before they saw Call, they looked carefree and happy, and he felt his stomach tighten. They didn't need him, not as a friend, not as a part of their apprentice group, not as anything but a cause of strife and argument.

Tamara caught sight of him first, and the smile slid off her face. "Call."

Aaron shut the door behind them and set down their books. When he straightened up, he was staring at the boots on Call's feet and the duffel in his hand.

"Where are you going?" Aaron asked.

"I was going to walk Havoc," Call said, indicating the wolf, who was darting merrily between them.

"And you needed to pack for a week?" Tamara pointed at his duffel. "What's going on, Call?"

"Nothing. Look, you don't need to — you don't need to know about this. That way, when Master Rufus asks you what happened to me, you don't have to lie."

Tamara shook her head. "No way. We're a group. We tell each other things."

"Why? So you can tell all our secrets?" Call asked, seeing Tamara flinch. He knew he was being a jerk, but he was unable to stop. "Again?"

"That depends on what you're doing." Aaron's jaw was set the way Call rarely saw it. Usually Aaron was so forgiving, so immensely *nice*, that Call often forgot that underneath, there was the steel that made him the Makar. "Because if it's something that's gonna put you in danger, then I'll tell the Masters myself. And you can be mad at me instead of her."

Call swallowed. Aaron and Tamara faced him, blocking the door. "They're going to kill my dad," he said.

Aaron's eyebrows went up. "What?"

"Someone — and I can't tell you who, you're just going to have to trust me — said that the Alkahest is missing. And since my dad went on the run, they're not going to put him in prison or give him a trial —"

"The Alkahest is gone?" Tamara echoed. "Your dad really stole it?"

"There's a mage prison?" Aaron asked, wide-eyed.

"Sort of. There's the Panopticon," Tamara said grimly. "I don't know that much about it, but it's a place where you're always watched. You're never alone. If your dad really did —"

"It doesn't matter," said Call. "They're going to kill him."

"How do you know that?" Tamara asked.

Call looked at her for a long moment. "A friend — a *real* friend — told me what he heard."

She blanched. "So what are you going to do?"

"I have to find him and get the Alkahest back before that happens." Call hitched his duffel higher on his shoulder. "If I return it to the Collegium, I can convince the mages that my dad's no threat to them — or to you. I swear, Aaron, my dad wouldn't hurt you. I *swear* he wouldn't."

Aaron rubbed a hand over his face. "We don't want your dad to get hurt, either."

"*Die*, not *get hurt*," Call insisted. "If I don't find him, he's going to be killed."

"I'm coming with you," Tamara said. "I can pack in ten minutes."

I don't want you to come. Call didn't say it. He wasn't even sure it was true. He was sure he was still angry, though. He shook his head. "Why would you want to do that?"

"This is my fault. You're right. But I can help you evade the mages while you look for your dad, and I can help you convince the Collegium to take back the Alkahest and stop hunting him. My parents are on the Assembly." She took a step toward her room. "Just give me ten minutes."

"You guys don't really think that I'm going to stay here while you both go on a mission, do you?" Aaron said. "Last time, you both saved me. Now I get to help with the saving part."

"You *definitely* can't come," Call said. "You're the Makar. You're too valuable to be running around looking for my dad, especially since everyone's worried he's going to hurt you."

"I'm the Makar," Aaron said, and Call thought he heard the shadow of all the things Aaron had overheard that summer in his words. "I'm the Makar and it's my job to protect people, not the other way around."

Call sighed and sat down on the couch. He pictured the long journey ahead of him, buses and walking and loneliness with no one but Havoc to keep him company. Nothing to distract from the voice in his head that said: *Your father is going to die. Your father might want you dead.* Then he thought about having Aaron and Tamara with him, Aaron's steady presence, Tamara's funny remarks, and felt reluctantly lighter. "Fine," he said in a rough voice. He didn't want to let on how relieved he was. "Just don't take too long. If we're going to go, we have to get out of here. Now. Before someone notices."

With a whine, Havoc flopped down on the floor, clearly disappointed by all the talking. Havoc was a wolf of action.

A few minutes later, Aaron and Tamara emerged with bags of their own.

"Good thing we made those rocks to protect Aaron from scrying," Tamara said, opening her hand and showing a small pile of them. "And good thing I like to practice."

Call stood up with a heavy sigh. "You're both sure about this?"

"We're sure, Call," Aaron said. Tamara nodded.

Havoc barked once, like he was sure, too.

↑ ≈ △ ○ ◉

The one gate of the Magisterium that stayed open all night was the Mission Gate, through which older students left and returned from missions and battles. Call and Aaron and Tamara sauntered along, trying to look as if they were on their way to the Gallery to eat candy or watch a movie. They passed Celia, Rafe, and Jasper deep in conversation, and some of the older students, laughing and chatting about their lessons.

The passageway forked, one path leading toward the Gallery, the other toward the Mission Gate. Aaron paused for a moment, looking around to make sure no one was watching, before ducking into the corridor that led outside. Tamara and Call hurried after him so fast there was a pileup, and they had to disentangle themselves from one another and Havoc. By the time they were done they were giggling, even Tamara and Call. Aaron looked pleased.

His pleased look didn't last long, though. They tiptoed down the passage. The air slowly became warmer, and Call could smell sun-warmed rock, leaf mold, and fresh air. The passage sloped up and he could see the stars beyond the Mission Gate.

Suddenly, they were blotted out. A slender figure rose up in front of them, smirking.

"Fancy meeting you here," Jasper said.

"That is such a tired villain line, Jasper, and you know it," said Call.

"Why are you here?" Aaron demanded. "Were you following us?"

"Because I knew that Call would do something eventually," Jasper said. "I knew he'd show his true colors. What did you expect me to do, nothing?"

"Yes, Jasper," said Tamara with heavy sarcasm. "See, normal people, who aren't psychopaths, don't automatically assume the worst of everyone."

Jasper crossed his arms. "Oh, really? Then tell me: Where are you going?"

"It's none of your business," said Call. "Go away, Jasper."

"Is this about a certain someone's dad who's gone on the run?" Jasper quirked an eyebrow at Call. "The mages wouldn't be happy at all if they knew you were going after him. Master Rufus —"

"Let's kill him," Call said. Havoc growled.

"Master Rufus?" Aaron looked alarmed.

"No, of course not Master Rufus! I meant Jasper," Call said. "Bury his body under a pile of rock. Who'd know?"

"Call, stop being ridiculous," said Tamara.

"Havoc could kill him," Call suggested. Havoc turned at the sound of his name, looking interested by the prospect. Although the Chaos-ridden wolf had grown over the summer, Call wasn't sure he could actually kill anyone, but he could sure take Jasper outside and chase him around the Magisterium a few times.

"And *I'm* supposed to be the psychopath?" Jasper grumbled.

Call wasn't sure what it meant that he'd gone full Evil Overlord on Jasper yet still couldn't manage to impress him.

Aaron raised his hand. For a moment Call thought that Aaron was going to settle them down, say that Call should quit threatening Jasper and they should all just go back to their rooms. Instead, black fire sparked between Aaron's fingers, a web of darkness. "Don't make me hurt you," he said, looking right at Jasper, chaos burning in the palm of his hand. "Because I really could."

Call was so astonished he couldn't even react.

Jasper blanched, but before he could say anything, Tamara

slapped Aaron none too gently on the shoulder. "Stop that," she said. "You can't just summon chaos whenever you feel like it."

Aaron closed his hand into a fist and the darkness winked out, but he didn't look any less terrifying.

Tamara pointed at Jasper. "We're going to have to take him with us."

"Take him with us? You're kidding," Call said. "He'll wreck the whole thing!"

She put a hand on her hip. "It's not a party, Call."

"And I'm not going anywhere with you," Jasper interrupted, starting to sidle along the cave wall. "I don't know what's going on, but I don't even care anymore. You've lost your minds. I'll forget I ever saw anything. I swear."

"Oh, no you won't," Aaron said. "You'll tell the mages on us the first chance you get."

Jasper looked mutinous. "I won't."

"Sure, you will," said Call.

Tamara took a stone out of her pocket and tucked it into Jasper's uniform. "Let's go."

"Agreed," said Aaron. He grabbed at the back of Jasper's collar. Jasper yelped and windmilled his arms. Aaron's expression was grim. "You're coming with us," he said. "Now march."

CHAPTER NINE

TRAVELING AWAY FROM the Magisterium was no easy task. They had to navigate through the forest to the highway, Tamara using the map on her phone to help. On the way, there was the possibility of running into elementals and Chaos-ridden animals. Plus there was the possibility of getting lost.

Still, the weather was nice, and with the sound of cicadas and Jasper's complaining ringing in his ears, Call didn't mind the walk. At least not until his leg started to stiffen up and he realized that, once again, he was going to hold the rest of them back. Even on a quest to save his own father.

If it had just been Aaron and Tamara tromping on ahead, Tamara carrying a heavy stick and shoving it in the dirt to propel her along like she thought she was Gandalf, Aaron's blond hair glowing in the moonlight, then Call might have complained. But the idea of Jasper having something else over him grated his last nerve. He gritted his teeth, hitched his backpack higher on his shoulders, and ignored the pain.

"Do you think they're going to throw you out?" Jasper asked conversationally. "I mean, helping the Enemy. Or at least a henchperson of the Enemy."

"My father is not a henchperson of the Enemy."

Jasper went on, ignoring Call. "Kidnapping me. Endangering the Makar . . ."

"I'm right here, you know," said Aaron. "I can make my own decisions."

"I'm not sure the Assembly would agree with that," said Jasper. They had passed out of the part of the forest where the trees were younger thanks to the fire and destruction wrought by Constantine Madden fifteen years ago. The trees here were towering and thickly branched. More moonlight spilled down through the leaves and danced along Havoc's fur. "Call, maybe you'll finally get your wish. You could actually get kicked out of the Magisterium. Too bad it's too late to bind your magic."

"Shut up, Jasper," said Tamara.

"And, Tamara, well, your family has been disgraced before. At least they're used to it."

Tamara smacked him on the back of his head. "Give it a rest. If you talk too much, you'll dehydrate."

"Ow," Jasper complained.

"Shh," Aaron said.

"I get it," Jasper said sourly. "Tamara already told me to shut up."

"No, I meant *everyone*, be quiet." Aaron crouched down behind the moss-covered root of a tree. "There's something out there."

Jasper immediately dropped to his knees. Tamara rolled up

her sleeves and got into a crouch, one of her hands cupped. Fire was already sparking in her palm.

Call hesitated. His leg was stiff, and he was worried that if he crouched down, he wouldn't be able to straighten up again, at least not gracefully.

"Call, get *down*," Tamara hissed. The light between her palms was growing into a shimmering square. "Don't be a hero."

Call almost couldn't hold back a sarcastic laugh at that.

The shimmering square rose, and Call realized that Tamara had shaped air energy into something that functioned like the lens of a telescope. They all leaned forward, as a valley below them sprang into view.

Looking through her magical lens, they could spot a circular clearing with small, brightly painted wooden houses spaced equidistantly around it. A large wooden building stood at the center. It had a placard over the door. To his surprise, Tamara's magical lens allowed Call to read the words on it. THOUGHTS ARE FREE AND SUBJECT TO NO RULE.

"That's what's written on the Magisterium entrance," he said, surprised.

"Well, on one of the entrances, anyway," said a voice behind him.

He spun around. A man stood amid the fallen leaves and ferns, dressed in the black uniform of a Master. Jasper gasped and scrabbled backward until he hit the trunk of a tree.

"Master Lemuel," he gulped. "But I thought you — I thought they —"

"Fired me from the Magisterium?"

None of them spoke for a long moment. Finally, Aaron nodded. "Well, yeah."

"I was offered a leave of absence, and I took it," Lemuel

said, scowling down at them. "Apparently, I'm not the only one."

"We're on a mission," Tamara said with vast sincerity and not a little annoyance. "*Obviously*. Otherwise, why would we have Jasper along?"

She really was a good liar, Call thought. He'd acted like it was a bad thing. But right then, he was glad.

Jasper opened his mouth to protest — or possibly tattle — when Aaron clapped him on the shoulder. Hard.

Master Lemuel snorted. "As if I care? I don't. Run away from the Magisterium if you want. Use your magic to get into nightclubs. Joyride on elementals. I don't have any apprentices to look after anymore, thank goodness, and I certainly have no intention of looking after any of you."

"Uh, okay," said Call. "Great?"

"What is this place?" asked Aaron, craning his neck to look around.

"An enclave of like-minded individuals," said Master Lemuel, making a shooing motion with his hands. "Now run along. Go."

"Who's there?" asked an older woman with freckled and sun-browned skin, wearing a saffron-colored linen dress. Her white hair was braided up onto her head. "Are you terrorizing those kids?"

"We know him," said Tamara. "From the Magisterium."

"Well, come on," the woman said, turning and beckoning them. "Come have a cold drink. Hiking through the forest is thirsty work."

Call looked over at Tamara and Aaron. If Jasper started complaining about being their prisoner, would Master Lemuel find it funny? Had he heard that the Alkahest was stolen? Call was sure he wouldn't find that part amusing.

"We should probably just get going," Tamara said. "Thanks and everything, but —"

"Oh, no, I won't take no for an answer." The woman hooked her arm with Aaron's, and Aaron, always polite, let her begin to lead him toward the encampment. "My name is Alma. I know what kind of awful food they feed you up at the Magisterium. Just stop in for a visit and then you'll be on your way."

"Uh, Aaron," Call said. "We're kind of in a hurry."

Aaron looked helpless. He clearly didn't want to be rude. Social pressure was, apparently, his kryptonite.

Master Lemuel looked more annoyed than pleased, so probably that meant it wasn't some kind of trap. With a sigh and a speaking look between himself and Tamara, he followed Alma and Aaron down a gentle sloped incline toward one of the houses with a small porch and blue-painted stars on the door. Inside, Call could see a little kitchen with long wooden shelves lined with hand-labeled bottles. A wood-burning stove smoked in the corner, a hammock swung in another, and a quaintly painted table with chairs was in the center of the room. The woman opened a cabinet, which was full of misting ice. She stuck her hand inside and came out with a pitcher of slushy lemonade, the glass cloudy with cold and several slices of lemon floating inside.

She placed a few mismatched glasses and started to fill them. Aaron snatched one, guzzled it down, then winced in pain.

"Brain freeze," he explained.

Call thought uncomfortably about gingerbread houses and

old ladies and didn't take a drink. He didn't trust Master Lemuel and he definitely didn't trust anyone who could put up with Master Lemuel either.

He did, however, sit down on one of the chairs and rub his leg. He couldn't remember anything bad about sitting in fairy tales.

"So, this place?" Tamara asked. "What is it?"

"Ah, yes," said the woman. "Did you see the sign above our Great House?"

"'Thoughts are free and subject to no rule,'" repeated Tamara.

The woman nodded. Master Lemuel had followed them to the house. "Alma, I know these children. They're not just trouble — they're the epicenter of trouble. Don't tell them anything you'll regret."

She waved vaguely at him and then turned back to the kids. She pointed at Havoc, who whined a little and moved behind Call's chair. "We study the Chaos-ridden. I see you have a wolf with you — a young one. The Enemy put chaos into both humans and animals, but while the chaos seemed to rob people of speech and intelligence, animals reacted differently. They continued to breed, so that the Chaos-ridden creatures of today never knew the commands of a Makar, because there wasn't one, until now."

She looked at Aaron.

"Havoc responds to Call, not me," said Aaron. "And Call isn't a Makar."

"That's very interesting to us," Alma replied. "How did you find Havoc, Call?"

"He was out in the snow," Call said, brushing the back of his fingers against Havoc's ruff. "I saved his life."

Tamara gave him an incredulous look, as though she thought that Havoc would have been fine without him.

"Havoc was born Chaos-ridden," said Alma. "There are no humans like that. Humans can't have chaos put into them; the human Chaos-ridden are made from the freshly dead."

Aaron shuddered. "That sounds gruesome. Like zombies."

"It is gruesome, in a way," said Alma. "There is an old alchemical saying: 'Every poison is also a cure; it only depends on the dose.' The Enemy managed to cure death, but the cure was worse than the original condition."

"Master Milagros says that," said Jasper, narrowing his eyes. "Were you a teacher at the Magisterium?"

"I was," said Alma. "At the same time that Master Joseph was there, experimenting with void magic. So were many of us. I helped with some of his experiments."

Tamara tipped over her lemonade glass. "You stood by as Constantine pushed chaos into people, into animals? Why would anyone do that?"

"The Order of Disorder," Call whispered. They had to be part of it. In the book, it had said they'd turned to researching Chaos-ridden animals. Where else would they find Chaos-ridden animals than in the woods around the Magisterium? They were the creators of the Alkahest.

Alma smiled at him. "I see you've heard of us. Haven't you ever asked yourself what Master Joseph and Constantine Madden were trying to do?"

"They were trying to make it so no one ever had to die," said Call.

Everyone looked at him oddly. "Way to pay attention in class," Aaron said under his breath.

"We are all beings of energy," said Lemuel. "When our

energy is expended, our lives end. Chaos is a source of endless energy. If chaos could be placed safely inside a person, he or she could feed off that energy forever. He or she would never die."

"But it can't be," said Aaron. "Placed safely inside a person, I mean."

"That's what we're still trying to determine," said Alma. "We're working with animals, because animals seem to react to chaos differently. Your wolf has chaos inside him — he was born with it inside of him — but he still has a personality, he has feelings, doesn't he? He's as alive as you are."

"Well, yeah," Call said.

"And he is absolutely, definitely, not ever going to snap and eat our faces," Jasper interjected. "Right?"

"Who can say?" offered Master Lemuel. He certainly appeared to be happier here than he had been as a teacher at the Magisterium, Call thought. Half of his mouth was turning up as though he might actually smile.

Jasper slid down in his chair. "Crud."

Tamara glanced around. "So if you're studying Chaos-ridden animals, do you catch them? Do you keep them in cages?"

Alma smiled and eyed Havoc in a way that Call didn't like. "So tell me about your mission. What's your assignment?"

"I thought you said you didn't care where we were going," Aaron said to Master Lemuel.

"I don't. I didn't say *nobody* would care." Lemuel's half smile turned into a full, malicious one. "It's not easy to run away from the Magisterium."

"Drew sure found *that* out," muttered Jasper.

Master Lemuel flushed. "Drew wasn't really trying to run away. Everything he said about me was a lie."

"Look, we know that," Aaron said, raising his hands in a gesture for peace. "And we *are* on a mission, just not one that everyone at school knows about. So if you could tell us the fastest way to the road —"

There was a commotion outside.

A middle-aged man with a bald head and big bristly beard rushed into the room. "Alma, Lemuel! The Masters from the Magisterium are coming this way. It's a search party."

Lemuel looked smugly at Call and the others. "Not running away, huh?"

"Just for the record," said Jasper, "these people kidnapped me and are forcing me to go with them on a stupid mission to —"

Tamara opened her hand. Jasper stopped speaking abruptly and started gasping for air. Tamara had apparently snatched the words from his mouth — quite literally — and taken the air he was breathing along with them. The adults hadn't seemed to notice, but Call was impressed.

"Stall, Andreas," said Alma calmly.

The bearded man rushed off in the direction he'd come.

Call leaped to his feet, heart in his throat. "We have to get out of here," he said.

Aaron scrambled up after him, and so did Tamara. Only Jasper remained seated, still breathing hard and glaring at the others. "We'll hide in the woods," said Aaron. "Please, just let us go and we'll never mention this place."

"I can do better than that," Alma said. "We'll hide you. But you have to do something for us in return."

Her gaze went to Havoc.

"No way," said Tamara, moving to put her hand on the wolf's side. "We're not letting you do whatever it is you're —"

"Do you promise he won't get hurt?" Call asked quickly, interrupting her. He didn't like to consider it, thinking of how his father had chained up Havoc, but he saw the covetous way Alma was looking at his wolf. He needed to agree, so he could stall for time until he found a way to get them all out of there, including his wolf.

"Call, you *can't*," Tamara protested, her fingers in Havoc's fur.

"Of course he can," said Jasper. "You think he's going to be loyal to anyone or anything? Let's just go back to the Magisterium."

"*Shut up*," said Aaron. "Call, are you sure —"

But Alma laughed. "You misunderstand. It's not Havoc we want, although he's very interesting. It's Aaron."

"Well, you *definitely* can't have Aaron," Tamara said.

"Without a Makar, we have so many theories, but no way to test them. We know you can't stay right now, Aaron, but make me a promise that you'll come back, and leave that wolf as collateral. When you return, all we need is a few hours of your time. And maybe when you see what you could do — how helpful to the world you could be as something other than a defense against an enemy with whom we're no longer at war — then maybe you'll decide to join us."

None of them spoke.

"The wolf will be fine," Alma said.

"Okay," Aaron said after a long moment. "I'll promise to come back, but you can't keep Havoc. You don't need collateral. You have my word."

"We trust you, Makar, but not that much. Quickly, children. Decide. We can hide you or we can turn you over to the mages. But you must know they'll trade Havoc to us in exchange for the four of you."

Call didn't doubt that — not at this point. "Fine. Same deal as before. But no experiments on him."

Alma looked well satisfied. "Good. Agreed. All of you, follow me." She led them out the back door of the cottage. They hustled across the green space between the buildings.

Call felt horribly exposed. He could see shadows moving through the trees circling the clearing and hear raised voices. The Masters, shouting their names. Hurrying after Tamara, he saw she had one hand clasped around Jasper's wrist, keeping him from running in the opposite direction. Call thought he heard Master Rufus's voice. He grabbed Havoc's collar and pulled him along faster. The wolf looked up at him as though he suspected something bad was about to happen.

If they ran into the woods, they'd be caught. Their only choice was to follow Alma — who was totally scary, who had once worked with Constantine Madden and Master Joseph, who wanted to experiment on Havoc, who probably qualified to have a pretty long Evil Overlord list of her own — and hope that she'd make good on her promise to hide them.

With a sigh, Call kept on going. Alma took a key ring with several keys out of a pocket of her saffron dress and unlocked the door to the central building.

Immediately, they were startled by the sounds of barking and keening and crying. The building they went into was lined on all sides with cages of various sizes, and in them were Chaos-ridden animals. From brown bears with wild swirling eyes to gray foxes to a single bobcat that roared as Call came into the room.

"This is the worst zoo ever," Jasper said.

Tamara's hand came up to cover her mouth. "So this is where you keep them."

Alma guided Call over to one of the cages. "Get your wolf inside. Quickly. I need to get you settled and then go deal with the mages."

"How do we know you're as good as your word?" asked Aaron, apparently pushed beyond the fear of offending.

"Makar, look at the creatures we have here," she said. "They were dangerous to obtain. They are dangerous to keep. But you are more dangerous than any of them. We wouldn't cross you lightly. We need your help."

Outside, voices got louder. Master Lemuel was arguing with another mage.

Taking a deep breath, Call put Havoc in the cage and let Alma lock it. She took the key and tucked it into her pocket, then led them to another room. It was windowless and full of boxes.

"Stay in here until I come back for you. It won't be long," said Alma before she shut the door. They heard the lock turn and then her footsteps receding.

Tamara whirled on Call and Aaron. "How could you agree to letting them take Havoc? He's our wolf!"

"He's *my* wolf," Call pointed out.

"Not anymore," Jasper said, examining his fingernails.

"And *you*," Tamara said to Aaron. "Agreeing to some stupid deal. Both of you are idiots."

Call threw up his hands. "What else were we supposed to do? We needed them to hide us — and now they have. If we break out — and get Havoc out, too — while they're talking to the Masters, we can sneak away without anyone knowing. And then Aaron doesn't have to come back."

Aaron opened his mouth to say something, but Call cut him off. "Don't say anything about keeping your promise. That wasn't a real promise."

"Fine," Aaron said.

"It's not going to be easy to break out your wolf. There's probably a magical lock on those cages," Jasper said.

"He's right," said Tamara.

"I have a plan," said Call, peering out through the keyhole in the door. "Aaron, can you get this door open?"

"If you are asking if I know how to pick locks," Aaron said, "I don't."

"Yeah, but you're a Makar," said Call. Through the keyhole, he could see the stuffy room full of cages, and Havoc curled up, looking miserable. "Makar it open or something."

Aaron looked at him as if he was talking nonsense. Then he spun around and kicked the door. It burst open, the hinges tearing.

"Or you could do that," Call said. "That works, too."

Jasper's body tensed, like he was thinking about making a break for it.

Tamara turned toward him. "Please don't leave. Just stay with us, okay? For a little while longer. I know this isn't fun, but it really is important."

Jasper looked at her, an odd expression on his face, as though she'd managed to say the one thing that could convince him not to run out of there and tell on them. Weirdly, that thing appeared to be *please*.

"Well, you're right about it not being fun," he said, leaning against the wall and crossing his arms over his chest.

Call went to the cages. As Jasper had predicted, the locks were inscribed with several interleaving circles of alchemical symbols he didn't recognize. And three keyholes. "Tamara, what does this mean?" he asked.

She peered over his shoulder and squinted. "It's warded against magic."

"Oh," he said. Back home, during the May Day Parade, he had liberated a naked mole rat and white mice, without magic, just ingenuity. After Aaron kicked open the door and got them into the main room, Call felt like he had to be the one to get the cages open. Somehow.

He grabbed hold of the bars, squinched up his eyes, and pulled as hard as he could.

"*That's* your plan?" Jasper said, bursting out laughing. "Are you kidding me?"

"We need a key," Aaron said, a small smile tugging at the corner of his mouth. "Or, well, a lot of keys."

One of the bears roared, sticking a paw through the bars of the cage and batting at the air. Its eyes were orange and burning, coruscating with chaos. Aaron looked at it with his mouth open. "I've never seen one of those before."

Call wasn't sure if he meant a bear or a Chaos-ridden bear, which he was willing to bet none of them had ever seen before.

"I have an idea," Tamara said, with a quick worried glance in the bear's direction. "We can't use magic on the locks, but . . ."

Call whirled to look at her. "What?"

"Give me something metal. Anything."

Call lifted a brass astrolabe off one of the desks and held it out to her.

In her hands, it started to melt. No, the more Call stared, the more he realized that the liquefying metal was floating *above* her hands. It formed into a red-hot roiling blob, blackening as it cooled in the open air and drifted toward the cage holding Havoc. When it got there, three tendrils of liquid metal snaked out into the keyholes.

"Send cold water at it," Tamara said, her whole body straining with concentration.

Call pulled water from the animals' dishes, forming it into a ball and using air magic to cool it.

"Quicker," she said, gritting her teeth.

He sent the water at what was left of the astrolabe. The metal hissed and the water evaporated into a cloud. Call jumped back, falling awkwardly against one of the cages.

When the cloud cleared, Tamara was holding a three-part key.

Havoc whimpered. Tamara pressed the key into the lock and twisted it; there were three distinct clicks — one, two, and then a third that echoed all around the room. The cage popped open and Havoc bounded out, sending the door swinging. Then, more clicks rang out as all the cage doors popped open.

"Maybe we shouldn't have unlocked *all three* locks," Call said into the unnerving silence that followed.

As the animals burst free from their cages, Jasper started yelling. The bear heaved its way up and out. Foxes, dogs, wolves, and stoats all poured out of their prisons.

"Go!" Call shouted at them. "Go and attack — I mean, go and *distract* the Masters! Lead them away from here!"

"Yes, distract," Tamara put in. "*Distract!*"

The Chaos-ridden animals rushed toward the door, barely paying attention to either of them. Aaron yanked the door open just in time for them to thunder through.

There were shouts from outside as well as growls and squawks. Call could hear people running and yelling.

Havoc danced up to Call, licking him vigorously. Call bent down to hug him. "Good wolf," he muttered. "Good wolf." Havoc nuzzled up against him, his eyes glowing yellow.

"Get *down*!" Tamara yelled, and reached up to yank at Jasper, who had climbed onto the desk and was trying to push open the window.

"I'm trying to help!" he protested.

Aaron leaned out the open door. "What if some of the Chaos-ridden attack one of the mages? What if someone gets hurt? Not all animals are like Havoc."

"Don't worry about the Masters," Call said. "Those animals didn't look in great shape. I bet most of them run for the forest the first chance they get."

"Like we should be doing," Tamara reminded him, heading for the door and pushing past Aaron. "Let's get out of here."

Keeping his head down and the fingers of one of his hands buried in Havoc's ruff, Call followed her. Aaron brought up the rear, keeping Jasper in front of him.

They emerged into a clearing and froze. The small outpost was completely overrun. Masters were running back and forth, trying to capture the Chaos-ridden animals fleeing in every direction. Jets of fire and ice were shooting through the air. Call was pretty sure he saw Master Rockmaple being chased around a tree by a Chaos-ridden golden retriever. Master North whirled, a gleaming ball of fire beginning to rise from the palm of his hand.

Alma suddenly lunged out of the small wooden house where she had given them lemonade. A whirlwind of air was whipping around her. She threw out her hand, and a tendril of air shot free and knocked Master North off his feet. His bolt of fire went wide, catching the leaves and branches of the tree over his head. It started to burn as Tamara took firm hold of Call by the collar and hauled him out of the clearing, into the woods.

They were all running, Tamara, Aaron, Jasper, even Call, limping a little but gaining a pretty good speed. Just as the sounds of the fighting behind them died down, Call heard a voice.

"I told Alma you were troublemakers," said Master Lemuel, standing ominously in their path. "She wouldn't listen."

Aaron stopped short, and the others nearly crashed into him. Master Lemuel raised his eyebrows.

"I'm going to tell you one thing," he said, "and you can believe me or not. But I dislike the Masters of the Magisterium more than I dislike you. And I don't want them to get what they want. Understand?"

They nodded in unison.

He pointed toward a narrow brook that ran through the trees. It was actually very pretty here, Call thought, which might have been something he would have appreciated under other circumstances.

"Follow that to the highway," Lemuel said. "It's the fastest way. From there, you're on your own."

There was a silence. Then Aaron said, "Thanks."

Of course Aaron would say thanks, Call thought, as they hurried toward the brook. If someone were hitting Aaron over the head, he would thank them for stopping.

They made their way along the brook for half an hour in silence before Jasper spoke up.

"So what's your plan now? It's not like we're safe once we hit the highway," Jasper said. "There's no buses, and we don't have a car —"

"I have a plan," Tamara said.

Call turned toward her. "You do?"

"I *always* have a plan," she said, raising her eyebrows. "Sometimes, even, a *scheme*. You should take lessons from me."

"This better be a really good plan," Aaron said, smirking. "Because you sure are talking it up."

Tamara pulled her phone out of her bag, checked it, and then kept walking.

CHAPTER TEN

THE FIRST SIGHT of the highway made Call shudder as he remembered the last time he'd crossed it, looking for Aaron. He recalled vividly the pain in his legs as he forced himself to hurry, the panic at the thought of Aaron in danger, and then the discovery that he wasn't the person he'd always thought himself to be.

Jasper squatted and petted Havoc's head when the wolf came up to him. For a moment, he didn't seem like such a jerk.

Then he saw Call looking and glared.

Call sat down on the ground, watching the occasional car whir by. Tamara was typing things into her phone. He wasn't sure if she was researching stuff for their quest or just e-mailing friends from home. Aaron frowned thoughtfully into the middle distance, the way heroes in comic books did. They could make a figurine of him looking like that.

Call wondered how Aaron would look when he found out that Call had lied to him — lied to him a lot.

He was still wondering about that when the sleek black town car pulled up.

The window rolled down and Tamara's butler, Stebbins, pushed back his sunglasses to show his pale blue eyes. "Get in," he said. "We've got to make this quick."

Jasper scrambled into the backseat. "Oh, sweet hydration." He grabbed a water bottle from one of the cup holders and guzzled the whole thing.

"That dog's not coming in here," Stebbins said. "He'll track dirt all over the seats and his nails could scratch up the leather."

"They're not your seats," Tamara reminded him, patting the cushion next to her. The wolf hopped into the car and then turned around, looking dubious.

Call got in next, pulling Havoc onto his lap. It was hard to believe that the wolf had once fit underneath his shirt. Now he was almost as big as Call himself.

Aaron got into the front.

"I assume this will be our usual deal," Stebbins said to Tamara, turning in his seat. "What's the address?"

Call told him, although he didn't know the number, just the road. Stebbins punched the location into his apparently non-magical GPS.

Then they were off.

"What's the usual deal?" Jasper asked Tamara under his breath.

"Stebbins drag races with my parents' cars," she told him, keeping her voice low. "I cover for him."

"Really?" Jasper asked, frowning at the guy in the front seat with what appeared to be new respect.

As they drove on, Call found himself dozing against the window until his head started knocking against the glass. They were heading down a dirt road.

He blinked. He knew exactly where they were. "Just pull up here," he said.

Stebbins stopped the car, squinting. "Here?" he asked, but Call was already opening the door. Havoc immediately ran around in circles, clearly relieved to be free.

The kids got out and Stebbins put the town car in reverse, probably glad to be rid of them.

"Are you kidding me?" Jasper said when they saw the landscape of cars. "This is a junkyard."

Call glared, but Tamara shrugged. "He is kind of right, Call."

Call tried to see the familiar area through her eyes. It was pretty bad. It looked like a parking lot, except that the vehicles weren't in tidy lines. Cars were haphazardly grouped together. Some had been driven in, but most had been towed and dumped wherever they fit. Rust bloomed along their hoods and along their sides, pocking the once-shiny chrome trim. Long grass had grown up around them, a telltale sign of how long they'd been abandoned.

"He keeps most of these for parts," Call said, feeling uncomfortable. He'd always thought of his dad as eccentric. But he had to admit that having a lot of corroding vehicles seemed a little bit worse than eccentric. Alastair could never use all the cars he'd collected, not even for parts since so many had rusted through, but he'd kept on collecting them anyway. "The good cars, the ones he's planning on restoring, are in the barn."

Tamara, Aaron, and even Jasper looked hopefully in the direction Call was pointing, but the ominous gray building didn't seem to give any of them any comfort.

A cold wind cut across the parking lot. Jasper shivered ostentatiously and hunched down into his jacket. He made a big show of rubbing his hands together as if they were climbing Everest and he was afraid of frostbite.

"Shut up, Jasper," said Call.

"I didn't say anything!" Jasper protested.

Aaron waved a peacemaking hand. "You really think your dad might be hiding out here?"

"It's not a place most people would look for him," Call said, no longer sure of anything.

"That's for certain," Tamara said, putting a depth of feeling into those words. She looked over at the farmhouse near the tree line, a gray clapboard building with a tilting, patched roof. "I can't believe someone lets him do this to their property."

"She's old," Call said. "It's not like her house is in great shape either. And he pays rent."

"Do you think he might stay in there?" Aaron asked hopefully. The yellow glow of the windows seemed inviting. "I mean, maybe she let him crash in her spare room."

Call shook his head. "No. When he comes here, he always stays in the loft of the barn. He keeps bedrolls up there and a camp stove. Cans of food, too. Maybe she would have seen him, though. He usually stops by."

"Let's go ask," Aaron said. "Is she one of those old ladies who bakes a lot?"

"No," Call said. He couldn't remember Mrs. Tisdale ever cooking anything. Aaron looked disappointed. Jasper just kept looking angry and staring up at the sky as if hoping to be saved by a helicopter or an air elemental, or maybe an elemental driving a helicopter.

"Come on," Call said, setting off toward the house. His leg wasn't just aching anymore; it felt like spikes of fire were shooting up through the bones. He clenched his teeth as he made his way up the front steps. He didn't want to make a sound of pain in front of Jasper, not one.

Aaron reached around him and knocked on the door. There were shuffling footsteps and the door opened a crack, revealing tangled gray hair and a pair of bright, pale green eyes. "Kind of short to be door-to-door salesmen, aren't you?" cackled an old woman's voice.

"Mrs. Tisdale," said Call. "It's me, Callum Hunt. I'm looking for my dad. Is he here?"

The door opened wider. Mrs. Tisdale was wearing a checked dress, old boots, and a gray shawl. "Why would he be here?" she demanded. "Think I decided to sell him for parts?"

As soon as she came into view, Havoc began to bark like mad. He barked like he wanted to rip Mrs. Tisdale's arm right off.

"He hasn't been home in days," Call said, catching hold of Havoc's collar and trying to pretend the wolf wasn't slavering a little. "I thought maybe . . ."

"And the mages haven't been able to find him," said Tamara. "They've been looking."

They all turned to her in shock. "*Tamara!*" Aaron said.

Tamara shrugged. "What? She's a magician. You can see it on her! You can smell the magic in this house."

"She's right," said Jasper.

"Quit sucking up, Jasper," warned Call.

"I'm not sucking up; you're just stupid," Jasper replied. "And that pet of yours is a monster."

Mrs. Tisdale looked from Havoc to Tamara to Call. "I suppose you all better come inside — all but the wolf."

Call turned toward Havoc. "What's wrong with you?"

The wolf whimpered but then caught sight of Mrs. Tisdale and began growling again.

"Okay," Call said finally, pointing to a spot on the lawn. "Stay here and wait for us."

Havoc sat grudgingly, still growling.

They shuffled into the house, which smelled like dust and cat, but not unpleasantly to Call. As much as it pained him that Jasper might have a point, it was good to be warm. She led them into the kitchen, where she put a kettle on the stove. "Now tell me why I shouldn't contact the Magisterium and tell them to come pick up some truant students."

Call wasn't sure what to say. "Uh, because my dad wouldn't want you to?"

"And because we're on a mission," Tamara said, although this time it didn't sound as convincing.

"A mission? To find Alastair?" Mrs. Tisdale took out five mugs from her cupboard.

"He's in danger," Aaron said.

"You left the mages, didn't you?" Jasper asked. "Like Call's dad."

"None of that matters." Mrs. Tisdale turned to Call. "Your father's in some kind of trouble?"

Call nodded vehemently. "We really need to find him. If there's anything you know . . ."

He could see the moment she relented. "He came by last week. Stayed a few days out in the barn. Paid up a couple of months in advance, too, which isn't like him. But I really don't know where he is now. And I don't like the idea of you four kids being out here by yourselves." She gave Jasper a sharp look. "I might have left the mages, but that doesn't mean I'm too proud to call the Magisterium."

"How about we stay over in the barn and we promise we'll go right back in the morning?" Call proposed.

Mrs. Tisdale sighed, clearly giving up. "If you promised not to cause any trouble . . ."

"Or the house," Jasper said. "Maybe we could stay in the house. Where it's warm and not creepy."

"Come on, Jasper," said Aaron, grabbing him by the arm. Jasper went quietly, as though he'd already decided that even Mrs. Tisdale was not on his side.

In the night air, the cars reminded Call eerily of skeletal creatures, like dinosaur bones jutting out of the earth.

Havoc padded behind them quietly. His pale eyes kept turning back toward the house and his tongue lolled as though he was hungry.

The others seemed to feel the same sense of foreboding. Tamara looked around with a shiver and summoned up a small ball of fire. It danced along the path to the barn in front of them, lighting up scattered license plates, tires, and cans full of bolts.

Call was glad when they reached the barn, with its red-painted door secured by a huge metal bar. Up close, it was easy to see that the metal had been oiled recently. Aaron set to work lifting aside the bar and sliding the door open.

The old post-and-beam barn was a familiar place to Call. It was where the good cars rested, each under oilskin tarps. It was where he and his dad had spent most of their time when they came down here. Call would bring a stack of books or his Game Boy and sit up in the loft while his father tinkered below.

They were good memories, but right then they felt as hollow as the skeletal landscape of cars outside.

"Upstairs," he said, and started toward the ladder. He put his foot on the lower rung and almost collapsed as a jolt of pain shot up his leg. He bit down on the noise he wanted to make but caught Aaron's sympathetic look anyway. He didn't glance over at Jasper, just reached to pull himself up with his hands, keeping the weight off his leg as much as he could. The others followed.

It was dark in the hayloft and Call blinked around for a moment, blind until Tamara appeared with her ball of fire dancing just over her head like a lightbulb in a cartoon. The other two followed, spreading out in the narrow room. There wasn't much to it — a desk, a camp stove, and two narrow beds with blankets folded at the bottoms. Everything was incredibly neat, and if Mrs. Tisdale hadn't told them, Call wouldn't have guessed that Alastair had been there recently at all.

Jasper flopped down on one of the beds. "Are we going to eat? You know, it's got to be breaking some law to take me captive and not feed me."

Tamara sighed, then looked over at Call hopefully. "There's a stove. Is there any food?"

"Yeah, some. Mostly canned stuff." Call reached under his dad's bed for the baskets he kept there. Cans of Chef Boyardee Ravioli, bottles of water, beef jerky, a utility knife, forks, and two large Hershey's bars.

Call sat on one of the beds with Tamara while Jasper glared from the other one. Aaron efficiently opened several of the cans of ravioli and heated them over the camp stove — kindled with magic — while Tamara spread out a map of the surrounding area she'd found among Alastair's things and glared at it with her nose wrinkled up thoughtfully.

"Can you read that?" Call asked, peering over her shoulder. He reached for the map. "I think that's a road."

She swatted at his hand. "It's not a road, it's a river."

"Actually, it's a highway," said Jasper. "Give me that." He held his hand out. Tamara hesitated.

"Where are you trying to go, anyway?" Jasper asked.

"We were trying to get here," said Call. "But now, I don't know."

"Well, if your dad isn't here, he must have gone somewhere," said Aaron, bringing over the heated cans of ravioli. They took them gingerly, wrapping cloth around their hands so as not to get burned. Call passed around forks and they started to eat.

Jasper made a face at the first bite, but then he started shoveling pasta into his mouth.

"Maybe we can get Mrs. Tisdale to tell us something," Call said, but a cold feeling was settling into his stomach. Alastair was clearly on the run, but where would he go? He didn't have close friends that Call knew of or any other secret hiding places.

Aaron and Tamara were talking in low voices, and Jasper had gotten hold of the map and was staring at it. Call put aside his half-eaten can of ravioli and got to his feet, heading over to Alastair's desk. He jerked the main drawer open.

As he'd expected, it was full of car keys. Single keys mostly, attached to leather fobs that showed the make of the car: Volkswagens, Peugeots, Citroëns, MINI Coopers, even an Aston Martin. Most were covered in dust, but not the key to the Martin. Call lifted it out of the desk — the Martin was one of his dad's favorites, even though he hadn't gotten it to run yet. Surely he wouldn't have been working on it while he was here, on the run for his life, though?

Maybe Alastair had been planning on driving the Martin? It was a kicky car to escape in, capable of handling sharp turns and maybe even outrunning mages. If so, Call thought it was possible that he'd gotten it to work. Sure, it would be illegal for one of *them* to drive it, but that was the least of his worries.

He went to the ladder with a sigh, and started the arduous process of going down it. At least, with the others still in the loft, he was free to take it slow and wince as much as he wanted.

"Call, where are you going?" Tamara called to him.

"Can you send some light down?" Call asked.

She sighed. "Why do I have to do it? You can make fire hover just as well as I can."

"You do it better," Call said in a way he hoped was persuasive. She looked annoyed but sent down a sphere of fire anyway, which hovered in the air like a chandelier, dropping embers occasionally.

Call pulled the tarp off of the Aston Martin. The car was blue-green in color and trimmed out in gleaming chrome, with ivory leather seats that were only a little bit ripped. The floor pan looked in good shape, too; his dad said that was usually the first thing to succumb to rust.

Call clambered into place in the driver's seat and slid the

key into the ignition. He frowned — he'd really have to stretch to reach the gas or brake. Aaron could probably do it; he was taller. Call turned the key, but nothing happened. The old motor refused to rumble to life.

"What are you doing?"

Call jumped and almost banged his head on the roof of the car. He leaned out the open door and saw Aaron standing by the driver's side, looking curious.

"Looking around," Call said. "I'm not sure for what exactly. But my dad was definitely poking around this car before he left."

Aaron leaned in and whistled. "This is a nice car. Does it start?"

Call shook his head.

"Check the glove compartment," Aaron said. "My foster dad always used to keep everything in his."

Call reached over and flipped the compartment open. To his surprise, it was full of papers. Not just any papers, he realized, lifting them out. Letters. Alastair was one of the only adults Call knew who carried on most of his correspondence via handwritten letters instead of e-mail, so the letters didn't surprise him.

What did surprise him was who they were from. He opened one and scanned to the bottom, to the signature there, a signature that made his stomach turn over.

Master Joseph A. Walther

"What? What is it?" Aaron said, and Call looked up at him. He must have had a shocked expression on his face, because Aaron stepped away from the car and yelled upstairs to the others: "He found something! Call found something!"

"No, I didn't." Call stumbled out of the car, the letters jammed under his arm. "I didn't find anything."

Aaron's green eyes were troubled. "Then what are those?"

"Just personal stuff. My dad's notes."

"Call." It was Tamara, hanging over the edge of the hayloft. Call could see Jasper behind her. "Your dad is a wanted criminal. He doesn't have 'personal stuff.'"

"She's right," Aaron said, sounding sorry. "Anything could be relevant."

"Fine." Call wished he'd been cleverer, wished he'd guessed his father's hiding spot instead of Aaron, wished he didn't have to share these letters with the others. "But I'm reading them. Not anyone else."

He kept the letters jammed under his arm as he climbed back up the ladder, Aaron on his heels. Jasper had figured out how the hurricane lamps worked, and the hayloft was full of light. Call sat down on one of the beds, and the rest of them clambered onto the other one.

It was weird, seeing Master Joseph's handwriting like this. It was spiky and thin and he signed every letter with his full name, complete with middle initial. There were nearly a dozen of them, dated over the last three months. And they were full of disturbing lines.

There's a way we can both have what we want.

You want your son brought back from the dead and we want Constantine Madden.

You don't understand the full power of the Alkahest.

We never saw eye to eye before, Alastair, but now you've lost so much. *Imagine if Sarah could be returned to you. Imagine if everything you lost could be returned to you.*

Steal the Alkahest, bring it to us, and all of your suffering will be over.

None of it made any sense. Alastair had been going to use the Alkahest to kill him, hadn't he? He'd wanted to destroy the Enemy of Death.

Call remembered the astonishment on his father's face as he'd struck the wall, remembered the feeling of overwhelming fury. What if he'd been wrong about Alastair? What if Alastair hadn't been lying when he said he wasn't going to kill Call?

But if Alastair wanted to get rid of him and get the soul of his *real* son back, that was just as bad. Maybe he didn't want to kill Call outright, but sticking his soul back in Constantine Madden seemed a lot like dying.

"What?" Tamara was leaning so far off the bed that she was nearly falling. "Call, what does it say?"

"Nothing," Call said grimly, folding up the most incriminating note and sticking it in his pocket. "It's a bunch of tips on how to grow begonias."

"Liar," said Jasper succinctly, snatching one of the letters off the bed. He started to read out loud, eyes growing wider. "Wait, these are . . . these are really, really, really not about begonias!"

It was horrible. Tamara and Aaron clearly hadn't believed him, but the look of betrayal on both their faces was almost as awful as Jasper's smug gloating. Worse, they read everything. Line after bizarre line — though to Call's relief, nothing in the letters referred directly to the fact that he possessed the soul of Constantine Madden. Who knew what they would have thought if they'd gotten ahold of the letter in his pocket?

"So, he really *has* the Alkahest and he's going to *give it* to the Enemy?" Jasper looked frightened. "I thought you said he'd been wrongfully accused."

"Look at this one," said Tamara. "Alastair must have agreed, because Master Joseph is writing about how he'll contact him and how they'll meet. It's supposed to take place two days from now."

"We need to go back to the Magisterium," said Aaron. "We have to tell someone. Call, I believed you about your dad, but maybe you were wrong."

"We can't risk the Alkahest falling into the hands of the Enemy," said Tamara. "It means Aaron could be killed. You see that, right, Call?"

Call looked at the fire burning in the lamps. Had he completely misunderstood what was going on with his father? He'd assumed his dad was a good person on the side of the Magisterium and the Masters, on the side of stopping Constantine Madden, whatever the cost. But now it seemed like maybe his dad was actually a bad person on Master Joseph's side after all, and was willing to do whatever it took to get the soul of his kid back. Which was not the worst thing from a certain perspective. But if Alastair decided to join up with Master Joseph, was Call morally obligated to let him do it or to stop him?

Call's head hurt.

"I don't want anything bad to happen to Aaron," Call said. That was the one thing he was sure about. "I never did."

Aaron looked miserable. "Well, we're not going to get anywhere tonight," he said. "It's late and we're all tired. Maybe if we sleep for a couple of hours, we can figure something out in the morning."

They looked at the two beds. Each was about big enough for one adult or two kids.

"I call that one," said Jasper. He pointed at Tamara and Call. "And I call Aaron, because you're creepy and you're a girl."

"I can sleep on the floor," Aaron offered, looking at the expression on Tamara's face.

"That doesn't help anyone but Jasper," said Tamara crossly, and got onto the leftmost bed. "It's fine, Call; we'll just sleep on top of the covers. Don't worry about it."

Call thought that maybe he should offer to sleep on the floor like Aaron had, but he didn't want to. His leg already hurt and, besides, he knew for a fact that there were sometimes rats hiding in the barn.

"Okay," he said, climbing in gingerly beside her.

It was weird.

In the other bed, Jasper and Aaron were trying to share a single pillow. There was a muffled cry as someone was punched. Call pushed the pillow on his bed over to Tamara and laid his head down on his crooked arm.

He closed his eyes, but sleep didn't come. It was uncomfortable trying to keep to one side of the bed, making sure that even his toes didn't stray over to Tamara's side. It didn't help that he kept seeing the words in the letters Master Joseph had written, painted on the backs of his eyelids.

"Call?"

He opened his eyes. Tamara was looking at him from a few inches away, her eyes big and dark. "Why are you so important?" she whispered.

He felt the warm gust of her breath on his cheek.

"Important?" he echoed. Jasper had started to snore.

"All those letters," she said. "From Master Joseph. I thought they'd be about Aaron. He's the Makar. But they were all about you. *Call is the most important thing.*"

"I mean . . . I guess because he's my dad," Call said, floundering. "So I'd be important to him."

"It didn't sound like that kind of important," Tamara said softly. "Call, you know you can tell us anything, right?"

Call wasn't sure how to answer her. He was still trying to decide when Havoc began to howl.

CHAPTER ELEVEN

Havoc, QUIET! SHHHHHH!" Call said, but the wolf kept on barking, shoving his snout into the gap between the barn doors and scratching the wood with his paws.

"What do you see, boy?" Aaron asked. "Is there something out there?"

Tamara took a step toward the wolf. "Maybe your dad came back."

Call's heart gave a wild thump. He ran to the door that Havoc was nosing at and pulled it back, opening the barn to the cold air outside.

Havoc darted past him. The night was quiet. The moon was a sliver in the sky. Call had to squint to see his wolf dart across the trampled grass toward the lines of wrecked cars, looking humped and unnatural in the darkness.

"What's that?" It was Jasper, his voice a scared whisper, pointing. Aaron stepped forward; they were all crowding around Call now, in front of the open barn door. Call looked where Jasper was pointing. At first he saw nothing; then, staring harder, he caught sight of something slipping around the side of one of the cars.

Tamara gasped. The thing was rising, seeming to grow from moment to moment, swelling right before them. It gleamed under the moon — a monster made of slick metal, dark and wet-looking, as if its surface were rubbed with oil. Its eyes were like two massive headlights, flashing in the darkness. And its mouth — Call goggled as its massive jaw unhinged, lined with rows of sharklike metal teeth, and then closed on the hood of an ancient Citroën.

The car made a horrible crunching sound. The creature threw its head back, swallowing. It bulged outward as the car disappeared into its vast maw. A moment later the car was gone and the creature seemed to grow more gigantic.

"It's an elemental," Tamara said nervously. "Metal. It must be drawing power from all those cars and junk."

"We should get out of here before it notices us," Jasper said.

"Coward," Call chided. "It's an elemental on the loose. Isn't dealing with it our job?"

Jasper threw his shoulders back and glared. "Look, that thing has *nothing to do* with us. We're supposed to defend *people*, but I don't want to die defending your dad's hoarding. He'll be better off without all these cars — if he's not executed for being in league with the Enemy, which is a big if — and we'll be better off out of here!"

"Shut up," Aaron said. "Just shut up." His hand rose from his side. The metal on his wristband glowed. Call could see what looked like a shadow starting to rise from his palm, half enveloping his hand.

"Stop!" Tamara grabbed Aaron's wrist. "You haven't been

taught to use the void properly. And the elemental's too big. Think of the size of the hole you'd have to open to get rid of it —"

Now Aaron looked angry. "Tamara —"

"Uh, guys," Jasper interrupted. "I get that you're arguing, but I think it just noticed us."

Jasper was right. The headlight eyes were gleaming in their direction. Tamara let go of Aaron as the creature began to move. Then, unexpectedly, she whirled on Call.

"What are we supposed to do?" she demanded.

Call was too surprised to be asked for instructions to answer. Which was fine, because Aaron was already talking. "We have to get to Mrs. Tisdale and protect her. If that thing has just stumbled on this place, then maybe it will eat some cars and go in peace. But if it doesn't, we have to be ready."

"Metal elementals are rare," Jasper said, grabbing up Tamara's pack. "I don't know a lot about them, but I know they don't like fire. If it starts coming for us, I'll throw up a fire screen. Okay?"

"I can do that," Tamara snapped.

"It doesn't matter who does it!" Aaron said, exasperated. "Now come on!"

They all started to run toward the farmhouse, Call lagging slightly behind, not just because his leg was hurting but also because he was worried about Havoc. He wanted to call out to him, make sure his wolf was safe, but he was worried it would call the elemental's attention. And he wasn't sure he could outrun it if it came to that. Already, Tamara, Aaron, and Jasper were outpacing him.

The creature was still moving, sometimes half-hidden by cars, sometimes horribly clear. It wasn't moving fast, more like a cat stalking its prey. Slowly it came, growing with each mouthful of metal it took.

As Call got closer to Mrs. Tisdale's house, he realized that something was wrong. Light was spilling out of the farmhouse, not just from the windows but also from the whole front. The door and part of the wall was missing. Wires and wood hung in the gaping hole that remained.

Aaron ran up the steps first. "Mrs. Tisdale!" he called. "Mrs. Tisdale, are you all right?"

Call followed, leg aching. The furniture was knocked over, a coffee table splintered. A love seat was on fire, flames rising from a blackened corner. Mrs. Tisdale lay on the floor, a terrible gash across her chest. Blood soaked the rug under her. Call stared in horror. Mixed in with the blood were gleaming bits of metal.

Aaron dropped to his knees. "Mrs. Tisdale?"

Her eyes were open, but she didn't seem to be able to focus her gaze. "Children," she said in a whispery, awful voice. "Children, they're after you."

Call remembered a little bit about healing magic. He'd seen Alex use it to heal Drew's broken ankle once, drawing up binding and healing powers from the earth. He bent down next to Aaron, trying to summon up what he could. If he could heal her, then maybe his magic was good for more than Alastair thought. Maybe *he* was good for more than Alastair thought.

Maybe he was good.

Pressing his fingers gently over her collarbone, he directed energy into her. He tried to feel it coming up from the ground, tried to think of himself as a conduit. But after a moment, she pushed his hand away.

"It's too late for that," Mrs. Tisdale said. "You're the ones who can still get away. You need to run. Call, I was there the night you thought you lost Havoc. I was the one who chained him up. I know what's at stake."

Call pulled back from her, reeling.

"What is she talking about?" Tamara asked. "What are you talking about, Mrs. Tisdale?"

"It's just an elemental," Aaron said. "We can get rid of it. We can help you." He looked up wildly at Tamara and Jasper. "Maybe we should call for help from the Magisterium —"

"No!" the old woman gasped. "Don't you know what that creature *is*? Its name is Automotones — it is an ancient and terrible monster — it was captured by the mages of the Magisterium hundreds of years ago." Blood had appeared at the corners of her mouth. She drew a ragged breath. "If it is here now, it's because those — those — *mages* released it to hunt you down. To kill you!"

With a shudder, Call remembered Master Rufus's lecture on the elementals trapped beneath the Magisterium. How terrifying they were. How unstoppable.

"To hunt *Alastair* down, you mean?" Jasper asked.

"It broke into this house," she hissed. "It demanded that I tell it where *you* were. Not Alastair. You four." Her eyes fixed on Aaron. "You had better run, Makar."

Aaron's face had gone blank with shock. "Run from the Magisterium? Not the Enemy?"

Her mouth curved up into a strange smile. "You can never outrun the Enemy of Death, Aaron Stewart," she said, and though she seemed to be speaking to Aaron, she was looking at Call. He stared back at her as her eyes went blank.

"Look out!" Tamara screamed.

The metal monster — Automotones — lurched into the house through the broken wall. It was truly huge now. It smashed upward with its flat, manhole-size hands, ripping away at the ceiling, tearing a hole between the upstairs and the bottom floor to clear a space for itself. Call yelped and fell sideways, narrowly missing being smashed by a falling dresser. The piece of furniture broke open on the floor, scattering clothes.

Suddenly a sheet of fire appeared, like a living wall of flame, scorching the floor and igniting what was left of the ceiling. Jasper was holding the fire in place with obvious effort as Automotones roared and snapped.

"Go," Jasper said to Call. "Run! I'll follow."

Call felt bad about having called him a coward. Pushing himself up from the floor, he staggered toward the back of the house.

Aaron and Tamara followed. Tamara had summoned a ball of fire, which glowed in her hand. She whipped her head back, braids flying, toward where Jasper stood.

"Come on, Jasper," Aaron called. "Now!"

Jasper released his wall of fire and ran toward them, the metal elemental racing after. Tamara threw her summoned flame at the monster's maw as Jasper staggered out onto the lawn with Call.

Jasper was clearly exhausted from the effort he'd put out raising the fire screen. He made it a few feet onto the lawn and then collapsed. Call took a step toward him but had no idea what to do. There was no way he could carry Jasper and run; he could barely run without the weight of a whole extra person on his shoulders.

Tamara ran over the lawn, Aaron just behind her. Behind them came Automotones. Rearing and clawing as the flames boiled around it — Jasper's fire had clearly caught some of the furniture alight, and now the curtains and probably the walls were burning. The whole farmhouse was going to go up like a torch.

"Jasper!" Call reached for Jasper's arm and tried to at least pull him upright. Jasper made it onto his knees and then let out a yowl of terror. Call spun around and saw the metal elemental rising up over them, blotting out the sliver of moon. Its hands were reaching down. They looked like huge metal crab pincers, about to close on Call and Jasper, about to slice them in half.

Call remembered being in his father's awful workroom the past summer, remembered the rage he felt and how he'd looked at Alastair and just *pushed*. Now he tried to summon up all the rage and fear and awfulness he was holding inside and *push* it at Automotones.

The monster flew back, emitting a noise that sounded like a rusty car being pulled apart. The noise turned to a raging growl as Automotones turned toward Tamara and Aaron. Aaron stepped in front of Tamara, raising his hand, but the monster swept him out of the way as if he were a pesky fly, and grabbed for Tamara, lifting her up into the air.

"Tamara!" Call started to run toward the elemental, forgetting for a second that it was terrifying, that it was huge, that it was deadly. In his mind he saw the metal pincer closing around Tamara, crushing her in its grasp. He was vaguely aware that Aaron was running and yelling, too, that Tamara was struggling but silent in the creature's claw. All of a sudden,

Automotones gave a lurch and a stumble. Tamara pulled free, tumbling onto the grass.

The elemental writhed around, and Call saw that Havoc had leaped onto its back, his Chaos-ridden claws sinking into the metal skin, teeth tearing. The noise of ripping metal filled the night.

But the creature shook itself, and Havoc lost his balance, legs scrabbling desperately at the air. He was holding on by his teeth and then wasn't holding on at all. He flew toward the house, toward the fire, whimpering as he fell.

Summoning air, heedless of the elemental or the fight, Call focused on his wolf. He concentrated on forming a soft cushion of circling wind to catch Havoc. Dimly, he heard the creature screeching close to him; dimly, he understood that he was putting the rest of them in danger to make sure his pet was unharmed, but he didn't care.

Havoc fell into Call's air magic as if it were a net, bouncing a little, his paws flailing, his coruscating eyes wide. Slowly, Call lowered the wolf to the ground, carefully, carefully —

That was when the elemental hit him. It felt like being smashed by a giant wave. He heard Tamara yell his name and then he was flying backward, hitting the ground with enough force to send a shock wave through his body. He rolled over, spitting out dirt and grass, and saw the metal elemental looming over him. It looked enormous, as big as the sky its body blotted out. Call struggled to get to his feet, his bad leg wobbling, but fell back into the grass. In the distance, he could see Tamara running toward them, ropes of fire swinging from her hands, but he knew she was too far away to get to him in time. Automotones was already swaying down toward him, its toothy jaws wide.

Call clutched at the dirt, trying to reach into it, to summon up earth magic, but there was no time. He could smell the stink of metal and rust as the elemental opened its mouth to swallow him.

"Stop!"

The elemental jerked its head back. Call swung around to see Aaron standing behind him, his hand outstretched. Shining in his palm was a cloud of oily darkness, spilling upward. The expression on his face was one Call couldn't remember seeing before. His eyes burned like brands and a grimace pulled his face into something that looked disturbingly like a smile.

The oily black nothingness flew from Aaron's hand and hurtled straight down Automotones's throat. For a moment, nothing changed. Then the creature began to vibrate, metal clanking against metal. Call stared. The elemental looked as if it were being crushed by a huge, invisible hand, its metal hide being sucked inward. It opened its mouth and Call saw the oily blackness fuming and bubbling inside it. He realized what was happening. The elemental was collapsing in on itself, each joint and screw, each plate and motor, drawn into the expanding void that Aaron had hurled down its throat.

There was a hand on Call's shoulder, and Aaron was drawing him up to his feet. The scary expression was gone from Aaron's face; he just looked grim, watching as Automotones gave a last howl and vanished into a speck of darkness that singed across the air.

"What happens to it?" Jasper asked, running up. "Where is it now? Is it dead?"

Call looked back at the burning building, at the wreckage of cars. He didn't care where Automotones had gone. The important thing was that they were all safe.

"It's in the void," Aaron said, his voice flat. "It won't come back."

"Come on," said Tamara. "We need to get away from the fire."

They began to make their way back toward the barn, Havoc running ahead of them. The air was filled with smoke, and the glow from the burning fire behind them turned the sky as light as day.

"What we need to do is go back to the Magisterium," Jasper said breathlessly. "Show them what we found. Call's dad has been in *direct contact* with the *Enemy's servants*, remember? He's going to bring them the Alkahest. We need help."

"We're not going back to the Magisterium," Aaron said. His voice was still the same, flat and rigid. Call had the sense that he was holding back whatever he was feeling, tamping it down hard. "*They* sent that thing after us."

"After Alastair, you mean," Tamara corrected. "You don't believe what that old woman said, do you?"

"Yeah, I do."

"She's got no reason to lie," Call agreed.

Now Aaron's voice started to crack a little. "If they didn't send it, why did it attack Mrs. Tisdale? Why did it attack us? It ought to have been given instructions not to hurt us."

"Maybe they decided that if they couldn't get us back, it was better to have us dead than in the Enemy's hands," said Jasper. They all looked at him in surprise. "It's the sort of thing the Assembly would do," he added, with a shrug.

"I thought you wanted to go back," Call said.

"I do. But you guys have messed up royally." Jasper rolled his eyes at Call like he was an idiot, an expression Call was very familiar with. "The longer we're away, the more convinced they're going to become that they have to cut their losses. Wipe out Aaron first, then wipe out us so there are no witnesses, and it's just a tragedy. If Constantine Madden got hold of Aaron, he could kill him — or he could brainwash him. Maybe they're afraid of that. Maybe they're afraid that losing Aaron to Constantine could lose them the war."

"Not having Aaron would lose them the war!" said Tamara. "He's the Makar!"

They had reached the barn. Jasper's face looked like cut stone in the flickering light. "I don't think you understand how they do math."

"Enough," said Call, turning to face the others. "You guys go back to school. I think I can stop my father, so long as I can get to him in time. I have to talk to him. I have to try. But this is getting too dangerous for you to come along."

They'll never get it, he thought. *My dad wants his son back. He thinks if he trades the Alkahest to Master Joseph, Joseph can fix me. Can make me Callum Hunt again. But Master Joseph's tricking him, trying to lure him in. He'll probably kill him once he gets the Alkahest.*

But Call couldn't tell them that, any of that.

You can't outrun the Enemy of Death.

"No way," Tamara said, crossing her arms over her chest. "It's not safe for you to go — it's not safe for any of us. You don't even know where Alastair's headed."

"I think I do, actually," Call said. He slid the barn door open and limped inside. The rest of them, even Havoc, waited in the doorway as he retrieved Master Joseph's letters. When he returned, he held one up to the light.

"There are numbers under Master Joseph's name," he said. "In every letter."

"Yeah, probably the date," Jasper said.

Call read the numbers off. "45. 1661. 67. 2425."

"That's not a date, except maybe on Mars," said Tamara, crowding closer. "It's . . ."

"It's coordinates," said Call. "Latitude and longitude. That's how my dad used to program the GPS in his car. It tells you how to find something. Joseph is telling my dad where he is."

"Then we know where we're going," said Aaron. "We just need to find something we can plug the coordinates into. . . ."

"Here," Tamara said, taking out her phone. But when she touched the screen, it didn't come on. "Oh. I guess I'm out of charge."

"A computer in any Internet café would work," said Call, folding up the papers. "But there's no 'we.' I'm doing this alone."

"We're not leaving you alone and you know it," Aaron said. He held up a hand against Call's protest. "Look, by the time we get back to school, your father could already have reached Master Joseph. There might not be enough time to do anything, even if we could convince the mages we knew what we were talking about."

"And if we go after Joseph and get the Alkahest back, then we go back in glory," Tamara added. "Besides, they already sent a monster after us. Until we know whether we can trust them, the only way is forward."

Call looked over at Jasper. "You don't have to come." He actually felt bad now for having dragged Jasper into this mess.

"Oh, I'm coming," Jasper said. "If monsters are hunting us, I am sticking with the Makar."

"How can the mages of the Magisterium be the good guys if they'd send a monster to murder us just for running away?" Aaron asked. "We're kids."

"I don't know," Call said. He was starting to worry that there weren't any good guys. Just people with longer or shorter Evil Overlord lists.

Tamara sighed and scrubbed a hand through her hair. "Right now, we need to find a town, somewhere where we can get new clothes and some food. We look like we set ourselves on fire and then rolled around in the mud. We don't exactly blend in."

Havoc, hearing the words *roll around in the mud*, began to do just that. Call had to admit Tamara was right. They were dirty, and not like actors in movies who had one artistic smear of dirt across a cheekbone. Their uniforms were ripped and bloody and soaked with oily metal elemental goop.

"I guess we start walking," said Jasper, sounding dispirited.

"We're not going to walk," said Aaron. "We're going to drive. There are three hundred cars here."

"Yeah, but most of the ones that haven't been eaten don't exactly *work*," Call pointed out. "And the few that *do* work don't have keys waiting for us."

"Come on," said Aaron. "I don't have a dad in prison for nothing. I think I can hot-wire one of these."

He strode off toward the field of cars with a confident set to his shoulders.

"That's our Makar," said Jasper. "Chaos magic *and* grand theft auto."

"I thought you said your dad ran off," Call said to Aaron, running after him. "And that you didn't know where he was."

Aaron shrugged. "I guess no one likes to admit their dad is in jail."

Right then an imprisoned dad didn't seem like the worst thing to Call, but he knew better than to say it.

Call helped Aaron select the least broken car he recalled Alastair buying. A Morris Minor, its swooping exterior a deep emerald green that contrasted with its red leather seats. It was one of Alastair's newer cars, manufactured in 1965, and unlike lots of the others, didn't need a new engine.

"It's still not fast," Call warned. "Like, we probably need to stay under forty miles per hour, even on the highway. And it doesn't have a GPS. He might have installed one eventually, but he didn't get around to it."

"What happens if we don't stay under forty miles per hour?" Tamara asked.

Call shrugged. "Maybe it explodes? I don't know."

"Great," Jasper said. "Can any of you numbskulls drive?"

"Not really," Aaron said, crouching down under the seat, cutting wires with Call's knife and wrapping them back together in a new combination.

"How can you know how to hot-wire a car but not drive one?" Jasper asked, heaving a massive sigh.

"That's a good question," Aaron muttered, sticking his head out from under the seat. He looked sweaty and a little shaky. "Maybe you should take it up with my dad. He didn't get around to teaching me before he got locked up."

"I've driven golf carts before," said Tamara. "How different could it be?"

The engine sprang to life, revving under Aaron's capable hands.

"I'll drive," said Call, whose father had shown him how —

sort of. He was in enough trouble that driving an unregistered, uninsured vehicle without a license was hardly going to make much of a difference. Besides, he was the Enemy of Death, an outlaw, a rebel — breaking the law should be the mere tip of his iceberg of evil.

Havoc barked, as if agreeing with him. Havoc had taken the front passenger seat and didn't seem inclined to let anyone else have it.

Aaron leaned against the hood, looking exhausted. He glanced in Call's direction, but his eyes didn't seem to focus. "It's weird, huh? Everyone expecting me to be a hero and my father a convicted criminal."

"Well, since we're tracking down my dad because he stole some kind of magical artifact, I'm not exactly in a position to judge." Call smiled, but Aaron didn't seem to notice.

"It's just — I don't know. Constantine Madden was a bad Makar. Maybe I'll turn out bad, too. Maybe it's in my blood."

Call shook his head, so surprised by the thought that at first he didn't know how to respond. "Uh, no . . . I don't think that's you."

"Come on, everyone, get in the car," Tamara said. "Aaron, are you okay?"

Aaron nodded, climbing unsteadily into the backseat. Jasper and Tamara loaded the Morris's trunk up with their remaining stuff. Thankfully, since they'd gotten out of bed to fight Automotones, their backpacks had remained safely in the barn.

Now all Call had to do was not crash. Alastair had let him drive before, steering one of the old cars when Alastair was towing it, or driving around the farm to park a new acquisition. But none of that was the same as driving all by himself.

Call got in and adjusted the driver's seat, shoving it forward so his shoes reached the pedals. *Gas*, he told himself. *Brakes*.

Then he adjusted the mirrors, because that's what Alastair always did in a new car — he hoped it would give Aaron and Tamara and even Jasper confidence that Call knew what he was doing. But the familiar movements made him think of his dad, and a helpless panic settled over him.

He was never going to be the person his father loved. That person was dead.

"Let's go," Jasper said, climbing into the backseat. Tamara climbed in after him. Apparently they'd decided to let Havoc keep shotgun. "If you even know how to drive."

"I know how," Call said, letting out the clutch and sending the car rocketing down the road.

The Morris Minor clearly needed new shocks. Every bump in the road threw the kids into the air. It also guzzled gas so fast that Call knew they were going to have to make a lot of stops. He clung to the wheel, squinted at the road, and hoped for the best.

In the backseat, Aaron fell into a kind of fitful sleep, not seeming to mind the roughness of the ride. He thrashed around a little but didn't wake.

"Is he okay?" Call called into the back.

Tamara touched the inside of her wrist to Aaron's forehead. "I don't know. He doesn't have a fever, but he's kind of clammy."

"Maybe he expended too much magic," Jasper said. "They say the cost of using void magic is high."

It took them twenty minutes to find the edge of a small town. Call pumped gas into the Morris while Tamara and Jasper went into the station to pay.

"Do you think he noticed how weird you looked?" Call asked when they came back. They were, after all, wearing burned, muddy clothes. And they were kids, all barely thirteen. Definitely too young to be driving cars.

Jasper shrugged. "He was watching television. I don't think he cared about anything except that we paid."

"Let's go," said Tamara, climbing into the back to sit next to the still-sleeping Aaron. "Before he thinks about it."

Tamara used the map to direct Call through the town until they came to a closed sporting goods store with a big, empty parking lot. Call very slowly and carefully pulled into a vacant spot. Aaron was still asleep. Tamara yawned.

"Maybe we should let him rest," she said.

"Yeah," Jasper said muzzily. "You're right. I am totally awake and alert in every way, but chaos magic is hard on Makars."

Call rolled his eyes, but he was as exhausted as the rest of them. He allowed himself to doze, leaning across the center console to pillow his head on Havoc. A moment later, he'd fallen into a fitful sleep. When he woke up, Aaron was awake and Tamara was asking him if he was okay and lemony daylight was filtering through the window.

"I don't know," Aaron said. "I feel a little weird. And dizzy."

"Maybe you need food," Call said, stretching.

Aaron grinned as Jasper and Tamara climbed out of the car. "Food does sound good."

"Stay here, boy," Call said to Havoc, scratching behind his ears. "No barking. I'll get you a sandwich."

He left the car window cranked open, in case Havoc needed fresh air. He hoped nobody tried to steal the car, mostly for the thief's sake. No regular person, even a car thief, was prepared for a surprise faceful of angry Chaos-ridden wolf.

The street had a few other shops, including a used-clothing store that Tamara pointed to with great enthusiasm.

"Perfect," she said. "We can pick up some new clothes. Aaron, if you don't feel up to it . . ."

"I'll be fine," he said. He still looked exhausted but managed to grin anyway.

"No amount of clothing is going to make that car of yours stand out less," said Jasper, who knew how to bring down any mood.

"We can buy it a scarf," Call told him.

The store was full of racks of used and vintage clothes, and all sorts of secondhand knickknacks that Call recognized from his dad's forays to antiques fairs and junk shops. Three Singer sewing machine stands had been turned into a counter. Behind it sat a woman with short white hair and purple cat-eye glasses. She glanced up at them.

"What happened to you four?" she asked, eyebrows going up.

"Mudslide?" Aaron said, although he didn't sound very certain.

She winced, as though either she didn't believe him or she was generally disgusted with them in her store, tracking mud and touching things with sooty fingers. Maybe both.

It didn't take too long for Call to find the perfect outfit, though. Jeans, like the kind he'd worn back home, and a navy blue T-shirt proclaiming I DON'T BELIEVE IN MAGIC with a squashed fairy in the lower right-hand corner.

Aaron started laughing when he saw it. "There is something seriously wrong with you," he said.

"Well, you look like you're on your way to yoga class," Call said. Aaron had picked out gray sweatpants and a shirt with a yin-yang symbol on it. Tamara had found black jeans and wore a big silky tunic that might be a dress over it. Jasper had somehow discovered khakis, a blazer in his size, and mirrored sunglasses.

The total for the clothes came to about twenty dollars, which had Tamara frowning thoughtfully and counting out loud. Jasper leaned past her and gave the cat-eye-glasses lady his most charming smile.

"Can you tell us where we can get sandwiches?" he asked. "And Internet?"

"Bits and Bytes, two blocks down Main," she said, and pointed at their heap of discarded, muddy green uniforms. "I'm guessing I can toss these? What kind of clothes are they, anyway?"

Call gave the clothes an almost regretful look. Their uniforms branded them as Magisterium school students. Without them, all they had were their wristbands.

"Karate uniforms," he said. "That's how we got dirty. Karate-chopping ninjas."

"In a mudslide," Aaron interjected, sticking to his story.

Tamara dragged them out of the store by the backs of their shirts. Main Street was mostly deserted. A few cars drove up and down, but nobody gave them a second look.

"Karate-chopping ninjas in a mudslide?" Tamara gave Aaron and Call a dark look. "Could you guys try to lay low?" She stopped in front of an ATM. "I've got to get some money out."

"Speaking of lying low, I've heard they can trace your ATM card," said Jasper. "You know, using the Internet."

Call wondered if he'd thrown away his phone for nothing.

"The *police* can," said Aaron. "Not the Magisterium."

"How do you know?"

"Well, we have to risk it," said Tamara. "That was all the rest of our cash, that twenty bucks, and we're going to need more gas and food."

Still, her hand shook a little as she took out the money and stuffed it in her wallet.

Bits and Bytes turned out to be a sandwich shop with a row of computers where you could rent Internet time, a dollar an hour.

Aaron went to buy sandwiches while Call logged in. He typed *latitude* and *longitude* into Google, which took him to a page that calculated both from an address. He pressed the reverse lookup button and entered the numbers he had.

Then he held his breath.

The map showed a location quickly enough, although there was no address associated with it, just the words *Monument Island, Harpswell, Maine*. According to the map, there were no roads on it and no houses. He doubted there was a ferry, either.

Even worse, when he typed in the directions, the computer said it would take fifteen hours to drive there. Fifteen hours! And Alastair had a head start. What if he was already there? What if he'd taken a plane?

For a moment, terrible panic overwhelmed Call. The screen in front of him flickered. The lights shuddered. Jasper looked in Call's direction, sneering.

"Maybe someone went through the Gate of Control too soon," he said under his breath.

"Easy." Aaron put a hand on Call's shoulder. Steadying him.

Call stood up abruptly, fighting for breath. "I've got to . . ."

"You've got to what?" Aaron looked at him strangely.

"Print," Call said. "I've got to print. The directions." He staggered over to the register. "Do you guys have a printer?"

The girl behind the counter nodded. "Three dollars a page, though."

Call glanced at Tamara. "Can we?"

She sighed. "It's a necessary expense. Go ahead."

Call sent the directions to print. Now all three of them were looking at him strangely. "Is something wrong?" Aaron said.

"It's in Maine," Call said. "Fifteen hours away by car."

Aaron looked up from his ham-and-provolone sandwich with a shocked expression. "Seriously?"

"Could have been worse," Jasper said, surprising Call. "Could have been Alaska."

Tamara glanced around and then back at Call. Her brown eyes were very serious. "You sure you want to do this?"

"I'm sure I have to," he said.

She took a bite out of her sandwich. "Well, eat up, everyone," she said. "I guess we're going on a road trip to Maine."

↑ ≈ △ ○ @

After lunch, they got back to the car, dumping their backpacks in the back. Call walked Havoc and fed him two roast beef sandwiches and then tipped a bottle of water so he could lap at it. The Chaos-ridden wolf ate and drank with surprising daintiness.

Call drove, with Tamara acting as copilot while Jasper and Aaron pillowed their heads on Havoc's furry back and napped. Jasper must have been pretty exhausted to deign to sleep on a Chaos-ridden animal. Hours passed like this.

"You know you can get arrested for going *under* the speed limit, too," said Tamara, her warm ginger ale in the cup holder beside her. She was unbraiding her hair, brushing it out as it blew around with the breeze of her open window. Tamara almost always kept her hair in braids, and Call was surprised by how long it was unbraided, black and shiny and hanging to her waist.

Call pressed his foot harder on the gas and the Morris lurched forward. As the speedometer needle started to edge up, the car began to shudder.

"Uh," Tamara said. "Maybe we should take a chance on the cops."

He gave her a quick smile. "Do you really think the Magisterium sent that monster after us?"

"I don't think Master Rufus would," Tamara said, hesitating. When she spoke again, the words came out in a rush. "But I'm not sure about anyone else. It just doesn't make sense to me. Call, if there was something you knew — you'd tell us, right?"

"What do you mean?"

"Nothing," she said, her fingers nimbly working her hair back into a single long braid.

Call focused on the road, on the blur of lines and keeping his distance from other cars.

"What's the next exit?" he asked her. "We need gas."

"Call," Tamara said again. Now she was playing with her wristband. He wished she'd stop fidgeting. "You know if there was something you wanted to tell me that was a secret, I'd keep it. I wouldn't tell anyone."

"Like you didn't tell anyone about my dad?" Call said, immediately regretting it. Tamara's eyes went wide and then angry.

"You *know* why I did that," she said. "He tried to steal the Alkahest! He was putting Aaron in danger! And things turned out even worse than we thought. He didn't have good intentions."

"Not everything is about Aaron," Call said, which made him feel even more terrible. It wasn't Aaron's fault he was who he was. Call was just glad Aaron was asleep again, his blond head resting on Havoc's fur.

"Then what is this about, Call?" Tamara said. "Because I have a feeling you know."

Words felt like they were clawing their way up Call's throat — he didn't know if he wanted to yell at Tamara or spill everything just for the relief of not keeping it bottled up anymore — when suddenly the car started shaking hard.

"Call, slow down!" Tamara said.

"I *am* slowed down!" he protested. "Maybe I should pull over —"

Suddenly and without warning, Master Rufus appeared, popping into existence between Call and Tamara in the front seat of the car.

"Students," he said, looking very displeased. "Would you like to explain yourselves?"

CHAPTER TWELVE

CALL AND TAMARA screamed. The car swerved, Call's hands heedless on the wheel. That made Tamara scream even harder. All the screams woke Jasper and Aaron, who added their voices to the screaming. Havoc started to bark. Throughout all the commotion, Master Rufus just floated in the center of the car, looking annoyed and — translucent.

That was the final shock. Call slammed on the brakes, and the car screeched to a stop in the middle of the road. Everyone suddenly stopped screaming. There was a dead silence. Master Rufus continued to be see-through.

"Are you dead?" Call asked in a shaking voice.

"He's not *dead*," Jasper said, managing to sound smug and annoyed even though he was clearly terrified. "He's calling from an ether phone. This is how it looks on the other end."

"Oh." Call filed away the knowledge that the thing he'd always called a tornado phone was actually called something else. He pictured Master Rufus holding the glass jar on his lap, staring into it balefully. "So you're somewhere else?" he said to Rufus. "Not . . . actually here?"

"It doesn't matter where I am. What matters is that you children are all in a great deal of trouble," Master Rufus said. "An enormous amount of trouble and also a great deal of danger. Callum Hunt, you are already on thin ice. Aaron Stewart, you are a Makar and you have responsibilities — responsibilities that include *behaving responsibly*. And you, Tamara Rajavi, of the three of you, I expected you to know better."

"Master Rufus," Jasper began, in his sweetest tattletale voice, "I'll have you know that I never —"

"As for you, Jasper deWinter," Master Rufus said, cutting him off. "Maybe I was wrong about you. Maybe you really are more interesting than I originally imagined. But the four of you must return to the Magisterium immediately."

Jasper looked horrified, probably for several reasons.

"Are you back at the Magisterium?" Call asked.

Master Rufus appeared highly peeved by that question. "Indeed I am, Callum. After spending most of yesterday and all of today fruitlessly searching for you children, one of you must have lost your protection against scrying. I see that you're in some kind of vehicle. Pull over, tell me where you are, and some mages will be along to get you shortly."

"I don't think we can do that," Callum said, heart pounding.

"And why not?" Master Rufus's eyebrows twitched with barely contained annoyance.

Call hesitated.

"Because we're on a mission," Tamara said quickly. "We're going to recover the Alkahest."

"I'm the Makar," Aaron said. "I'm supposed to save people. They're not supposed to save me — they resent having to save me. And I've been told plenty that I can't succeed doing stuff alone, so Call is here to be my counterweight. Tamara is here because she's clever and crafty. And Jasper is . . ."

"Comic relief?" Call ventured under his breath.

"I'm your friend, too, you idiot!" Jasper burst out. "I can be clever!"

"Anyway," Aaron said, trying to recover the situation. "We're a team and we're getting the Alkahest back, so please don't send any other elementals after us."

"Send any other elementals after you?" Master Rufus sounded genuinely confused. "What on earth do you mean?"

"You know what I mean," Aaron said in that flat voice he used when he was angry and trying not to show it. "We all know. Automotones nearly killed us, and he came from the Magisterium. You released him to hunt us down."

Now Master Rufus looked shocked. "There must be a mistake. Automotones is here, our prisoner; he has been for hundreds of years."

"It's not a mistake," Tamara said. "Maybe the other mages didn't tell you, because we're your apprentices. But it absolutely happened. Automotones murdered a woman, too. Burned her house down."

Tamara's voice shook.

"These are lies," Master Rufus said.

"We're not lying," Aaron told him. "But I guess that means you trust us about as much as we trust you."

"Then you're being lied to," said Master Rufus. "I don't know — I don't understand yet — but you must come back to the Magisterium. It's more important now than ever. This is the only place where I can protect you."

"We're not coming back." Surprisingly, Jasper was speaking. He turned to Call. "Hang up the phone."

Call stared at ghostly Rufus. "I, uh, don't know how."

"Earth!" Tamara yelped. "Earth is the opposite of air!"

"Right. I, uh —" Call reached down and grabbed Miri out of the sheath on his belt. Metal had earth magic properties. "Sorry," he said, and plunged the knife into ghostly Rufus.

Rufus disappeared with a pop, like a burst bubble.

Tamara screamed.

"I didn't kill him, did I?" Call said, looking around at everyone's shocked faces. Only Havoc seemed unmoved. He'd gone back to sleep.

"No," Jasper said. "It's just, most people just use the earth power to shut down the connection. But I guess that's a lot of restraint to expect from you, weirdo."

"I am not a weirdo," Call grumbled, sheathing his blade.

"You're a little weird," Aaron said.

"Oh, yeah, well, who lost their protective rock?" Call demanded. "Who forgot to transfer it to their new clothes?"

Tamara groaned in frustration. "That's how the mages found us! Jasper, did you?"

Jasper held up his hands, flummoxed. "*That's* what that rock was? No one told me!"

"Now isn't the time to worry about this," Aaron insisted. "We made some mistakes. The important thing is that we hide from the mages as best we can."

Call went to pull the car back onto the main road, when he realized the engine had stalled out.

Aaron had to spark the wires all over again, while they held their collective breaths, since there were no more cars to take if the Morris conked out on them. A few moments later, though, Aaron had it running once more.

Tamara didn't have any more stones, so they took turns passing around the ones they had, so the mages might not scry the right person at the right time.

Call drove for the rest of the day and through the night, with the other kids sleeping in shifts. Call didn't sleep, though. At each rest stop, he acquired more and more coffee until he felt as though his head was going to spin around like a top and then pop right off.

The landscape had changed, becoming more mountainous. The air was cooler, and pine trees took the place of mulberry and dogwood.

"I could drive for a while," Tamara offered, coming out of a Gas and Grub in Maine. Dawn was breaking by then and Call had been caught at least once driving with a single eye open.

Aaron had bought a Butterfinger and a Honey Bun and was mashing the candy bar into the pastry to make a bizarre sugar hot dog. Call approved. Jasper ate pretzels and stared.

"No," Call said, taking a swig from his coffee. One of his eyes twitched a little, but he ignored it. "I've got this."

Tamara shrugged and handed the directions to Jasper. It was his turn to navigate.

"I refuse," Jasper said, taking a long look at Call. "You need to sleep. You're going to drive into a ditch and we're going to die, all because you won't take a nap. So take a nap!"

"I'll set an alarm," Tamara offered.

"I could stretch my legs," said Aaron. "Go ahead. Lie down in the backseat."

Now that they mentioned it, Call was feeling kind of fuzzy-headed. "Okay," he said, yawning. "But just for twenty minutes. Dad used to say that that was the ideal amount of time for a nap."

"We'll take Havoc for a real walk," Tamara said. "See you in twenty."

Call climbed into the backseat. But when he closed his eyes, what he saw was Master Rufus, his eyes going wide as Call drew Miri and stabbed the image of him. His expression had reminded Call of the way his father had looked, right before Call used magic to slam him against a wall.

Despite being exhausted, Call couldn't stop his brain from showing him those images over and over again.

And as soon as he shoved those images away, new ones rose up to take their place. Images of things that hadn't happened yet, but might. The look of betrayal on Aaron's face when he discovered who Call really was, the look of fury on Tamara's. Jasper's smug certainty that he'd been right about Call all along.

Finally, he gave up and got out of the car. Early-morning sunlight dappled the grass, and the music of distant birdsong hung in the air. Aaron and Tamara and Havoc were gone, but Jasper was sitting at a worn old picnic table. Sparks flew from his fingers as he set fire to a pinecone and then watched it turn to embers.

"You're supposed to be asleep," Jasper said.

"I know," Call told him. "But I wanted to talk to you about something, while the others aren't here."

Jasper narrowed his eyes. "Oh, going behind your friends' backs? This should be interesting."

Call sat down at the picnic table. The wind had picked up and it was blowing his hair into his eyes. "When we get to the destination on the map, hopefully, my father is going to be there and he's still going to have the Alkahest. But I need to talk to him — alone."

"About what?"

"He'll listen to me, but not if he thinks a bunch of apprentices are going to attack him. And I don't want Aaron getting too close, in case my dad *does* try to hurt him. I need you and Tamara and Aaron to keep back, at least until I finish my conversation."

"Why are you telling me this?" Jasper still looked suspicious, but not unconvinced.

Call couldn't tell him the truth — that it was easier to lie to Jasper than to his friends. "Because you care about protecting Aaron a lot more than you care about protecting me."

"True," said Jasper. "He's the Makar. You're just . . ." He looked curiously at Call. "I don't know what you are."

"Yeah, well," Call said. "That makes two of us."

Before Jasper could say anything else, Tamara and Aaron appeared from between the trees, Havoc bounding around excitedly beside them.

Call slid off the bench. "What's he so happy about?"

"He ate a squirrel." Tamara sounded disapproving.

As Call headed toward the car, he bent down to pet Havoc's head and whispered, "Good dog. Excellent hunting instincts. We eat squirrels, not people, am I right?"

"Never too early to start molding his character," Aaron said.

"That's what I was thinking." Together Call and Aaron helped heave a reluctant Havoc into the backseat. Jasper and Tamara clambered in after him, and Aaron took the passenger seat.

The moment they all sat down, the doors of the car slammed shut in unison.

"What's going on?" Tamara demanded. She scrabbled at her door, but it wouldn't open. None of their doors would budge. "Start the car, Aaron!"

Aaron reached across Call for the wires, trying to get a spark. Nothing happened. No sound of the engine turning over. He did it again, and again. Sweat started to prickle along Call's back. What was going on?

From the backseat, Jasper shouted, "I tried to use metal magic and sparks hurt my hand instead."

"It must be warded," said Tamara.

Something swooped in front of the windshield. Call yelled and Aaron jerked back, wires dropping from his hands.

Two huge air elementals had appeared in front of the car. One of them looked like a six-legged horse, if horses were about twice the size they normally were. The other one resembled a brontosaurus with wings. Both were bridled and saddled: Master Rockmaple was riding one, and Master Milagros the second.

"We are in so much trouble," said Jasper.

Master Milagros slid from the back of her six-legged horse and stalked over to the car. She lifted her hands, spread her fingers, and hurled from her palms long threads of glimmering metal wires. They wrapped around the front of the car and within seconds, it was tightly secured.

As she performed her metal magic, Milagros looked through the windshield at the kids. She shook her head disapprovingly, but Callum thought she looked a little bit as if she found the whole thing . . . funny.

She whirled around without a word to them and marched back to the elementals. She tossed a rope of metal to Rockmaple and climbed back up onto her own elemental, securing her rope to the pommel of the saddle.

"Oh, my God," said Tamara. "We've got to get out of here."

She threw herself against her door, but the car was already rising into the air like the basket below a balloon. Everyone in the car shrieked as maps and empty soda cans and candy bar wrappers flew off the dashboard and out of the cup holders and rattled around inside the car.

"What are they doing?" Call yelled over the sound of the wind.

"Taking us to the Magisterium — what do you think?" Jasper yelled back.

"They're going to fly us to Virginia? Won't someone normal, you know, notice?"

"They're probably using air magic to block us from view," Tamara said. Then she yelped as the car swung out over the forest below. All Call could see beneath them were miles of green trees.

"In movies, people pretend to be sick to get their jailers to let them out," Aaron told them. "Maybe one of us could try throwing up — or frothing from the mouth."

"Like we're rabid?" Call asked.

"We don't have time to argue," Tamara said, reaching into her satchel, clearly completely panicked, and coming out with a little bottle of clear liquid. "I have hand soap. Quick, Jasper, drink it. You'll definitely froth."

"I am *not* drinking that," Jasper said. "I am a deWinter. We do not froth."

Aaron squinted at the air elementals pulling their car like a sled, as though he was reconsidering his own plan. "I'm not sure they'd hear us if we shouted anyway."

"Wait," said Call, turning in his seat. "I've watched my dad work on cars my whole life. You know what goes really early? The floor pan. Look down. It's rusted, right? All we have to do is kick."

For a moment, they all just stared at him. Then Tamara started kicking the floor with a vengeance. Havoc leaped up onto the seat, whining as Aaron climbed over the passenger seat to help. After three kicks, his booted foot went right through.

"This is going to work!" Jasper shouted, as much with surprise as with anything else.

A few more kicks and they were able to peel back the floor of the car. Tamara looked over at Call and then Aaron.

"Ready?" she asked.

"I've got Havoc," Call said.

"Wait, who's got me?" Jasper asked, but Call ignored him and, grabbing hold of his wolf and his backpack, jumped out into the dark nothingness below the car. Havoc yipped, limbs flailing, tail cycling.

Above him, Call saw Tamara leaping out, her hair flying up in the blue sky. A moment later, he saw what he thought was Aaron shoving Jasper through the hole. Then Aaron appeared, falling through the air.

Call drew on the air, weaving an invisible net of magic

around and beneath him. His fall slowed, and Havoc stopped barking as they descended steadily into the woods below.

Call hit the ground on his back, but the impact was light. He let go of Havoc, who rolled to his feet, his eyes wild. Call wasn't sure exactly where they were and cursed himself for, in his panic, not remembering the map. But a moment later he realized that he couldn't have found their place on it anyway. Even if they'd had it, it would have been useless.

Beside him, Havoc whined, looking up in the sky, as though he might be forced to fly again at any moment. He barked as Tamara drifted down gracefully, her dark braid floating up around her head. She alighted on a fallen log, a huge smile on her face. "That was amazing," she said. "I always thought I liked fire magic the best, but air —"

WHAM! Jasper slammed down onto a pile of pine needles. A moment later Aaron touched down beside him, his arms crossed, looking furious.

"You let me fall," Jasper moaned.

"I did not," Aaron said defensively. "He said he could do it himself! He said he'd be fine!"

"Seems okay to me," said Call. Tamara shot him a quelling look and ran over to Jasper, who pushed himself half upright.

"Ow," Jasper muttered, collapsing again. "Ow ow ow."

Tamara was leaning over Jasper, who was milking the attention for all it was worth.

"The pain," he said. "The agony."

"Aaron, don't you have a first-aid kit in your backpack?" Tamara said.

"Yeah, but I left my backpack behind." Aaron scanned the sky. "How long do you think before they notice they're hauling an empty car?"

"Probably not very long," Tamara said. "We need to hide."

"Right," Aaron said. "Stand back, Tamara, Jasper." He reached out a hand and caught Call's wrist. "Call. Stay."

Puzzled, Call stayed, as Tamara, Jasper, and Havoc moved a few feet away. Aaron looked exhausted — Call suspected they all did. The aftereffects of the air magic were beginning to catch up with him, flattening out the adrenaline that had been keeping him going. No twenty-minute nap was going to help. He felt as though he might fall over.

Aaron took a deep breath and raised the hand that wasn't holding Call's wrist. His fingers shone with a black glow. The darkness spilled down like acid, spreading across the ground. Dissolving it.

Call could feel the pull and tug inside him that meant Aaron was drawing on him to work chaos. Aaron's eyes were closed, fingers digging into Call's skin.

"Aaron?" Call said, but Aaron didn't react. Soil was churning at their feet, like a whirlpool. It was hard to see what was happening, but the force of it shook the ground. Tamara held on to Jasper to keep upright.

"*Aaron!*" For the first time, Call could imagine how the Enemy of Death's brother, Jericho, had died. Constantine might have gotten so caught up in the magic he was doing that he forgot about his brother until it was too late.

Aaron wrenched his grip free of Call's arm. He was breathing hard. The dust of disturbed earth had begun to settle, and Call and the others could see that Aaron had torn a chunk of the ground free, hollowing out a sort of hole, hidden from sight by an overhang of grassy rock.

"You made us a dirt cave," Jasper said. "Huh."

Aaron's sweaty hair was stuck to his forehead and when he

looked at Jasper, Call thought that he might be seriously considering disappearing him into the void.

"Let's rest," Tamara said. "Call, I know you're in a hurry to get to Alastair, but we're all tired and the air magic wiped us out." She did look a little gray; so did Jasper. "Let's hide out until we all have our strength back."

Call wanted to object, but he couldn't. He was just too tired. He crawled into the cave and flopped down on the ground. He wished for a blanket . . . and that was his last thought before he dropped into sleep, falling as quickly and as deeply as if he'd been struck in the back of the head.

When he woke, the sun was setting in a blaze of orange. Tamara was slumbering beside him, one hand in Havoc's fur. On Tamara's other side, Aaron was tossing fitfully, his eyes closed. Jasper slept, too, his jacket wadded up as a pillow beneath his head.

Call heard a rustling sound outside the cave. He wondered if it was some kind of animal.

Digging around in his pack, he found a half-eaten candy bar and made short work of it. He wasn't sure how long he'd been resting, but he knew he felt more awake and alert than he had since they'd embarked on this mission. A strange calm settled over him.

I should leave them, he thought.

They'd come far enough. He'd never had friends like this, friends who were willing to risk everything to help him. He didn't want to reward his friends by leading them to their doom.

Then Call heard another rustling, closer this time. It didn't sound like an animal, more like a herd, moving slowly and quietly through the brush.

He revised his plan rapidly.

"Tamara, wake up," Call whispered, poking her with his foot. "Something's out there."

She rolled over and opened her eyes. "Mrmph?"

"Out there," he repeated softly. "Something."

She poked Aaron and he got Jasper up, both of them yawning and groaning at being awoken.

"I don't hear anything," Jasper complained.

"Let's check it out," Aaron whispered. "Come on."

"What if it's the mages?" Tamara said quietly. "Maybe we should just hunker down?"

Call shook his head. "If they come in here, there's nowhere to run. We're literally backed against a wall."

No one could deny that, so they got their stuff and, tugging Havoc along, emerged from the cave. Night was falling.

"You've lost it," Jasper said. "There's nothing out here."

But then they all heard it, a rustling that came from two places at once.

"Maybe the mages found us," Aaron said. "Maybe we could —"

But it wasn't a mage that stepped out of the foliage.

It was a Chaos-ridden human who emerged, slack-faced and staring with coruscating eyes that spun with colors like a kaleidoscope. He was huge, dressed in ragged black clothes. Looking more closely, Call realized they were the remains of a uniform. A ripped, old, mud-stained, blood-soaked uniform. There was an emblem over his heart, but in the gloom, Call couldn't make out what it was.

Jasper had gone papery white. He'd never seen one of the Chaos-ridden before, Call realized.

Call had only long enough to be horrified when another one stepped out to his left. He spun, clutching Miri in his hand, just as a third surged out of some undergrowth to his right. And then another, and another, and another, all pallid and sunken-eyed, a flood of Chaos-ridden coming from all sides.

The Enemy's army outnumbered them.

"W-what do we do?" gasped Jasper. He had grabbed up a stick from the forest floor and was brandishing it. Tamara was shaping a fireball between her hands. They were steady but her expression was panicked.

"Get behind me," Aaron ordered. "All of you."

Jasper moved behind him with alacrity. Tamara was still working on her fireball, but she was already behind Aaron. Most of the Chaos-ridden were massed on the opposite side of the clearing, staring at them with their whirling eyes. Their silence was eerie.

"I won't," Call said. He didn't feel afraid. He didn't know why. "You can't. I'm your counterweight and I can tell you're not rested enough. You just used chaos magic. It's too soon to do it again."

Aaron's jaw was set. "I have to try."

"There's too many of them," Call argued as the army began to advance. "The chaos will consume you."

"I'll take them down with me," Aaron said grimly. "Better this than the Alkahest, right?"

"Aaron —"

"I'm sorry," Aaron said, and ran toward them, skidding across pine needles. Tamara looked up from her fireball and screamed.

"Aaron, duck!"

He ducked. She threw the fire. It arced over Aaron's head, landed among the mass of the Chaos-ridden, and exploded.

Some of the Chaos-ridden caught fire, but they kept coming. Their expressions didn't change, even when they fell down, still burning.

Now Call was more afraid than he could remember being. Aaron was nearing the first line of the enemy army. He held his hand up, chaos beginning to whirl and grow in his palm like a tiny hurricane. It swirled upward —

The Chaos-ridden reached Aaron. They seemed to swallow him up among them for a moment, and Call's stomach dropped into his shoes.

Call started to stumble toward them — and halted. He could see Aaron again, standing stock-still, looking bewildered. The Chaos-ridden were walking around him, making no move to touch him at all, like water parting around a rock in a stream.

They marched past Aaron, and Call could hear Jasper and Tamara breathing harshly, because the Chaos-ridden were moving in their direction now. Maybe they wanted to take out the weak ones before starting on Aaron. Call was the only one with a knife, although he wasn't sure how much Miri would help. He wondered if he'd die here, protecting Tamara and Jasper — and Aaron. It was a heroic way to go, at least. Maybe it would prove he wasn't what his father thought.

The Chaos-ridden had reached them. Aaron was trying to push his way through, trying to reach his friends. The first of the Chaos-ridden, the huge man with the spiked wristbands, came to a stop in front of Call.

Call tightened his grip on Miri. Whatever else, he would go down fighting.

The Chaos-ridden spoke. Its voice sounded like a croak,

rusty from disuse. "Master," it said, fixing its whirling eyes on Call. "We have waited for you for so long."

The first Chaos-ridden knelt down in front of Call. And then the next Chaos-ridden knelt, and the next, until they were all on their knees and Aaron was standing among them, staring at Call across the clearing with a look of disbelief.

CHAPTER THIRTEEN

MASTER," SAID THE leader of the Chaos-ridden (or at least that's what Call assumed he was). "Shall we kill the Makar for you?"

"No," Call said quickly, horrified. "No, just — stay where you are. Stay," he added, as if he were talking to Havoc.

None of the Chaos-ridden moved. Aaron began walking toward Call, boots crunching on pine needles. He navigated his way gingerly among the kneeling army.

"What," said Jasper, "is going on?"

Call felt a hand on his shoulder. Whirling around, he saw it was Tamara. She was staring at the Chaos-ridden; she ripped her gaze away from them and fastened it on Call. "Tell us what this all means," she said. "Tell us what you are to them."

It was there in her voice — even if she didn't know the answer already, she strongly suspected it. Call had thought Tamara would look angry, figuring this out. But she didn't. She looked incredibly sad, which was worse.

"Call?" Aaron asked. He was standing only a couple of feet from Call now, but it felt like a long way away. He stood there uncertainly, trying not to look around him at the Chaos-ridden, who remained on their knees, awaiting a command. Call looked over them, some of their bodies young and some old, but none of them beneath fourteen years of age. None of them younger than he was.

Tamara shook her head. "You were mad at me for lying to you. Don't lie to us now."

There was a torturously terrible pause. Jasper was staring (and still grasping his stick, as if that would protect him). But Aaron was looking at Call hopefully, as if he expected Call to be able to clear all of this up, and that was the worst.

"I'm the . . . Enemy of Death," Call said. The Chaos-ridden made a noise — a sort of long sigh, all of them at once. None of them moved, but it served as an awful testament to what Call was saying. "I'm Constantine Madden — or whatever's left of him."

"That's not possible," Aaron said, speaking slowly, as if he thought Call had hit his head too hard. "The Enemy of Death is alive. He's at war with us!"

"No, Master Joseph is," said Call. He stumbled on, through the explanation he'd been given, the one he didn't want to understand. "The Enemy of Death was dying at the Cold Massacre. He pushed his soul into the body of a baby." He swallowed. "That baby was me. My soul is Constantine Madden's soul. I *am* Constantine."

"You mean *you* killed the real Callum Hunt and took his place," Jasper accused. Fire ignited in his palm, spreading up the bark of the stick he held until the tip of it burst into flame.

It was probably the best display of fire magic Jasper had ever achieved, but he barely seemed to notice. "Quickly — we have to destroy him before he kills us all, before he kills the Makar. Aaron, you have to run!"

Aaron remained exactly where he was, though, staring at Call with a mix of disbelief and misery. "But you can't be," he said finally. "You're my best friend."

The Chaos-ridden leader lurched to his feet. All the other Chaos-ridden rose as well, like an army of puppets. They began to march toward Jasper, passing around Call as if he weren't there.

"*Wait*," Call shouted. "Don't! Everyone stop."

Nothing happened. The dead-eyed warriors kept coming. They weren't moving fast, but they were moving steadily toward Jasper, who wasn't backing away. The flame in Jasper's hand still burned and there was a terrible look in his eyes, as though he was ready to die fighting. It was a far cry from the Jasper who had complained throughout the trip, the Jasper who whined over minor injuries. This Jasper appeared fearless.

But Call knew it wouldn't do Jasper any good. However fearless he was, he couldn't hold his own against hundreds of Chaos-ridden. Call had been terrified before when they had obeyed him; now he was terrified that they *wouldn't*.

"Stop!" he shouted again, in a ringing voice. "You, who are born of chaos and the void, stop! I command it!"

They lurched to a stop. Jasper was breathing hard; Tamara was at his side, light burning in her palm. Aaron had moved toward them as well. His heart lurched. His friends, ranged against him.

"I didn't know," Call said, hearing the pleading in his own voice. "When I came to the Magisterium, I didn't know."

They all stared at him. Finally, Tamara spoke. "I believe you, Call," she said.

Call swallowed and went on. "Most of the time, it doesn't even seem possible. I'm not going to hurt anyone, okay? But, Jasper — if you go for me, the Chaos-ridden are going to kill you. I don't know if I can stop them."

"So when did you find out?" Aaron demanded. "That you were — what you are?"

"At the bowling alley, last year," Call said. "Master Joseph told me, but I didn't want to believe him. I think my dad always suspected, though."

"And that's why he threw such a fit when you didn't flunk out of the Magisterium," Jasper said. "Because he knew you were evil. He knew you were a monster."

Call flinched.

"That's why he wanted Master Rufus to bind your magic," said Aaron.

Call hadn't realized how much he had wanted Aaron to contradict Jasper, until he didn't. "Listen, here's the part I couldn't explain, because it wouldn't have made sense before. My dad doesn't want to hurt Aaron with the Alkahest. He wants to use it to fix me."

"Fix you?" Jasper said. "He should kill you."

"Maybe," Call said. "But he definitely doesn't deserve to die for it."

"Okay, so what do you want, Call?" Aaron asked.

"The same things I wanted before!" Call shouted. "I want to get the Alkahest and give it back to the Collegium. I want to save my father. I don't want to have any more awful secrets!"

"But you don't want to defeat the Enemy of Death," said Jasper.

"I *am* the Enemy of Death!" Call yelled. "We have already defeated the Enemy! I'm *on your side.*"

"Really?" Jasper shook his head. "So if I said I wanted to leave, would you tell the Chaos-ridden to stop me?"

Call hesitated for a long moment, with Tamara and Aaron watching him. Finally, Call said, "Yeah, I'd stop you."

"That's what I thought."

"We're too close to the end," Call tried to explain. "Too close to my dad. He still has the Alkahest. He's still going to give it to Master Joseph. And Master Joseph won't use it to kill me; he wants me alive. He'll kill my dad, he'll kill Aaron, then who knows what he'll do after that. We *have* to finish."

He stared at them, willing them to understand. After a long, long moment, Tamara gave a tiny nod. "So, what next?" she asked.

Call turned to the Chaos-ridden. "Take us to Master Joseph," Call commanded. "Escort us there, don't hurt any of us, and do not tell him we're coming."

The Chaos-ridden began to move, flanking Call. Aaron, Tamara, and Jasper were being moved along, herded, surrounded. They walked in a narrow path surrounded by corpse-like bodies; it reminded Call of biblical paintings of the Red Sea parting. There was nowhere to go but in the direction the Chaos-ridden went and no pace to walk but the pace they set.

They marched through the dark forest in dead silence, the crackle of pine needles underfoot. Havoc marched along happily, at home with others of his kind. With every step, Call felt a terrible loneliness overtake him. After this, there would be no return to the Magisterium. There would be no more friends; no more lessons from Master Rufus; no more meals of lichen in the Refectory or games with Celia in the Gallery.

At least Havoc would come with him, although Call wasn't sure where they'd go.

They walked for what felt like a long time, long enough for Call's leg to ache intensely. He could feel himself slowing down, could feel the majority of the Chaos-ridden slow to keep pace with him.

So, basically, *he* was setting the pace.

Aaron stepped to his side. "You were going to be my counterweight," he said, and only when he said it in the past tense did Call realize with a sinking heart how much he'd wanted to do it.

"I didn't know," he said. "When I offered."

"I don't want to have to fight you," Aaron went on. Jasper and Tamara were walking up ahead, Tamara speaking urgently to Jasper. "I don't want to, but that's what's going to happen, isn't it? That's our destiny: to kill each other."

"You don't really believe I want to kill you, do you?" Call said. "If I wanted to kill you, I could have. I could have killed you in your sleep. I could have killed you a million times over. I could have chopped your head right off!"

"That's convincing," Aaron muttered. "Tamara!"

She dropped back to walk with them. Jasper continued to stalk ahead, a few Chaos-ridden alongside him.

"Why did you say what you said back there?" Aaron asked. "That you believed Call."

"Because he tried to flunk out of the Magisterium," said Tamara. "He really didn't want to go. If he'd known he was Constantine Madden, he would have tried to get on the

Masters' side, to spy on them. Instead, he just pissed all of them off. Besides," she added, "Constantine Madden was famously charming, and Call obviously isn't."

"Thank you," Call said, wincing at the pain in his leg. He wasn't sure how much longer he could go on without resting. "That was heartwarming."

"Also," Tamara said, "there are some things you can't fake."

Before Call could ask her what she meant, his foot hit a root and he stumbled, falling to his knees. The Chaos-ridden halted abruptly, those in front of Jasper turning and stopping him with their hands to his chest.

Call groaned and rolled over, trying to stand.

One of the Chaos-ridden lifted him, holding him as easily as Call himself might have held a cat. It was embarrassing and, even more embarrassingly, a relief. "We will carry you the rest of the way, Master," the Chaos-ridden told him.

"That's probably not the best idea," Call said. "The others —"

One of the Chaos-ridden grabbed hold of Tamara, slinging her over his back. She struggled in its grasp. "Call!" she shouted, panicked.

Two of them hauled Aaron off his feet, while a fifth lifted a kicking and screaming Jasper into the air.

"We will carry them all," the Chaos-ridden holding Call told him, but that didn't seem to calm them down any. "We can move more swiftly this way."

Call was so surprised that he didn't give any orders at all, even as the Chaos-ridden's steps came more swiftly. They began to lope and then run, Havoc alongside them. They ran and ran, covering so much ground that Call couldn't imagine himself walking it.

This close, Call had expected the Chaos-ridden to smell like rot. They were supposed to be the dead, after all, reanimated by void magic. But their odor was more mushroomy, not unpleasant, just strange.

Aaron looked uncomfortable. Tamara looked exhilarated and terrified in equal measure. But Jasper's expression was unreadable to Call, a blankness that might have been fear or despair or nothing at all.

"Call, what are they doing?" Tamara shouted over to him.

Call shrugged awkwardly. "Carrying us? I think they're trying to be helpful."

"I don't like this," Aaron said, sounding like he was on a particularly dizzying ride.

Faster the Chaos-ridden went, magic propelling them forward, through the woods, over fallen leaves, through streams and over stones, through brush and ferns and bramble. Then, as quickly as they began, the Chaos-ridden halted their march.

Call found his feet, dropped down on the sand of a beach, the slivered moon above them casting a silver path over the water.

The Chaos-ridden began to move in more tightly, the path between them narrowing as they made their way down the beach. Call could hear the ocean, the lap of the waves.

Three rowboats were tied to poles out in the water, rolling gently with the tide. If Call squinted, he could make out a stretch of land in the distance, visible only because it interrupted the reflection of moonlight.

"Evil Island?" Jasper asked.

Call snorted, surprised that Jasper had said something. He

was probably being serious, Call decided, as this seemed an unlikely time for him to acquire a sense of humor.

"Chaos-ridden," Call said, "how do we get across?"

At his words, three of the Chaos-ridden waded into the sea. First, they were up to their thighs in the water, then it was at their waists, then their necks, then it covered their heads completely.

"Wait!" Call shouted, but they were gone. Had he just put them to death? Could they die?

A moment later, pale hands rose from the sea, untying the rope binding the boats. And then, pulled by unseen hands, the boats floated toward shore. The Chaos-ridden rose from the depths, their faces impassive as ever.

"Huh," Aaron said.

"I guess we get in," Tamara said, going to one of the boats. "Aaron, get in the boat with Call."

"How does that make sense?" Jasper demanded.

Tamara looked at the Chaos-ridden. "So the Makar can't get drowned before Call stops them."

Jasper opened his mouth to object and then shut it again.

Call climbed gingerly into the boat. Aaron followed him.

Jasper settled himself in the second boat and Tamara took Havoc and went to the third.

The Chaos-ridden dragged them out to sea.

For all the driving Call had done with Alastair, the only boats he'd been on were ferries carrying a vintage car or some other antique object back from some semi-remote location where Alastair had purchased it. That and the little boats that navigated the tunnels of the Magisterium.

Call had never been so low in the water, out on the open sea. The waves were black in every direction, the spray icy on his cheeks and salty enough to sting his mouth.

He was scared. The Chaos-ridden were terrifying, and the fact they listened to him didn't make them any less monstrous. His friends wanted to get away from him — maybe even hurt him. And still ahead were his father and Master Joseph, both unpredictable and dangerous.

Aaron was sitting hunched up at the prow of the boat. Call wanted to say something to him but guessed that anything he had to say wouldn't be welcomed.

The Chaos-ridden walked along, under the sea, pulling the boats with them. Call could see their heads beneath the waves.

Finally, the patch of land ahead of them resolved into a landscape. The island was small, not more than a few miles across, and densely covered in trees. The Chaos-ridden pulled the small craft up the beach with their wet hands. Call clambered out of the boat, Aaron after him, and joined Tamara and Jasper on the shore. Tamara had been holding on to Havoc by his ruff; Havoc barked and scampered over to Call. They all watched as wave after wave of the Chaos-ridden came up on shore like drowned pirates from a ghost story.

"Master," the leader said, when they were all assembled. He had stationed himself near Call, like a bodyguard. "Your tomb."

At first Call misheard him. *You're home*, the thing had seemed to say for a single hopeful moment. But those weren't the words at all.

Call stumbled, nearly falling in the sand. "Tomb?"

Aaron gave him a strange look.

"Follow," said the Chaos-ridden leader, setting off through

the woods. The rest of the army crowded around, their bodies dripping, and herded Call and the others toward a path. It wasn't lit, but it was wide, with white stones that caught the light marking the edges.

He wondered what would happen if he ordered the Chaos-ridden to walk single file. Would they do it? Did they have to?

Then, with that thought in his head, he began to have other giddy and strange imaginings of what he could command the Chaos-ridden to do. Line dance. Or hop on one foot. He imagined the entire advancing army of the Enemy of Death, hopping into battle on a single foot.

A small, crazed giggle escaped his mouth. Tamara looked over at him, worriedly.

Nothing like your Evil Overlord cracking up, he thought and then had to tamp down another completely inappropriate burst of nervous laughter.

That was when the path took a sudden turn and he saw it — a massive building of gray stone. It looked old and weathered by years and sea air. Two crescent-shaped doors formed the entrance; set high on one of the doors was a knocker in the shape of a human head. The archway was carved with words in Latin. ULTIMA FORSAN. ULTIMA FORSAN. ULTIMA FORSAN.

"What does it mean?" Call wondered aloud.

"It means 'the time is closer than you think,'" said the leader. "Master."

"I think it means something about the last hour," Tamara said. "My Latin isn't great."

Call looked at her, puzzled. "It means 'the time is closer than you think.'"

Jasper looked surprised. "That's right. It does."

"Call, why'd you ask if you already knew?" Aaron said.

"Because I didn't know until he told me!" Call said, exasperated. He pointed at the leader of the Chaos-ridden. "Didn't you hear him?"

There was another horrible silence. "Call," Tamara said slowly. "Are you saying those *things* are talking to you? We knew you were talking to them but haven't heard them talking back."

"Mostly him," Call said, jabbing a finger toward the leader, who looked impassive. "But yeah. I can hear them talking and — didn't you hear him back in the clearing? When he called me 'master'?"

Tamara shook her head. "They're not saying words," she said quietly. "Just mumbling and groaning."

"And making weird sounds like muffled screams," put in Aaron.

"It sounds like they're speaking perfect English to me," said Call.

"That's because you're like them," Jasper spat. "Their souls are all hollowed out and they're nothing inside and neither are you. You're nothing but the Enemy."

"The Enemy made these creatures," Aaron said, stuffing his hands in his pockets. "He would have had to understand them because they served him. And you understand them because . . ."

"Because I *am* him," said Call. It wasn't anything they didn't know, just another horrible piece of proof. "I'm so creepy I'm creeping myself out," he muttered.

"Master," said the leader. "Your tomb awaits."

He clearly expected Call to step up to the huge mausoleum and walk right in. And Call was going to have to. This was their destination. This was where Master Joseph was going to meet Alastair.

Call squared his shoulders and started toward the door. Havoc bounced along beside him, clearly in his element. Behind Havoc came Aaron, Tamara, and Jasper.

"Oh, my God," he heard Tamara say in a horrified voice. It took him a second to realize what she was reacting to. What he had taken for a door knocker in the shape of a head was actually a real, severed human head, mounted on the door like the head of a deer.

It had belonged to a girl, a girl who didn't look much older than the rest of them. A girl who must have been killed recently; she would barely look dead at all if it wasn't for the fact that the skin around the base of her neck was cut raggedly across. Her mahogany hair, blown by the wind, whipped around her oddly familiar face.

Tears sprang to Tamara's eyes, rolling over her cheeks. She wiped them with the back of her hand but otherwise didn't even seem to notice that they were falling. "It can't be," she said, walking closer to the door.

Call felt like he'd seen the girl's face before — but where? Maybe at the party at the Rajavi estate? Maybe she was one of Tamara's friends? But why would her head be displayed here, like a grisly trophy?

"Verity Torres," Jasper said quietly, the words coming out almost like a whisper. "They never found her body."

Call was struck by how lost Aaron looked, shivering in his thin shirt. Staring at the last Makar who'd defended the Magisterium. If he'd lived a generation earlier, this would've been him. His head nailed up there as a terrible warning.

"No." Aaron blinked hard, like he could dispel the vision in front of him. "No, it can't be her. It can't."

Call felt like he was going to throw up.

Then the eyes on the head opened to show milky marbles without pupil or iris.

Tamara gave a little cry. Jasper put a hand over his mouth.

The dead lips moved, and words came out. "As my name means truth, I assure you I am what remains of Verity Torres. Here sleep the dead, and the dead guard them. If you desire entrance, three riddles I will ask you. Answer them correctly and you may go inside."

Call looked at the others helplessly. He'd been counting on the fact that he was Constantine Madden to get them into the building, but the head of Verity Torres obviously didn't recognize him.

"Riddles," Tamara said in a quavering voice. "Fine. We can do riddles."

"What do you call something that's not behind you?" the girl asked in an odd voice that didn't quite line up with the way her mouth moved.

"Oh, no, that's not funny," Call said. "That's not a good joke."

"What are you talking about?" Aaron asked. "What's the answer? In front?"

Tamara looked even more upset. "*Ahead*," she said. "A head. Get it?"

Verity Torres laughed a croaky little laugh. There was no laughter in her eyes, though; they stayed white and blank.

"Who did this to you?" Aaron asked suddenly. "*Who?*"

"It had to be Master Joseph," said Tamara. "Constantine

had already left the battlefield by then. He was in the caves at the Cold Massacre —"

"Busy stealing other people's bodies to live in," Jasper interrupted. And even though the words cut, Call was staggered with relief that Constantine Madden couldn't have done this horrific thing; that he had been busy being reborn as Callum. Of course, the Enemy had done other terrible things. But not this.

"That wasn't a true riddle," the head said, ignoring Aaron's question. "That was just for practice."

"We've got to get out of here," Jasper said, babbling with terror. "We've got to go."

"Go where?" Aaron demanded. "There's hundreds of Chaos-ridden behind us." He squared his shoulders. "Ask away."

"So we begin," Verity said. "What begins and has no end, yet is the ending of all that begins?"

"Death," Call said. That one was easy. He was glad. *Good at riddle*s was nowhere on the Evil Overlord list.

There was a clicking, grinding noise, a bolt on the inside of the door sliding back.

"Now the second riddle. I wear you down, yet you will mourn me once I fly. You can kill me, but I will never die."

The Enemy himself, Call thought. But that wasn't a good riddle answer, was it?

They exchanged looks. It was Tamara who spoke.

"Time," she said.

Another scraping noise. "And now the last," said Verity. "Take it and you will lose or gain more than all others. What is it?"

Silence. Call's mind was racing. *Lose or gain, lose or gain.* Riddles were always about something bigger than they seemed to be. Love, death, wealth, fame, life. There was no sound but the distant moaning of the Chaos-ridden and Call's own breath. Until a sharp, shaking voice cut through the quiet.

"Risk," said Jasper.

The head of Verity Torres let out a disappointed sigh, those terrible eyes closed, and there was a last clicking noise. The door swung open. Call could see nothing beyond it but shadows. He was shaking suddenly, colder than he'd ever been in his life.

Risk.

He looked back at Aaron and Tamara, took a deep breath, and stepped over the threshold.

The tomb was dimly lit by stones along the wall that reminded Call of the glowing rocks inside the Magisterium. He was able to pick out a corridor leading to what looked like five chambers.

Turning back, he glanced at the assemblage of horrible, staring figures with their coruscating eyes. The leader fixed his gaze on Call.

Call tried to make his voice firm. "Remain here, children of chaos. I will return."

They bent their heads as one. Disturbingly, Call saw that Havoc was among them. His wolf had also bent his head. A wave of sadness overwhelmed him — what if Havoc had only stuck by him because he'd had to? Because that was what he'd been created to do? The idea was more than Call thought he could bear.

"Call?" Tamara called. She was partway down the hallway, Aaron and Jasper beside her. "I think you better come see this."

He looked back at the army. Was he being ridiculous, not bringing at least one of them to protect him? He pointed to the leader. "Except you. You come with me."

Trying to push Havoc out of his thoughts, he limped inside the mausoleum. The leader of the Chaos-ridden followed him, and Call watched as he shut the doors carefully behind them, blocking out the outside world.

The leader turned around and looked expectantly at Call, awaiting instructions. "You're going to follow me," Call said. "Protect me if anyone tries to hurt me." A nod. "Do you have a name?"

The Chaos-ridden shook his head.

"Fine," Call said, "I'm going to call you Stanley. It's weird if you don't have a name."

Stanley had no reaction to this, so Call turned and started down the hall. He was halfway along the corridor when he heard Tamara call his name again. "Call! You *need* to come see this."

Call hurried to catch up with her. He found her with Aaron and Jasper, huddled in front of an alcove. As he and Stanley approached, they moved aside, letting Call have a clear view.

Inside the alcove was a marble slab . . . and on top of the marble slab was the body of a dead boy with a mop of dark brown hair. His eyes were shut, his arms at his sides. His body was perfectly preserved, but he was clearly dead. His skin was waxy white, and his chest didn't rise or fall. Though someone had dressed him in white funeral clothes, he still wore the wristband marking him as a student in his Copper Year.

Carved on the wall behind him was his name: *Jericho Madden*. Piled around the body was an assortment of strange objects. A ratty-looking blanket beside a bunch of notebooks and dusty tomes, a small glowing ball that seemed to be almost depleted of its charge, a golden knife and a ring emblazoned with a sigil Call didn't recognize.

"Of course," Tamara whispered. "The Enemy of Death wouldn't have built a tomb for himself. He didn't think he was going to die. He built this place for his brother. Those are his grave goods."

Aaron stared in fascination.

Call couldn't speak. He felt something twist inside him, the yearning ache of something he'd hoped to feel when he saw his mother's handprint in the Hall of Graduates. A connection to love and family and the past. He couldn't stop staring at the boy on the slab and remembering the stories he had heard: This was the brother Constantine had wanted to resurrect, the brother whose loss led him to experiment with the void and create the Chaos-ridden, the brother whose death had caused him to make death itself his enemy.

Call wondered if he would ever love anyone that much, to forswear everything else for him, to want to burn down the world to get him back.

"They were so young," said Aaron. "Jericho had to be our age. And Verity was just a little older. Constantine never even made it out of his twenties."

The Mage War had consumed all of them like a fire. It was horrible to think about — but at the same time, Call had never heard anyone say Constantine's name with such compassion before.

Of course it was Aaron. He had compassion for everyone.

"Over here," said Jasper. He'd wandered a little farther down the corridor and was staring into another alcove. The strange glowing stones along the walls cast an eerie light over his face. "Someone we know."

Call knew who they would find before he got there. A skinny boy with stick-straight brown hair and freckles, his blue eyes closed forever.

Drew.

He remembered Drew's body the last time he'd seen it, and the way Master Joseph had enchanted it to close up its wounds, even though Drew was already dead. His body looked healed now, even if his spirit was gone.

He had grave goods, too, folded clothes and favorite games, a horse statuette and a photograph of him with one arm around a smiling Master Joseph and the other around someone else — someone who'd been cut out of the picture.

Call was about to pick up the photo and take a closer look when he heard muffled and distant voices coming from below them.

"Do you hear that?" he whispered, walking away from Drew's body and down the hallway.

Stairs receded into the gloom — they looked as though they'd been carved from solid rock, and it took Call a moment to realize that they must have been formed by magic.

The time is closer than you think.

Call crept down the steps. The others followed more cautiously. He reached the bottom stair and looked around the cavernous, shadowy room. The darkness down here was deeper, the glowing rocks set into the walls more spread out.

And then he saw it. The final body — Constantine himself. He was lying on a slab of marble, arms crossed over his chest. He had dark brown hair and sharp features; he might have been handsome if it wasn't for the livid burn marks that covered the right side of his face and disappeared down into his collar. They weren't as bad as Call had imagined, though, hearing the story of the Enemy's burned face and the mask he'd worn. Constantine mostly looked normal. Horribly normal. He could have been anyone walking down the street. Anyone at all.

Call took a step closer. Stanley lurched along behind him.

"What do you see?" Aaron whispered from farther up the stairs.

"Shhhh," Call whispered back, moving to Constantine's body. "Stay there." He could still hear voices coming through the walls. Whispering ghosts? His imagination? He wasn't sure of anything anymore. He couldn't stop staring at the body. *That's me*, he thought. *That's the face I grew up with first, before I became Callum Hunt.*

Dizziness flooded him. He stumbled back against the wall, into a shadowed nook, just as an unseen door slid back and Master Joseph entered the room, followed by Call's father.

Call's heart thundered in his chest. They were too late to stop Alastair.

CHAPTER FOURTEEN

MASTER JOSEPH LOOKED exactly as he had the last time Call had seen him: the same staff, the same uniform, and the same manic glint in his eye.

"You have the Alkahest, good," he said to Alastair. "I knew that we'd be better off working together. Really, we both want the same thing."

Alastair, on the other hand, looked exhausted. His clothes were dirty; he wore old jeans and a beat-up anorak. He had beard stubble on his chin. "We do not want the same thing. I just want my son back."

My son. For a second, when Call had first seen his father, he'd felt a rush of relief. A sense of familiarity. Now he felt like he'd been punched in the chest. He knew who his father wanted back, and it wasn't him.

Master Joseph's gaze flickered toward the thick shadows where Call and Stanley stood. Call froze, trying to be as still as possible. He didn't even want to breathe for fear that he'd be noticed. Aaron and the others must have sensed that something was wrong, since they stayed safe in the stairway. As usual, Stanley took Call's lead and remained still as well.

Alastair followed Master Joseph's gaze to where Call and Stanley stood in the dim light. "Chaos-ridden. You shouldn't just leave them around like that."

"Every tomb needs sentries," Master Joseph said. Maybe it was normal to find random Chaos-ridden wandering around the tomb of Constantine Madden. Maybe he was just distracted by Alastair. "Your boy is dead. But he can rise again. You've raised Constantine, who was the greatest mage of our time, perhaps of any time, and who will be again. Once restored to his own body, he will be able to draw your son's soul back into his body. If you've truly repaired the Alkahest, then all we need is Callum."

"I need a demonstration that the Alkahest won't kill him outright," Alastair said. "I told you I wouldn't bring him to you unless I knew he'd be safe."

"Oh, don't worry," Master Joseph said. "I made sure Callum would be joining us."

Alastair took a step toward Master Joseph, and Call saw that Alastair was wearing the Alkahest on his left hand. It glittered as he moved his fingers, looking just like it had in the picture. "What do you mean?"

"I mean that he left the Magisterium looking for you, of course. Trying to save you from the wrath of the mages. I knew where he'd go, so I left him a trail to lead him straight to us. I even sent an escort to bring him safely here. I promise you, Alastair, I take great pains for his safety. He means far more to me than he does to you."

Call's heart thundered in his chest. He thought of the letters — the latitude and longitude carefully sketched out in each one, the mention of the specific date of the meeting, a meeting happening in just enough time for them to make it. Call had thought he'd been lucky, that he'd been one step ahead of the adults. But he'd been playing right into Master Joseph's hands.

For a moment, Call lost his nerve. He was just a kid. His friends were just kids, even if one of them was the Makar. What if they were in over their heads? What if they couldn't help?

Alastair started speaking, and for a moment, Call couldn't even focus.

"I can assure you you're wrong," Alastair was saying. "Callum means far more to me than he ever will to you. Stay away from him. I don't know if he's the greatest mage of his generation or any of that — but he's a good kid. No one has broken him the way you broke the Madden brothers. I remember them, Joseph, and I remember what you did to them."

Call felt an ache in his chest. Alastair didn't *sound* like he hated Call, even though he'd come here to trade for a new son.

"Stop waving the Alkahest around. You know that thing can't hurt me," Master Joseph said, raising his staff. "Much as I wish I had the ability to use chaos magic, I don't, so there's no point in threatening me with it. The only reason the Chaos-ridden listen to me is because Constantine commanded it."

"I'm not here to threaten you, Joseph," Alastair said, taking a step toward the body of Constantine Madden.

Master Joseph frowned. "All right. Enough. Give me the Alkahest. I'd like to reward you, but don't think for a moment

that I would hesitate to kill you if you resist me. Very conve-
nient, dying in a tomb. Won't have to go far to bury you."

Alastair took another careful step toward the body.

Master Joseph raised his hand and a dozen thin cords of
what looked like silver sprang out of the darkness. They
wrapped around Alastair, binding him the way a spider binds
a fly before feasting on it. Alastair yelled in pain, struggling to
free his gauntleted hand.

Call had to do something. "Stop!" he shouted. "Leave my
father alone! Stanley, do something! Get him!"

Both Master Joseph and Alastair stared as it became clear
that they'd mistaken Call, standing at the bottom of the stairs,
for one of the Chaos-ridden. Stanley began to lurch toward
Master Joseph, but Call's command had been so imprecise that
he wasn't sure what the Chaos-ridden might actually do.
Master Joseph certainly didn't seem worried; he was ignoring
Stanley as if he wasn't there.

Instead, he began to smile.

"We're coming down," Aaron whispered. Call turned his
head without meaning to and saw Tamara, Jasper, and Aaron
moving down the stairs. He motioned them back.

"Ahhh, Callum, so glad you could make it," said Master
Joseph. "I see you brought friends, although I can't quite see
which ones. Is that loyal Makar with you? What a pleasant surprise."

Stanley had nearly reached where Master Joseph stood. *We
could win the war*, Call thought. *If I order Stanley to kill you, the
war will be won.*

But would it? Could the war ever be won for the side of
good if the Enemy was still alive?

"Call?" Alastair said, looking horrified. "Get out of here!"

Tamara and Jasper stumbled down to the last step. They were both clearly astonished by the sight of the Enemy's body and who was standing beside it. Aaron tried to get past them, but Tamara and Jasper moved to block him.

"Let me through," Aaron protested. He craned his neck to see what they were looking at.

"Not a chance," said Tamara in a harsh whisper. "Call's father has the Alkahest. That thing could kill you."

"Dad's right. You all need to leave," Call said. "Get Aaron somewhere safe."

He could see the indecision on their faces, and he was torn, too — he didn't want to put them in danger, but he also wasn't sure he could be as brave without them.

"Look," Jasper exclaimed. Stanley had reached Master Joseph; he grabbed him by the wrists and tugged them behind his back, holding Master Joseph trapped.

Master Joseph didn't move; he was acting like it wasn't happening. Like he wasn't being held against his will. Like Call hadn't just immobilized him. Instead, he just stared across the room, his intense eyes burning holes in Call.

"There is no need for this, Callum," said Master Joseph. "Constantine, I am your most devoted servant."

"I heard what you said to my father," Call told him. "And I'm not Constantine."

"And you heard what your father said to me. What he was prepared to do. Your only true home is here, with me."

Call moved to where his father stood. Alastair, the copper gauntlet firmly on his hand, was still struggling against the cords that bound him. He flinched away when he saw Call coming toward him. "Call!" he barked. "Stay away from me!"

Call hesitated. Was his father afraid? Did he hate Call?

"We'll untie him," Tamara murmured, as she and Jasper slipped away and went to Alastair.

"You should do as Call says. Leave!" shouted Alastair, as Tamara bent down to inspect the silver cord that bound him. It was magical and knotless. Call hoped she'd know how to undo it, because he didn't have the first idea. "Take him out with you! None of you are safe here, Call least of all."

"You mean Aaron least of all. Give us the Alkahest," said Jasper, relentlessly practical. "Give it to us and we can all leave together." He put a hand on Tamara's arm. "Don't free him until he gives it to us."

Master Joseph's focus remained on Call. "Did you think it was funny?" he asked. "The head of Verity Torres? The riddles? You were the one who came up with the design of this place, of the entrance. Of course, it wasn't going to be *her* head back then, but it's quite a funny improvisation, don't you think?"

Call didn't feel like laughing. He'd been so sure that it was a good thing he could figure out some of the riddles. But apparently he was good at these riddles because he was a guy who thought severed heads were hilarious.

"Just give Jasper the Alkahest, Dad," Callum yelled, losing patience with all of this.

But Alastair turned his head away as if he didn't want to look at Call. He was clutching the Alkahest to his body, wrenching himself away when Tamara tried to touch him. "Leave me with it!" he shouted. "Get yourself away from here! Take Call and the Makar with you!"

Aaron had moved to stand beside the body of Constantine Madden and was staring down at it, stricken. Call limped toward him; he could imagine what Aaron was thinking: that these were the hands that had killed Verity Torres, that had slain a thousand mages. The hands of a Makar, like Aaron's own.

"The Enemy died thirteen years ago," Aaron said flatly. "How can he look like he isn't dead at all? How can they all look like this?"

"You think this is a mere tomb," said Joseph.

"It sure looks like one," said Call. "What with all the bodies and all."

"This was your ultimate stronghold against death," Master Joseph continued. "Here is where you taught yourself to use the void to preserve bodies, suspended, unliving but unchanging. Here you preserved your brother's body for the day you would raise him again. Here I used the same magic to preserve your body —"

"It's not my body!" Call shouted. "What is it going to take for you to give up? I don't remember anything! I've never seen this place before! I'm not who you want me to be, and I won't ever turn into him!"

Master Joseph smiled, wide. "It took me years to help you perfect your magic, back at the Magisterium. When we worked alone with chaos, together. Behind your master's back. You used to get frustrated and shout at me just like this. *I'm not what you want me to be.* That's what you said to me then. Once we put your soul back into your body, I believe you'll remember more. Maybe this life will be the one that seems like a dream." He tried to move forward, but Stanley hauled him back. "But even if you never remember, you can't change your nature, Constantine."

"Don't call him that," said Aaron, in a voice like ice. "People change all the time. And this is sick. This whole thing is sick.

Constantine Madden put his soul into Call's body; fine, no one can change that. Leave Call alone. Let the dead stay dead."

Master Joseph's face twisted. "Spoken as someone who has suffered no true loss."

Aaron whirled. He was as Call had seen him only a few times before, no longer Aaron. He was the Makar, the wielder of chaos. His palms began to blacken. "I know plenty about loss," he said. "You don't know anything about me."

"I know about Constan — about Call," said Joseph. "Don't you want your mother back, Call? Don't you want her to live again?"

"Don't you dare talk about Sarah!" It was Alastair. Either he'd torn away the metal ropes or Tamara and Jasper had freed him. Either way, he was still wearing the Alkahest.

He ran at Call.

In that heart-stopping moment, Call knew he was going to die. He remembered the chains his dad had readied in the basement of his own house, remembered the words that Master Joseph had shown to Call, carved in the ice by his own mother's hands with the same blade that Alastair had thrown at him: *KILL THE CHILD*.

Finally, thirteen years later, Alastair was going to do it.

Call didn't move. If his own father really hated him this much, if Alastair was prepared to end his life, then maybe he really was too much of a monster to live. Maybe he *should* die.

Everything slowed down around Call: Aaron, Tamara, and Jasper running toward him but too far away to reach him in time, Master Joseph struggling and shouting in the Chaos-ridden's grasp.

"Let go of me, I command you," Call heard Master Joseph

say — and to Call's numb shock, Stanley released him. The old mage darted toward Call, throwing himself on top of Call to protect him from his own father. Call's knees buckled and he went to the ground, Master Joseph pinning him down.

But Alastair didn't pause. He ran past Call and Master Joseph and straight to the preserved body of the Enemy of Death. There, he stopped. "Joseph, did you really think you could tempt me to betray *my own son*? As soon as I got your messages about trying to put his soul inside this villain's corpse, I knew what I had to do." With that, he raised the Alkahest, gleaming and beautiful in the dim light, and brought it down hard, slamming his metal-clad hand over Constantine Madden's heart.

Master Joseph screamed, pushing off Call, who coughed and rolled to his knees, staring.

Light shone from underneath the skin of the Enemy of Death — and where it shone, the body around it began to blacken, as from fire. Alastair howled with pain as the Alkahest turned scarlet with heat. He was screaming as his hand pulled free, covered all over with red burns.

"Dad!" Call staggered to his feet. The room was full of a burning stink and smoke that stung his eyes.

"No! NO!" Master Joseph cried out, picking up his staff and flinging himself toward Constantine's body. He yanked the Alkahest free, yelling in pain as his hand closed on the hot metal. Still, he didn't drop it. Instead, he swung his staff and magic exploded from it, surrounding the Enemy, trying to halt the force that was devouring Constantine's body. Energy crackled in the room as he cast his preservation spell again and again.

Call limped forward and then stopped, overcome by a wave of dizziness. The edges of his vision were starting to turn dark. *What's happening to me?* he thought as he slid down to his knees. He felt no pain, but his body was shaking, as though he was being destroyed along with Constantine.

"Run, Call!" Alastair shouted, clutching his burned arm. "Get away from the tomb!"

"I — can't," Call gasped, and then there were figures around him, Aaron and Tamara and Jasper, and someone was trying to help him to his feet but his legs wouldn't work. "Go," he whispered. "Go without me."

"Never." A hand gripped his arm and he realized it was Aaron's.

"What's happening to him?" Jasper's frightened whisper was drowned out by Master Joseph's cries; Constantine Madden's chest was collapsing inward, like a balloon with the air sucked out of it.

"Seize the Makar and his friends!" Master Joseph shouted at Stanley. "Kill everyone but Callum!"

The Chaos-ridden began to lurch toward them. Call heard Tamara's frightened cry and felt her arms around him; all of them were trying to pull him toward the steps, but he was dead weight. He slid from their grasp and hit the floor in front of the steps.

Then everything seemed to vanish, the voices of Call's friends fading into silence. All he could do was try to keep breathing as a roiling darkness rose in front of his eyes, a pure blackness he had seen before only when it had come from Aaron's hands, the lightless darkness of the void. Chaos filled him, his thoughts shredded by it, his responses overwhelmed by the power expanding inside of him.

Slowly breath ebbed back into Call's body. He raised his head, his face wet.

The room was in chaos. Stanley had obeyed Master Joseph's command and attacked Call's friends. He loomed over Tamara, who was backing away, summoning fire. She threw it, but it only seemed to singe the Chaos-ridden. It left a burned scorch along Stanley's chest, but he barely seemed to notice.

Aaron jumped on Stanley's back, his arm circling the Chaos-ridden's neck, tightening as though he was attempting to pull Stanley's head right off. Jasper was using air and earth magic together to throw dust in Stanley's eyes. Stanley thrashed around but seemed more annoyed than damaged.

Alastair and Master Joseph were struggling over the Alkahest. Master Joseph cracked him across the face with his staff. Alastair staggered back, his face bloody.

"Leave him alone," Call shouted, crawling toward his father.

Master Joseph spoke a word and Alastair's legs gave out. He fell to the floor.

Constantine's body was partially burned away, his chest concave and blackened. Call could see the burned bones of his rib cage through his charred skin. A fresh wave of magic washed over him suddenly, pushing him back into immobility. It felt as if he were watching something unreal, happening at a great distance.

"Call." Tamara's voice cut through the fog in Call's mind. "Call, you have to do something. Order the Chaos-ridden to stop."

"There's something wrong with me," Call whispered, spots dancing in front of his vision. The pressure inside him was still expanding, pushing outward against the limits of his control.

He didn't know what it was, but it felt as if it were going to break him apart.

Tamara's grip on him tightened. "There's nothing wrong with you," she said. "There never has been. You're Callum Hunt. Now tell that *thing* to stop attacking us. It will listen to you over Master Joseph. You can stop it."

And so Call brought up one hand, meaning to thrust it forward to hold off Stanley, meaning to tell the Chaos-ridden leader to stop. But as he raised his hand, the pressure inside him broke through the thin shell of his control, like an explosion in slow motion. He stared in shock as his fingers flexed and opened, and for the first time ever, Callum Hunt summoned chaos into the world.

Darkness exploded from the palm of his hand. The shadows rose, circling Stanley, surrounding him with ribbons of blackness. The Chaos-ridden turned tortured eyes toward Call, and Call could see the feeling of betrayal in them. Stanley began to shriek, and Call understood the cries as words, each one stabbing into his ears: *Master, you made me — why do you destroy me?*

The shadows collapsed inward, crushing Stanley out of existence.

The darkness spread its tendrils as if in search of other prey. It reached out, spreading toward the others, reaching toward Tamara, toward Jasper, toward Master Joseph — who turned on his heel and ran, clutching the Alkahest, vanishing through the door in the wall that he and Alastair had come through. Alastair tried to stop him, but it was too late. The door slammed shut behind Joseph, locked.

Call couldn't seem to stop the chaos magic. It flowed out of him like a river, and he felt himself flowing away with it. He remembered what it had felt to fly without a counterweight, to drift away without human cares.

He felt Aaron's hand on his back, pinning him in place, forcing him to focus. "Call, *enough*."

And somehow, that allowed Call to turn off the torrent. He couldn't reverse it, but at least it was no longer pouring out of him like his lifeblood. Shaking, he looked around. The chaos he had unleashed had become living shadows, shadows that were tearing at the edges of the room. Darkness was spreading inexorably, eating away at the walls of the tomb at the pillars that held up the roof, gnawing at the mortar that held the bricks of the underground room together until they started to loosen and fall to the floor.

"We need to get out of here!" Alastair turned away from the doors Master Joseph had escaped through and dashed to the foot of the stairs, gesturing for the others to follow him. "All of you, come on!"

Tamara rose to her feet, pulling Call with her. Along with Jasper and Aaron, she and Call began to race toward Alastair and the steps. Nearby, a piece of roof gave way, and rock tumbled to the ground, exploding at their feet. They swerved, nearly colliding with a patch of spreading black shadow. Jasper yelled and jumped back.

The darkness shot toward them; Aaron thrust his hand out, and a beam of black light shone from his palm: It struck the shadow and enveloped it. Call looked at Aaron in amazement.

"Chaos stops chaos," Aaron explained.

"I can't do chaos magic," Call whispered.

"It looks like you *can*," Aaron observed, and there was

something in his voice, a dark amusement and maybe something less comfortable.

Tamara's face was smudged. "It's devouring this whole tomb. Aaron, can you hold it off until we get out?"

"I think I can," Aaron said, looking around at the shadows, at the crawling magic that deepened them, drawing off everything it touched into the void. "But Call released a lot of chaos energy — I don't know."

"Just go," Call said. He felt better without the chaos in his head, cluttering up his thoughts, but he could still feel something simmering inside of him, something that hadn't been there before.

"Callum —" Alastair began, but Call cut him off.

"Dad, I need you to get them out of here. Now."

"What about you?" Tamara asked. "Don't get some idea about staying behind."

Call looked Tamara in the eye, willing her to believe him, to trust him just this once. "I won't. Go. I'll be right behind you."

What's something that's not behind you? Call thought grimly. *Ahead. A head. Get it?*

Tamara must have seen something in Call's face, because she nodded once. Jasper was already moving past Alastair. Aaron looked less sure, but with chaos magic burning away the walls around them, he had his hands full. He threw out more and more magic, pushing back the void as they made for the stairs.

Call had only a few moments before Alastair noticed he wasn't following.

Call drew Miri from her sheath and went to where the remains of Constantine Madden rested on the marble slab.

CHAPTER FIFTEEN

CALL RACED UP the stairs as quickly as he could go, cursing his leg for slowing him down when the very walls were crumbling away into nothingness. All around, darkness was lapping at his heels, as if it wanted to pull him into its endless embrace. Chaos magic that he'd unleashed but had no idea how to constrain.

"Call," Alastair was shouting from the corridor, hands thrust up to hold the ceiling above them with magic. "Call, where are you? Call!"

He ran to his father, rocks spinning above them, rocks that would have collapsed had his father not come back for him. "Here," he said, out of breath. "I'm right here."

"We're going together now," Alastair said. He put out his arm and Call saw that his father's burned hand had been healed — not completely, but the bubbling black marks were just sore-looking red skin now. "Healing magic," Alastair explained at Call's surprised look. "Come on — lean on me."

"Okay," said Call, letting his father slide an arm around Call's shoulders and help him make his way past the bodies of Drew and Jericho, past Verity's laughing head and out onto the grass where Jasper, Tamara, and Aaron were standing. Aaron had both hands raised and was obviously doing all he could to hold back the chaos magic that was trying to rip the tomb apart. The moment he saw Call and Alastair he collapsed to his knees, letting go.

Blackness roared up like ash pouring out of a volcano. Call and Alastair stopped, Call leaning hard against his dad, as they watched the final resting place of the Enemy of Death be devoured by chaos magic. A thick, oily darkness covered the building, tendrils snaking along the outside like ivy. But as Call stared, he realized that it wasn't really black — it was something darker, something that his eye was translating into the comprehensible, because what he was seeing was *nothing*. And where nothing touched, the building simply wasn't, until what they were looking at was the flattened earth where a tomb had once been, Verity's strange and terrible laughter still hanging in the air.

"Is it gone?" Jasper asked.

Aaron gave him a tired look. "The tomb went to the same place I sent Automotones."

"Automotones?" Alastair looked shocked by that pronouncement. "But he's trapped in the deepest pits of the Magisterium."

"He *was*," Call said. "The Magisterium sent him after us."

Alastair inhaled in a way that he did only when he was angry or surprised or both. He took a few steps away from the rest of the group, obviously trying to clear his head. Call hitched his backpack higher on his shoulder. He was exhausted.

Master Joseph had gotten away — and worse, he'd gotten away with the Alkahest, the very device they'd come to keep out of their hands. The massed army of Chaos-ridden had vanished. Master Joseph must have commanded them to take him back to shore. He'd probably taken all the rowboats, too, just to be a jerk.

Suddenly, Call remembered that Havoc had been with the Chaos-ridden, that Havoc was Chaos-ridden, and so, if Master Joseph could command the rest of them, he could probably command the wolf, too.

"Havoc!" he shouted, panic reigniting in his chest. "Havoc!"

How could he have let his wolf stay outside the tomb? He'd left Havoc behind like Havoc was just a dog, when Havoc was way more than that.

Call rushed along the path back toward the beach, leg aching, nearly in tears, calling for his wolf. It was one more thing he wasn't ready for, one more thing he couldn't bear.

"Call!" his father shouted. Call turned and saw Alastair looking weary, walking up the path with Havoc at his heels. Call stared. His dad's unburned hand was buried in the wolf's fur, and there was ash on the wolf's pelt, but he didn't look otherwise harmed. "He's okay. You rushed off before we could tell you, but he tried to get back into the tomb. We had to stop him, but it wasn't easy."

"Your father held him back," Aaron said.

Havoc took a few steps toward Call. Call held his arms out and Havoc bounded into them, licking his face.

"That's a way more touching reunion than you had with me," Tamara said. She was going over Aaron's cuts and scratches, using earth magic to heal the worst of them. She'd already fixed Jasper's bloody lip.

Call patted Havoc on the head. "I should have known Master Joseph wasn't going to kidnap you. He only likes dead things and weird things."

"We're all weird," Tamara pointed out. She examined Aaron. He'd used what must have been immense amounts of chaos magic without a counterweight and, although he was still standing, he looked on the verge of collapse. "Well, you're not actively bleeding anymore, but I don't know enough healing magic to check to see if you have anything sprained, or broken, or —"

"Is anyone going to talk about the fact that Call's a Makar?" Jasper said, cutting into the discussion.

Everyone looked horrified. "Jasper!" said Tamara.

"Oh, sorry," Jasper said. "I didn't realize we were pretending it didn't happen." He turned to Call. "Did you know you were a Makar before? Oh, wait, never mind, I forgot I can't trust anything you say."

"He didn't know," said Alastair. "Chaos magic was locked into Constantine's body and when the body was destroyed, the chaos magic was released. It must have been attracted to Call's soul. When Constantine became a Makar, it was because there was a danger to his brother. Jericho was attacked by a rogue elemental in the caverns, and Constantine — made it disappear."

Tamara looked at him narrowly. "How do you know that?" she said.

"Because I was in the same apprentice group that he was," said Alastair. "There were five of us. Sarah, Declan, Jericho, Constantine, and me. Rufus was our Master."

Aaron, Tamara, and Jasper all goggled at him. "They say Constantine got perfect scores on the Trials," said Jasper. "Perfect scores."

"We were the best in our year," said Alastair. He sounded tired and distant, like he was talking about something that had happened a million years ago.

"You were friends with Constantine? Good friends?" Aaron said. Despite being messy and bloody and dirty, he looked ready to defend himself, to defend them all.

"He and Jericho and Sarah were my best friends," said Alastair. "You know how apprentice groups are."

"Speaking of which," Tamara said, casting a worried glance at Aaron, "we need to figure out how to get this apprentice group out of here."

"Nice segue," Call muttered. Tamara gave him a dirty look.

"Water magic," Alastair said, and started to walk down to the edge of the beach. "Gather up some wood. We'll spell together a raft."

Suddenly, the whole beach lit up as if a spotlight had been shone on it. Call staggered back, clutching his backpack, fingers digging into the straps. He heard Jasper yell something, and then mages were flying above them.

Master North, Master Rockmaple, Master Milagros, and Master Rufus hovered in the air.

"Dad," Call shouted, rushing to his father. "They're going to kill you — you have to go. I can try to hold them off!"

"No!" Alastair cried against the wind. "I deserve punishment for taking the Alkahest, but I'm not the one who's in the greatest danger —"

"CALLUM," Master Rufus said. "TAMARA. AARON. ALASTAIR. JASPER. DO NOT STRUGGLE."

And with that, air swirled around Call, thickening and lifting them into the sky. Despite what Master Rufus said, Call still struggled.

"We must have been hidden from them by the tomb," Tamara said. "It must have been enchanted the way the Magisterium is — to prevent scrying. But now that it's gone, they found us."

"Don't hurt us!" Jasper shouted. "We surrender!"

Master North raised his hands and out of clouds came three long eel-like air elementals. They were large and placid, until they unhinged massive jaws. He saw one swallow Aaron, gulping him down into its gullet. A moment later, the second elemental was racing toward him, large maw waiting.

"Aaaaugh!" Call yelled as he tumbled inside it. He was expecting to land in the stomach of a creature, but where he fell was soft and shapeless and dry, the way he imagined lying on clouds might feel — even though he knew that clouds were actually just a bunch of water.

Havoc rolled in after him, looking really freaked out. The Chaos-ridden wolf howled and Call hurried over to try to calm him down. Call wasn't sure Havoc was going to get used to flying. Then Alastair came rolling in, hands still up, as though he was in the middle of readying a spell.

The elemental began to move, swimming through the sky, following the mages back to the Magisterium. Call could tell where it was going, because he could see through the creature in places. It was opaque and cloudy in some spots, translucent in others, and completely transparent in a very few spots. But wherever he touched, the elemental seemed like a solid thing.

"Dad?" Call said. "What's going on?"

"I think the mages want to be sure we don't get away, so they created a prison *inside* an elemental. Impressive." Alastair sat down on the cloud belly of the creature. "You four must be quite slippery."

"I guess," Call said. He knew what he had to say to his father, what he'd wanted to say since he'd first seen Alastair's notes to Master Joseph. "I'm sorry about what happened. You know, this summer."

Alastair glanced over at Havoc, who was trying to pull up his paws at once and slipping around. Call followed his glance and remembered that he wasn't sorry about everything.

"I'm sorry, too, Callum," Alastair said. "You must have been very frightened by what you saw in the garage."

"I was afraid you were going to hurt Havoc," Call said.

"Is that all?"

Call shrugged. "I thought you were going to use the Alkahest to test out your theory about me. Like, if I died, then I was really —"

Alastair cut him off. "I understand. You don't need to say anything else. I don't want anyone to overhear us."

"When did you start to suspect?"

Call saw the weariness in Alastair's face as he answered, "For a long time. Maybe since I left the cave."

"Why didn't you say anything — to me, at least?"

Alastair looked around, as though evaluating if the elemental might be eavesdropping on them. "What was the point?" he said finally. "Better you not know, I thought. Better you never know. But we can't speak about this anymore now."

"Are you mad at me?" Call asked in a small voice.

"For what happened in the storage room?" Alastair asked. "No, I'm angry with myself. I suspected Master Joseph had been in contact; I worried he already had his hooks in you. I thought that if you knew more, you might be tempted by the idea of power. And after he began writing to me, I was afraid of what he wanted to do to you. But I forgot how frightened you must have been."

"I thought I'd really hurt you." Call let his head fall against the softness of the elemental's side. The adrenaline was quickly draining out of his system, leaving only exhaustion behind. "I thought I was as terrible as —"

"I'm fine," Alastair said. "Everything's fine, Callum. People don't start wars by losing their tempers or losing control of their magic."

Callum wasn't sure that was true, but he was too exhausted to argue.

"You never should have come to the tomb, Callum — you know that, right? You should have left things to me to handle. If Joseph had actually been able to do what he planned — who knows what he might have done to you." Alastair shuddered.

"I know," Call said. If his soul had moved into Constantine's body, maybe all the memories he had of being Callum would have been gone, which, when he let himself think about it too much, seemed like it might be a fate much, much worse than death.

But the farther they flew, the more exhausted he felt. He remembered the way Aaron had been after using chaos magic on Automotones.

I'm just going to shut my eyes for a moment, he told himself.

When Call woke, it was because there were arms around him and he was moving. Being carried, he realized, over the rocks outside the Magisterium. He cracked an eye and looked around.

Morning light stung his eyes. He guessed it was probably around breakfast time. Master North and Master Rockmaple were behind him, watching from their places astride massive air elementals. They looked dour and stern. Havoc, Tamara, Aaron, and Jasper were following Master Rufus down a path to a gate set into the wall of the Magisterium. Alastair was following them, and he was carrying Call the way he hadn't since Call was very young, with Call's head against his shoulder.

The backpack. Call grabbed for it, and realized his dad was carrying that, too, slung over one shoulder. He breathed a sigh of relief.

"Do you want me to put you down?" asked Alastair in a low voice.

Call didn't say anything. Part of him wanted to be set down on his own imperfect feet. Another part thought this was probably the last time his dad would ever carry him.

The stones had given way to a grassy patch beside the Magisterium. They were in front of two doors that had been hammered out of copper. The hammering had been done in a way that left swirls and coils in the metal that looked like flames.

Above the door were the words: HE WHO LOVES NOTHING UNDERSTANDS NOTHING.

Call took a deep breath. "Yeah," he said.

His dad set him down on his feet and the usual pain shot up his leg. Alastair handed him his backpack and Call slung it over one shoulder.

"I've never seen this door before," Tamara said.

"This is the Assembly entrance to the Magisterium," said

Master Rufus. "It never crossed my mind that any of you would have occasion to use it."

Over the time he'd been at the Magisterium, Call had cycled through many feelings about it. He'd started out being afraid, then it had come to seem like home, then it had been a refuge from his father, and now, again, it was a place he wasn't sure he could trust.

Maybe Alastair had been right after all. Right about everything.

Master Rufus tapped his wristband against the doors, and they opened. The corridor inside didn't look like any of the other Magisterium corridors, with the usual rock walls and packed dirt floors. This corridor was made of polished copper, and each few steps along the way took Call past a symbol for an element — air and metal, fire and water, earth and chaos — with words in Latin running underneath.

Rufus reached a point on the wall that looked exactly like every other point along the wall. He tapped his bracelet again, and this time a door-size piece of metal slid back to expose a room beyond. It was a bare room made of rock, with a long stone bench that ran around the walls.

"You'll wait in here," he said. "Master North and Master Rockmaple will return shortly to escort you to the meeting room. The Assembly is gathering now to determine what to do with you."

Tamara gulped. Her parents were Assembly members. Jasper looked terrified, and even Aaron seemed uneasy.

"I'll take Havoc," said Rufus, and held up a hand before Call could protest. "He'll be perfectly safe in your rooms, which is more than I can say if he's brought with us. The Assembly is not overfond of Chaos-ridden animals."

He snapped his fingers and Havoc trotted over to his side. Call gave Havoc a dark look of betrayal.

"Alastair," said Rufus. "Come here for a moment."

Alastair appeared surprised, then approached Rufus. The two men looked at each other. Rufus's change in expression was subtle, but Call thought he could note in the Master's face that the Alastair he saw was very different from the man Call saw when he looked at his dad. It seemed like he was seeing a boy, maybe Call's age, with dark hair and mischief in his eyes.

"Welcome back to the Magisterium, Alastair Hunt," Rufus said. "This place has missed you."

When Alastair looked back at Master Rufus, there was no anger in his expression. He only looked drained, which made Call's stomach clench. "I haven't missed it," he said. "Look, this whole situation is my fault. Let the kids go back to their rooms and bring me in front of the Assembly. I don't care what they do."

"Good plan," said Jasper, rising to his feet.

"Sit down, deWinter," said Master Rufus. "You're lucky Master Milagros isn't here. She was thinking about having you all dangled over the Bottomless Pit."

"The *what*?" asked Call. Jasper sat down hastily, as Master Rufus leaned forward to say something to Alastair, something Call couldn't hear. Master Rufus backed away with Havoc and tapped his wristband once more against the wall. The door slid shut, sealing them into the room.

Call took a deep breath. He was glad he was going to speak in front of the Assembly. He needed to stay; he needed to explain before someone else explained on his behalf. He needed to show them what they wouldn't otherwise believe.

Looking over at Jasper, Call tried to guess what he might say to the Assembly. He would definitely bring up the kidnapping — so Call had to just talk first, to get out what he needed to before guards dragged him away. Jasper looked back at him with thoughtful dark eyes.

"What are we going to say?" he said. "I mean, what's your plan, about telling the Assembly?"

"We tell them the truth," said Call. "We tell them everything."

"Everything?" Aaron looked startled. Call felt his stomach tighten further. Had Aaron been prepared to lie for him?

"Call's right," said Alastair. "Think about it practically. The worst thing we could do in there is contradict one another. Only if we tell the exact truth will we all be telling the same story."

"I don't know why we're listening to the advice of a wanted criminal," Jasper muttered.

"We're all wanted criminals, Jasper," Tamara snapped, and patted Call's shoulder. "It'll be okay," she said.

"Yeah, better comfort old evil pants over there," Jasper said. "He's fragile. His daddy princess-carried him in here."

"Oh, lay off," Aaron said. "You get mean every time you're nervous."

Call looked over at Jasper, surprised. Was that true? In Call's experience, Jasper was unpleasant most of the time, but Call certainly knew what it was like to have a mouth that ran away from you. Call said lots of stuff before he thought better of it.

He didn't want to think he had anything in common with Jasper, especially something about Jasper he didn't like.

Constantine Madden was charming, Tamara had said.

The door opened and Master North came in. "The Assembly will see you now," he said.

Be charming, Call told himself. *If you're Constantine, then make something useful out of it. Be charming.*

They all got to their feet and followed Master North down the copper corridor and through an archway into a massive circular room. Call had been there before but hid his start of recognition — he'd been sneaking around the Magisterium when he'd happened upon a mage meeting here. Now probably wasn't the time to bring up the fact that he'd eavesdropped.

Jewels decorated the cavern's walls, formed into the shapes of constellations. The center of the room was dominated by a massive circular wooden table with a hollow core. It looked as though it was made from a slice of tree trunk, but the tree would have to have been enormous — bigger than the biggest redwood. Call couldn't help wanting to run his fingers over the surface of it.

Around one side of it sat Assembly members in their olive green suits, alternating with the mages of the Magisterium in black. They looked like a set of chess pieces.

Master North gestured with his hand, and a section of the table lifted away like a slice of cake being cut out. He gestured for Call and the others to walk through the gap in the circle. After a moment's hesitation, Alastair went first and the kids followed him. The moment the last of them — Jasper — was inside the circle formed by the table, the section that had been lifted away slammed back into place. Call and his friends were trapped inside the circle of the table, completely surrounded by the Assembly.

Call looked around at the adults' smug faces. Well, maybe they didn't all look smug. Master Rufus, Master North, Master Rockmaple, and Master Milagros looked tense, and Tamara's parents seemed worried. Other than the teachers and the Rajavis, the only Assembly member Call recognized was Alex's stepmother, Mrs. Tarquin. She sat looking regal as a queen, her silver hair piled on top of her head. No one introduced themselves.

"Where to even begin," said an elderly man in an Assembly uniform. "Never since Constantine Madden have we had such a disruption, such a blow to the Magisterium and all that it stands for, as we have had this past week."

"Hurting the Magisterium was never our intention," said Tamara.

"Really?" The old man leaped on her statement like a cat on a mouse. "Do you know how demoralizing it is to the other apprentices to hear that our Makar has run away from the Magisterium? Did that occur to you, Aaron Stewart?"

"I didn't run away, Assemblyman Graves," Aaron said, standing up straight. He was still wearing the outfit he'd gotten from the thrift shop, though it was covered in dirt and blood now. He was a thirteen-year-old kid and his stupid haircut had grown out some, but when he spoke, everyone looked at him. Call could see the expressions of the Assembly members softening. They wanted to listen to Aaron. That was what Constantine had possessed; that was what Tamara meant when she said *charming*. "This summer, I talked to many members of this Assembly and many mages in the community. All of them stressed to me that I was the only weapon that would stop the Enemy. Well, it seems to me that I owe it to everyone to make sure I don't hide away in the Magisterium when I'm needed."

There was a brief silence, and Graves cleared his throat. "Your enthusiasm is admirable, but if you really did think you were needed to take down Alastair Hunt, why did you not deal with him when you caught up to him? Why is he still with you?"

A flame of anger lit in Call's chest.

"It's not like that," Tamara said. "You have to hear the whole story."

"Tamara Rajavi, we would have thought that after what happened to your sister, you would have better sense," chided Master North. Tamara's face crumpled. The flame in Call's chest burned hotter.

"And you, Callum Hunt," said Master North. "We allowed you into the Magisterium even though your scores were pitiful, and this is how you repay us? Consider your application to be the Makar's counterweight dismissed, and count yourself lucky if that's all that happens to you."

Master Rufus's hands were clenched. Call felt as if he were choking down boiling water.

"You don't have the right to punish any of us," Jasper said, eyes blazing. "You sent an elemental to kill us!"

"Jasper!" Master Milagros looked horrified. "Do you understand where you are, what this is? Lying is not going to help you."

"He's not lying," Call said. "And we know the Magisterium doesn't care about the truth. What happened to Master Lemuel? He didn't really hurt Drew, so why wasn't he allowed to come back? Why does he have to squat with some animal-experimenting weirdos in the woods?"

Master Rufus sighed. "He chose not to come back, Call."

Call bit his tongue.

"Lying certainly won't help your parents' bid to get back on the Assembly," Mrs. Rajavi said to Jasper in a low voice, then turned to Alastair. "And where is the Alkahest?" she demanded. "Why don't I see it on the table?"

"Master Joseph has it," Alastair said flatly. Call winced. If he wasn't particularly charming, he knew who to blame for not teaching him better.

"Master Joseph?" Mrs. Tarquin spoke coolly. "The Enemy of Death's second-in-command? The one who first led him down the path of evil?"

Graves rose to his feet. "You children let this traitor deliver the Alkahest to the Enemy? We should lock up Alastair and lock up all of you with him —"

"The Enemy of Death doesn't have the Alkahest," said Call. "He doesn't have anything. No thanks to all of you."

Graves narrowed his eyes. "How do you know so much about what the Enemy has and doesn't have?"

"*Callum*," Alastair cautioned.

But Call wasn't going to stop. He'd prepared for this moment. He reached into his backpack and gripped a handful of hair. Choking back rage and nausea, he pulled Constantine Madden's severed head out of his backpack.

He slammed the head down on the table in front of Master Graves. There was no blood; the wound in Constantine's neck looked cauterized where Call had sliced it with Miri. The Enemy's face was smeared with ash, but it was still very recognizably Constantine Madden.

"Because my dad killed him," Call said. "He used the Alkahest."

The Assembly was entirely silent. Mrs. Tarquin made a choked noise and turned her face away. Master Rufus looked uncharacteristically shocked. Assemblyman Graves looked as though he was about to have a heart attack, and the Rajavis were both staring at Tamara as though they'd never seen her before.

Into the silence, Aaron spoke, his voice higher, cracking a little. "You *cut off* his *head*?"

Call supposed it wasn't exactly charming. The head was faced toward the Assembly members and they were staring at it with a mixture of horror and trepidation, as though they were expecting it to speak. Call noticed that an orange Life Saver and a piece of fuzz were stuck to the Enemy's cheek, but he didn't want to draw more attention to them by reaching over and flicking either off.

"I thought that maybe we'd need proof," Call said.

"I *touched* that backpack!" Tamara said. "That is the grossest thing I have ever —"

Alastair began to laugh, and once he started, he couldn't seem to stop. Tears rolled over his cheeks. He wiped his eyes and sagged against the table with the force of hilarity. He tried to talk, but he wasn't even able to get out words.

Call hoped that the sight of Constantine Madden's head hadn't permanently unhinged anyone, least of all his dad. Lots of people in the room looked a little bit unhinged.

"Callum," said Master Rufus, recovering himself first. "How did Alastair come to slay the Enemy of Death?"

"He tricked Master Joseph into bringing him to where Constantine was," Call said, careful not to lie. "Then he used the Alkahest on the Enemy. After that, Constantine was dead." Call didn't mention he'd also been dead *before* that.

"There were a bunch of Chaos-ridden around. We helped fight them off, but when we did, the tomb was destroyed."

"And the Alkahest was lost?" Master Milagros asked.

Call nodded. He was pretty sure the Assembly was supposed to be asking more questions, but they looked too shell-shocked to interrupt. "We think Master Joseph escaped with it as the place was falling apart."

At least Alastair's laughter had finally trailed off.

"What happened to the Enemy's body?" asked Master North.

"It disappeared with the rest of the tomb. Chaos, uh, devoured it."

Master Rufus nodded.

"That's not what happened," Jasper said, shaking his head. "You're leaving important stuff out."

Call felt his father tense, Alastair's fingers digging into his shoulder. He could see Tamara had caught her breath and Aaron was looking daggers in Jasper's direction.

"And what is that?" asked Assemblyman Graves, looking as if he was reeling from innumerable shocks.

"The reason the tomb was destroyed is because of Call," Jasper said. *Because Call is the Enemy of Death. Because Call is Constantine Madden reborn and just as Constantine destroyed the Magisterium, Call destroyed the tomb. Bind his magic; kill him.* Call stared in frozen horror as Jasper went on. "Call used void magic to keep back the Chaos-ridden. It got kind of out of control, because it was the first time he'd ever used it." Jasper gave them all a smug look, like he knew how much they'd been panicking. "That's right. Call is a Makar, like Aaron. Now we have two."

Call let out a sigh of relief. The Assembly members were staring at Jasper as if he'd grown a second head.

Finally, for real, Jasper had surprised him.

At that moment, Anastasia Tarquin rose to her feet. Her back was straight, her silver hair glimmering. She stared directly at Call as she spoke. "The Enemy is dead at last," she said. "Thanks to you five" — her hand swept out, indicating Call, Alastair, Tamara, Jasper, and Aaron — "Verity Torres and the many lost in the Cold Massacre have finally been avenged."

Call thought of Verity's head nailed to the door of the tomb and swallowed hard.

Mrs. Tarquin's words seemed to snap Assemblyman Graves out of his shock. "Anastasia is right," he declared. "The Treaty is rendered null. The Alkahest must be retrieved, but for the moment, this is a time of celebration. The war," he said, "is over."

The rest of the Assembly members began murmuring, smiles broadening across their faces. Master Milagros began to applaud, and it caught on wildfire-fast, the Assembly members and Masters rising to their feet to clap for them. Tamara looked surprised, Jasper smug, and Alastair relieved. Then Call looked over at Aaron. Aaron wasn't grinning. He had an odd, conflicted expression on his face as though he was wondering, knowing what he knew about Call, if he was doing a terrible thing by hiding it.

But maybe Aaron wasn't thinking that. Maybe he was exhausted and not thinking about anything at all.

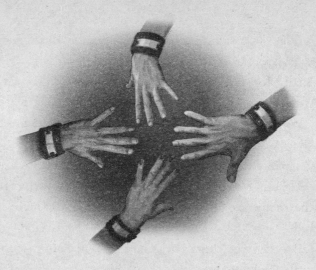

CHAPTER SIXTEEN

AFTER THAT, THINGS happened quickly. Alastair was squired off by Master Rufus to sleep in a spare Master's room. The kids were sent to their common rooms to bathe and rest, meaning that Call was a) separated from Jasper and b) reunited with Havoc, both of which he regarded as good things.

No sooner had Call, Tamara, and Aaron spilled back into their common room to collapse in exhaustion on sofas and chairs than Alex Strike arrived, bearing food from the Refectory — wooden plates and bowls piled high with different sorts of mushrooms and lichen and tuberous puddings, from stuff that tasted like nachos to purple goop that Tamara thought resembled salted caramel to a mushroom that tasted exactly like a breaded chicken finger.

After eating his fill, Call stumbled to his bed and collapsed, exhausted. He didn't dream — or if he did, he didn't remember.

When he woke up the next day, he realized that his sheets were gritty with smoke and dirt. He couldn't remember the last time he'd had a real bath and decided he'd better take one before Master Rufus got a good look at him and dunked him in one of the Magisterium's silty pools.

Looking down at Havoc, he realized his wolf was in even worse shape. Havoc's fur had turned an entirely different color from filth.

The washroom was a grotto off the main hallway and shared by two different rooms of apprentices. It had three chambers — one with toilets, one with sinks and mirrors, and one with warm pools that bubbled gently and streams of water that poured down over you like warm rain if you stood in the right place. Walls of rock cleverly separated all of the individual bathing areas, so that multiple people could bathe at the same time without having to see one another with their clothes off.

Call went over to one of the pools, hung his towel on a hook, stripped off the filthy civilian clothes he'd fallen asleep in and climbed in. The water was so hot it was almost uncomfortable at first, until his muscles relaxed. Then it felt amazing. Even his leg felt good.

"Come on in," he told Havoc.

The wolf hesitated, sniffing the air. Then he took a suspicious lick of the water. Once, this would have annoyed Call, but now he found the idea that Havoc didn't automatically do what he wanted to be a huge relief.

"Call?" he heard someone say. It was a voice coming from the other side of the rock wall of his bath. A very familiar girl's voice.

"Tamara?" His voice went a little squeaky. "I'm taking a bath!"

"I know," she said. "But there's no one else in here and we need to talk."

"I don't know if you know this," he said. "But mostly people take baths with their clothes *off*."

"I'm on the other side of a wall!" she said, sounding exasperated. "And it's really humid in here and making my hair frizz, so could we just talk?"

Call pushed his own wet black hair out of his face. "Okay, fine. Talk."

"You called me a liar," she said, and the hurt in her voice was unmistakable.

Call squirmed. Havoc looked at him sternly. "I know," he said.

"And then it turned out that you were an even bigger liar," she said. "You lied about everything."

"I lied to protect my dad!"

"You lied to protect yourself," she snapped. "You could have told us you were the Enemy —"

"Tamara, *shut up*."

"Call, I hate to tell you this, but the bathroom is not exactly full of people listening in. It's just us."

"I'm not the Enemy of Death." Call glowered at his reflection in the water. Black hair, gray eyes. Still Callum Hunt. And yet not.

"You could have told us the truth about what Master Joseph said to you, and you didn't."

"I didn't want you to hate me," Call said. "You're my best friend."

Tamara made a dubious noise. "Aaron's your best friend, *liar.*"

"You're my best girl friend," said Call. "I didn't want either of you to hate me. I need you both."

When Tamara spoke again, she sounded less angry. "So I guess what I wanted to tell you is that I don't want us ever to lie to each other again."

"But we can still lie to other people?" Call looked at Havoc, who wiggled his ears.

"If it's important," Tamara said. "But not to each other and not to Aaron. We only tell each other the truth. Okay?"

"Okay," Call said, and Havoc barked.

"Call," said Tamara. "Is there someone in the bathtub with you?"

Call sighed. He hadn't expected his truth telling to bite him back so quickly. "Havoc," he admitted.

"Call!" Tamara said. "That is *so disgusting.*"

Then she started to laugh. After a second, Call was laughing, too.

↑ ≈ △ ○ @

Once Tamara left and Call finished up his bath, he headed back to his room in his robe and pulled on a uniform. When he reemerged, Aaron was already there, clean, dressed, and eating what looked like a very pale pear.

"What *is* that?" Call asked him.

Aaron shrugged. "Magic cave fruit. One of the Silver Year apprentice groups grew it. Tastes a little like cheese, but also like an apple. Want one?"

Call made a face. Behind Aaron, he saw that their table had a big pile of the weird fruit, some drinks and candy from the Gallery, and what looked like a few homemade cards. A single eyeless fish floated in a glass bowl.

Aaron followed his gaze. "Yeah, some people were worried about us. Those are 'get well' presents, I guess."

"'Get back here' presents," Call said.

Aaron grinned. A few minutes later, Tamara came out of her room. Her hair wasn't frizzed at all: It was in smooth dark braids, and she'd put them up around her head like a crown. Gold earrings hung from her ears, swinging when she moved. She smiled at Call and when she did, he felt his gut twist. He looked away quickly, without quite knowing why.

"Ready to go to the Refectory?" she asked them.

Aaron took a last bite of the magic cave fruit, folding the core in half and eating it. He glanced down at Havoc, fluffy from the bath. He smelled a little bit like green-tea soap and looked unhappy about it.

"Hey, puffball," he said.

The Chaos-ridden wolf, striker of terror into the hearts of Iron Year students, looked up with swirling, chagrined eyes. Call reached down to pat his head.

"We'll get you some sausages in the Refectory," he promised. "You deserve to celebrate, too."

They headed out into the hallway, only to find Jasper there waiting for them.

"Uh, hi," Jasper said. "I was just about to knock on your door. Everyone in my apprentice group is being super weird and staring at me. I mean," he added, "I am a hero, so I can see how that would be awkward for them."

"You're definitely something," said Aaron.

Jasper shrugged. "Anyway, I didn't want to go to the Refectory by myself."

He fell into step with them as they made their way down the hall, chatting to Tamara. It had actually started to feel like Jasper just belonged with them, which seemed like a bad sign to Call. On the other hand, he couldn't be mean to Jasper when Jasper was, against all odds, keeping his secret.

But sometimes Jasper cut his gaze over and Call wondered if the secret would get too tempting. If Call annoyed him — and Call was absolutely sure that he would eventually annoy Jasper, just as he was sure that Jasper was likely to annoy him — could Jasper continue to keep his mouth shut? If he was trying to impress another student, could he really resist temptation?

Call swallowed down the cold lump in his throat. "You're not going to tell anyone, right?"

"Tell anyone what?" Jasper asked with a half smile.

There was no way Call was going to say it out loud. "The thing!"

Jasper raised an eyebrow. "So long as it continues to benefit me."

"We need to agree," Tamara said firmly. "No one says anything about Call. We don't know who we can trust around here."

Jasper didn't answer her, and there was no way to make him, no way to extort a promise, and even if they were able to make him promise, no reason to believe he would keep his word.

Call was practically in a panic when they arrived in the Refectory. They were late, so it was already full. Smells of grilled onions and barbecue sauce filled the air, although kids were carrying plates piled high with grayish puddings, lichen, and mushrooms. Call's mouth began to water despite his having just eaten.

After the first few apprentices spotted them, words were murmured and everyone's heads went up. The whole Refectory fell silent. Call, Tamara, Aaron, and Jasper stood awkwardly in the doorway, feeling the weight of hundreds of eyes on them. People they knew, people they didn't. *Everyone* was staring.

Then the room exploded into applause. Students Call didn't recognize at all were whistling and clapping and standing up on their chairs, chanting and yelling that the war was over.

Master Rufus climbed atop the Masters' table, looming over them all. He clapped his hands together and an instant silence fell — students were still moving their mouths, still applauding, but nothing was audible but Master Rufus.

"Today we welcome back to the Magisterium four students who have achieved an almost unprecedented victory in the history of the Assembly," he said. "Jasper deWinter; Tamara Rajavi; our Makar, Aaron Stewart; and our *newest* chaos magician, Callum Hunt. Please welcome them back."

The silence spell dissipated just long enough for a deafening roar of applause to sweep through the room.

"The Enemy of Death, he who sought to make himself and his minions immortal, he who would have defeated death itself, has now met death. We have not one but two Makars in this generation of mages. Every student here has contributed in some small way to this. We are truly lucky."

People whistled and clapped. Across the room, Alex Strike winked at Call from under the fall of his messy brown hair.

"Now, we should remember that while the war is over, we have not yet achieved peace. The Enemy might be gone, but his minions remain. There are battles yet to be fought, and as mages of the Magisterium, it will be your job to fight them."

This time there was a much more subdued murmur of applause. Good.

Master Rufus is right, Call thought grimly. *Even more right than he knows.*

"Now. Call, Tamara, Aaron, and Jasper," said Rufus, turning toward the four of them. "Raise your wristbands. In them you will find a new stone, a tanzanite, representing the greatest of victories achieved in the cause of the Magisterium."

Call jerked his wrist up and stared. It was true. There was a purple-blue stone glimmering on his wrist. Beside it was another new stone. A black stone, representing his new status as a Makar, a user of chaos magic.

Jasper pumped his fist skyward and whooped. Suddenly, the room was full of people shouting: *"The Enemy is dead! The Enemy is dead!"*

Only Tamara and Aaron didn't chant along with them. They looked at Call — Tamara with worry and Aaron with disquiet. They, Jasper, and Alastair were the only ones who knew, Call thought. The Enemy of Death was no more dead than he'd been before. You couldn't kill a monster when you were that monster.

Rufus lowered his hands, a gesture that seemed to unlock the students from their places. Everyone started running toward Call and his friends, pelting them with claps on the back and questions about the Enemy and the battle. Call whirled around in a sea of bodies, trying to keep his balance.

Kimiya was hugging Tamara and crying. Alex was shaking Aaron's hand. And then Celia was in front of Call, her eyes rimmed with red, reaching for his arm. Relieved, he turned toward her, thinking that at least she would be normal.

Moments before she planted a massive kiss right on his mouth.

Call's eyes went wide. Hers were closed as she leaned into him. They stood like that for a moment. Call was aware that people were staring at them — Tamara looking shocked, and Aaron, standing near her, started to laugh. Call was pretty sure Aaron was laughing at the fact that Call, having no idea where to put his hands, was waving his arms around like a squid underwater.

Finally, Celia pulled back. "You're a hero," she said, her eyes shining. "I always knew it."

"Um," Call said. So that had been his first kiss. It had been . . . soft?

A blush started on her cheeks. "I should go," she said, and ducked into the crowd.

"*Look* at Jasper," Aaron said, coming up next to Call and clapping him on the shoulder. "What a show-off."

At that moment Jasper sailed by, carried around on Rafe's shoulders as people cheered and sang "For He's a Jolly Good Fellow." He had a huge grin on his face.

Call smiled, too, immediately feeling a lot better. There was no way Jasper was going to say anything anytime soon, not if it meant giving up all of this. Call's secret was safe.

"Excuse me," Master Rufus said, pointing to Call. "I need to borrow you for a moment. That is, if you're not too busy."

Call swallowed a groan of humiliation. Had Master Rufus

seen Celia kiss him? Was he going to say something embarrassing about it? Call desperately hoped not.

Master Rufus led him over to a table in a far corner, a table blocked by a rock outcropping from the view of the rest of the Refectory. At the table, a tall, dark-haired, clean-shaven man was eating a plate of mushrooms like his life depended on it. Alastair.

Call couldn't remember any other parent being allowed inside the Magisterium, twice no less, but then the circumstances of his father being there were pretty unusual.

"It's been a long time since I sat in this Refectory," Alastair said, taking a big swig of some greenish juice that Call had never dared to try. "This is the lichen of my youth."

"Uh, yeah," Call said, wondering if the stuff had some kind of addictive properties, given the way his dad was tucking into it. "It's not so bad after a while."

"Mmmm," Alastair said. Then, after swallowing a final forkful, he stood. "Call, I can't stay, but Master Rufus agreed that the both of you could walk me out."

"Okay," Call said. "But do you have to go right away? Right now?"

"I'm afraid I do. There's still some business with the Assembly. Some more questions to answer. And I have left my affairs in some disorder. But I will see you over the winter holidays and we'll have lots to talk about then."

Call sighed, but after all the terrible things his father had said about the Magisterium, he wasn't surprised he was ready to leave so fast. Call wondered if he'd visited the Hall of Graduates and looked at his wife's handprint — Call wasn't sure if he was allowed to think of her as his mother anymore — but he couldn't bring himself to ask.

They walked together in silence out of the Refectory and down the long corridors that led to the front gates of the Magisterium, Alastair's hand on Call's shoulder, Master Rufus a few paces behind them.

At the doorway, Alastair turned and put his arms around Call, hugging him tightly. Call froze a little as his dad's hand smoothed his hair down. He wasn't a touchy-feely guy, Alastair, but Call could hear his dad swallow as he pulled back from Call and looked down at the band on his wrist. He raised Call's hand gently.

"Constantine Madden had this same black stone in his wristband," he said, and Call winced inside. "But he never had this." His thumb moved to the purple-blue stone. "The tanzanite. This stone indicates ultimate bravery. The only other person I ever knew who bore the tanzanite was Verity Torres."

"I'm not a hero," Call said. "But I'm not going to be like Constantine. I promise."

Alastair let go of Call's wrist and smiled one of his rare, crooked smiles. "You put yourself in a lot of danger, staying behind in the tomb," he said. "But I will never forget the look on Assemblyman Graves's face as long as I live."

Call couldn't help smiling. Alastair gave him one last touch on the shoulder and began to make his way toward the long black car waiting for him on the cleared dirt outside the gates.

"Take care of yourself," Master Rufus called.

Alastair paused and looked back at Rufus, then at Call. "Take care of my son."

Master Rufus nodded. Then, with a half wave to both of them, Alastair ducked inside the car. It drove away, the tires squeaking on the gravel.

Call turned around to head back to the Refectory, but Master Rufus stopped him with a quick hand. "Call," he said, "we ought to talk."

Call turned, full of cold dread. He wondered what Alastair had told him. "Uh, okay. What about?"

"There is something I did not want to say to you in front of the other students."

Call tensed. That couldn't be good.

"Call, there is a spy in the Magisterium. It could be someone on the Enemy's side. Working for Master Joseph now, most likely. Or it could be someone with a distrust of chaos mages."

"What do you mean?"

"You may remember from your Iron Year lectures about the origins of magic that not all parts of the world are welcoming to Makars. Some mages believe that no one should ever work with chaos magic — and that those who can should be stopped or killed."

Call vaguely recalled something about that, something about Europe not being Makar-friendly. "Why would you think there's a spy, though?

"*Automotones.*" Rufus spat the name. "The mages here would never have sent a deadly elemental to retrieve you. He was too powerful and too violent. And if we had sent him, we would never have sent him with orders to hurt any of you, even Alastair. Someone here sent him with orders to kill the Makar. We thought that meant Aaron, but now that you're a Makar, no doubt that same person wants you dead, too."

A cold shudder went through Call. Whoever had sent the elemental after them hadn't been worried about Call's safety.

Which meant it *couldn't* have been one of Master Joseph's minions, since Master Joseph had thrown himself in front of Call to keep him alive. Which meant Master Rufus was right.

"Go back to the Refectory," Master Rufus said. "Your friends are waiting for you. We have time enough to discuss the future when your classes begin. Tomorrow. You're back just in time to go out with the other Copper Years on their second mission."

"Second mission?" Call asked, astonished.

Master Rufus nodded. "Yes, finding seven speckled frogs in the surrounding forest."

"You've got to be kidding me!" Call said. "We killed the Enemy of Death. Doesn't that count for anything?"

"Of course it does," Master Rufus said with a rare, small smile. "It counts as your *first* mission. You won't have to do any makeup work. Now get going."

"Tomorrow," Call echoed. He started back through the passageways of the Magisterium, past glowing crystals and rock formations, his mind a swirl of uneasy thoughts.

"Callum Hunt," said a voice.

It was a voice he knew well. Call stopped in place, looking up until his gaze lit on a glowing lizard partway up the wall, regarding him with half-lidded eyes. Warren's long tongue lashed through the air.

"The end is closer than you think, *Makar*," the elemental said.

Then he darted away, leaving Call to stare after him.

ABOUT THE AUTHORS

Holly Black and **Cassandra Clare** first met over ten years ago at Holly's first-ever book signing. They have since become good friends, bonding over (among other things) their shared love of fantasy — from the sweeping vistas of The Lord of the Rings to the gritty tales of Batman in Gotham City to the classic sword-and-sorcery epics to *Star Wars*. With Magisterium, they decided to team up to write their own story about heroes and villains, good and evil, and being chosen for greatness, whether you like it or not.

Holly is the bestselling author and co-creator of The Spiderwick Chronicles series and won a Newbery Honor for her novel *Doll Bones*. Cassie is the author of bestselling YA series, including The Mortal Instruments and The Infernal Devices. They both live in Western Massachusetts, about ten minutes away from each other. This is the second book in Magisterium, following *The Iron Trial*.

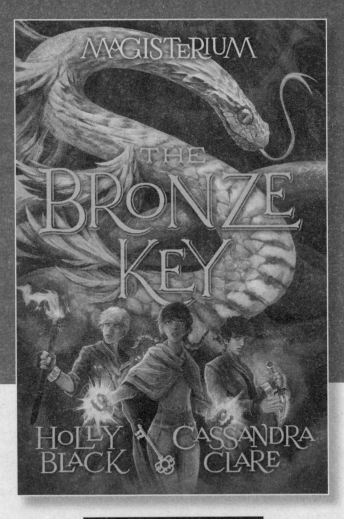